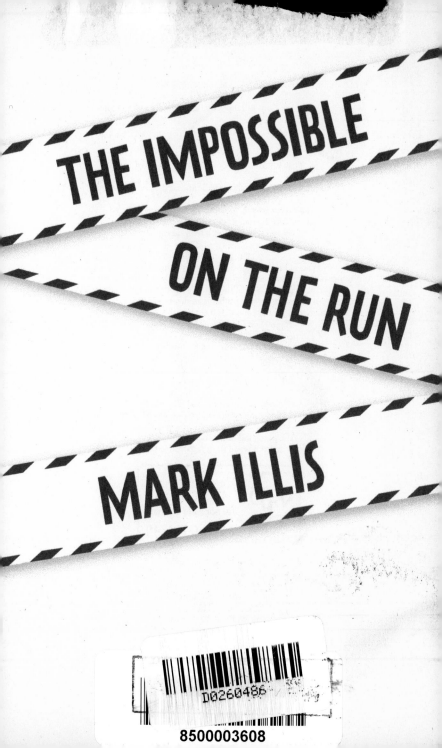

# THE IMPOSSIBLE

## ON THE RUN

## MARK ILLIS

QUERCUS CHILDREN'S BOOKS

First published in Great Britain in 2018 by Hodder and Stoughton

3 5 7 9 10 8 6 4 2

Text copyright © Mark Illis, 2018
Illustrations copyright © Bimpe Alliu, 2018

The moral rights of the author and illustrator have been asserted.

A CIP catalogue record for this book
is available from the British Library.

ISBN 978 1 786 54012 6

Typeset in Joanna MT by Hewer Text UK Ltd, Edinburgh
Printed and bound in Great Britain by Clays Ltd, Elcograf S.p.A.

The paper and board used in this book
are made from wood from responsible sources.

**MIX**
Paper from
responsible sources
FSC® C104740
FSC
www.fsc.org

Quercus Children's Books
An imprint of
Hachette Children's Group
Part of Hodder and Stoughton
Carmelite House
50 Victoria Embankment
London EC4Y 0DZ

An Hachette UK Company
www.hachette.co.uk

www.hachettechildrens.co.uk

For Sam

Also by Mark Illis:

The Impossible

# DAY ONE

**1.17 p.m.**

So here I am, balancing on a small stepping-stone in the middle of the river, swaying, wondering how the hell I'm going to get over the next stone which has mostly crumbled away. My three best mates are all lined up on the bank watching, like they bought tickets especially to see me get humiliated, like they're just waiting for someone to come round with popcorn. I lift my right foot and my left leg starts shaking, and I'm standing here like I'm demonstrating some sort of totally made-up yoga pose. Wobbling Loser. Asha's laughing at me.

And what am I doing? I'm searching for the egg that I don't even, if I'm honest, want to find.

Just one hour ago, everything was fine. One hour ago I was in my bedroom writing my blog, and, OK, you could argue I was pretty much a weird, friendless loner, but apart from that I was fine, I was absolutely fine.

My clumsy fingers slipped and scrambled over the keyboard, like I had to get this done quickly or someone would stop me.

**THE ANNIVERSARY**

**Some of you people who I speak to on here every day, some of you get it, but most of you don't, most of you think I'm lying or stupid or mad, but I'm not any of those things because it's all true. One of these days you'll find out and I'll say Told you so.**

That was a bit rubbish. A bit childish. It was just missing the words: *So there!* at the end of the paragraph. I didn't care, I'd edit it afterwards. I kept writing, fingertips chik-chakking over the keyboard.

**If you're wondering what I'm talking about then just scroll down and read pretty much any of my posts from the last year. They'll tell you about the egg that turned up in Gilpin almost exactly a year ago which turned out to be – and I promise you I know how this sounds – alien.**

**It's true. I was there.**

**The government doesn't want you to believe any of this – and I know how that sounds too – but my friend Asha started glowing like the sun and she got brighter and brighter till she was in danger of exploding.**

**My friend Grace could only speak in questions, and after a while even those started drying up.**

**My best mate Max turned into a ghost and basically evaporated.**

**My second-best mate Josh was, sort of, tattooed by the universe.**

A guy we know called Matt – he died when his blood boiled inside his body.

True.

And me? I met my fifty-year-old self. Knocked at my door, came in, said, 'I'm you.' And he was basically OK, but he was also a pompous old git and he wasn't a war correspondent like I want to be, or anything remotely interesting. He worked for a magazine called Card, which is basically all about cardboard.

I mean, cardboard. I actually wish I was making this up.

So I've been a bit anxious ever since then, a bit careful. My mum says I'm paralysed by choice. I don't know about that. I just worry, whatever I do, that it's going to lead to cardboard.

I mostly stay indoors, in my bedroom, talking to you, my invisible readers who mostly hate me.

And meanwhile the Anniversary is here. One year since the alien egg which most of you don't even believe in arrived.

And, along with the Anniversary, there's the nightmares.

I'm asleep, I'm sure I'm asleep, but I'm aware of this thing, this cold, still presence in the darkness. I lie motionless, trying not to breathe, but I feel it turning, looking at me.

I wake up gasping, panting, thrashing around under my duvet.

**It's the same nightmare every night for a month. And it doesn't really feel like a nightmare. It feels like a thing that's actually happening.**

**The cold, still presence. Turning towards me.**

**So I've only got one thing on my mind.**

**Is the egg coming back? Is it going to poison every teenager in Gilpin again?**

I finished the blogpost, read it, decided not to post it. The problem with my blog is that it sounds like the diary of a mad person. Even the title – *The Secret Diary of H* – sounds like something a mad person might come up with. And yet I keep going. Keep writing, keep spilling this crazy stuff on to the screen. Because I'm still trying to be a reporter I guess, a war correspondent, still trying to summarise impossible, horrible events, still trying to convince people that it honestly in real life all happened.

I stood up, drummed my knuckles on my desk a bit, then sank into my beanbag. Couldn't get comfortable. Then I was sitting at my desk again, staring at the laptop screen, with homework and two empty mugs and a stray pair of pants all shoved to one side, and then all of a sudden – and I didn't even remember standing up this time – I was pacing in my small room, up and down, and Mum was shouting up the stairs.

'Hector, are you pacing again?'

Back to my desk.

Sod it. I knew I was never going to get round to editing it, and I did want my voice to be heard, even if that voice sounded like it belonged to someone with serious mental health issues.

I clicked SUBMIT and the blog was posted. That's pretty much how I do social media these days – reluctantly, abruptly, angrily. I got up quickly, like I was backing away from the computer. My bed's on a platform with my desk underneath it. I climbed halfway up the ladder to my bed, slid my legs between the rungs and lowered myself carefully so I was hanging upside down like a bat. It was an experiment. I'd read somewhere that when you get more blood in your brain it clarifies things, gives you a clean, sharp image of the world. Probably worth a try. A clean, sharp image of the world sounded good to me.

Upside down.

It was an unusual view of my room. Desk, beanbag, red curtains.

I'd had pirate curtains until last year, got rid of them a few months ago. That was one small improvement in my life. My back stretched, my thighs and my stomach tightened, and it started to hurt behind my knees, where I was gripping the ladder.

Couldn't think of many other improvements. Last year my best mate Max saved my life and then died. My brother Jason's gone missing. Asha dumped me ages ago, mostly because you can't go out with someone who won't leave their room except to go to school. And Josh and Grace have pretty much given up coming to see me. I miss all of them, more than I can say in words. Max, Jason, Asha, Josh, Grace. Sometimes I actually feel sick and I think I need to call a doctor but then I remember.

No, it's OK, I'm not sick. I'm just sad.

Was there more blood in my brain? I wasn't sure, but I thought I'd give it a few more minutes.

There was a noise downstairs, the front door banging open. I jumped and nearly fell head-first on to the floor. I could've died. The top of my skull could have crumpled like the top of a soft-boiled egg.

People were coming in. Who? The army? Government agents? Scientists? They might have been spying on my computer, they might know exactly what I was writing, as I was writing it, so now they were raiding my home.

I knew this was paranoid and slightly crazy and basically stupid even as I was thinking it, but I still thought it. Couldn't help myself. For the last year, ever since the alien egg turned up, my brain had been in a paranoid, slightly crazy, basically stupid kind of state.

Funny how you can be aware of it, but at the same time completely unable to do anything about it.

My mum was in the hall saying something which must have involved the words *Go on up* because now there were feet drumming on the stairs and before I could do anything other than turn my upside-down head in the right direction the door burst open and three people who definitely weren't the army or government agents or scientists burst through it.

Asha stared at me.

Josh stared too, let out a short sharp, one-syllable laugh, 'Ha!' then bent over, bangles jangling, to look at me from a different angle.

Grace also stared, but she didn't say anything, she just raised an eloquent, upside-down eyebrow.

I wanted them to go away. Yes, I missed them, but that didn't mean I actually wanted to see them. I mean I did want to see them, obviously, but I also didn't because I had an uneasy, vague but very strong feeling that if we all got together again, then bad things would happen.

Also, a part of me was wondering if there was any way at all to be dignified in this situation.

'Jesus!' Asha was holding her nose. 'Your bedroom stinks. Are you drinking your own piss? Are your toenails a foot long? You've gone full hermit, haven't you?'

'This is an intervention, mate.' Josh was pulling my window open. 'We're here to rescue you.' He turned to me and grinned. 'You're welcome.'

'We've left you to it,' Grace said, her voice all soft and reassuring, 'all this time, because everyone has their own way of coping—'

Josh interrupted. 'Except you're obviously not coping.'

'But it's the Anniversary,' Grace continued, 'and you've been blogging about these nightmares. So—'

This time Asha interrupted her: 'So, long story short, we decided it was time we came and gave you a slap,' she said. 'Literally, if necessary. I'm volunteering right now.'

I slid my legs out of the ladder, wriggled into a sort of handstand, then fell on to my feet and got up slowly, because

I suddenly had a feeling I might faint. No dignity involved at all, and no extra clarity either.

I held up both hands, like I was planning to physically shove them out of my room, back on to the landing, back down the stairs, right out of my house.

'No,' I said. 'No, no, no.'

'No what exactly?' said Grace.

'No to whatever you've got in mind!' I was trying to keep my voice steady, but not entirely succeeding. I was pretty sure I knew exactly what they had in mind.

'Come on, bud.' Josh's tone was coaxing, the sort of voice you might use with a stubborn toddler. 'We've been down to Max's house without you loads of times in the last year. This time we want you with us.'

I shook my head. 'Why would you even think about going back there? If you know about the nightmares then you know it could be coming back.'

'It's a whole nip-it-in-the-bud situation,' Asha said, impatiently. 'Obviously. If we find anything, we call in Colonel Doofus straightaway, he removes it before it does any spooky stuff, no one gets hurt.'

I was still shaking my head. 'No.'

'Hector.' Grace pushed her blue fringe off her forehead, looking at me with her steady, serious gaze. 'It's been a year. It's the Anniversary. It's time.'

## 1.53 p.m.

#Anniversary **So we're all here, all basically holding our breath. Bracing ourselves. Waiting.**

We sat outside *Love Bites* in the square. The same square where there'd been a riot a year earlier when Colonel Douglas, who was basically a fascist and didn't even try to hide it, had started rounding up all the teenagers in town. Why? Because every single teenager in Gilpin started having weird, scary, sometimes life-threatening mutations. And there was nothing good about it. No one turned into a superhero. Douglas and his sidekick Professor Kirby, aka Colonel Doofus and Professor Patronising, wanted us all stashed in some sort of prison, where they could watch us, study us, and quite possibly dissect us.

I was sitting opposite Grace, who had short blonde hair and a fringe that changed colour from month to month. Asha was leaning back in her seat like she was in charge. Josh had whipped cream on his nose from his hot chocolate.

'You've got to come with us,' he said. 'Obviously.'

I sipped my coffee, and stared at my phone. Sent my melodramatic tweet. 'Back to Max's house to search for an egg that will turn the whole entire town insane?' I said, glancing up at him. 'Yeah, you're right I've got to come with you for that. Except, oh, hang on, you're not. I haven't got to do anything.' Back to my phone.

'You're all kinds of stupid, aren't you?' said Asha.

I didn't feel like that needed an answer.

Connor and his twin sister Ruby went by. I sort of envied

them. They were twelve when the alien egg showed up last year, too young to be affected, and they seemed fairly relaxed now, even though they were thirteen and therefore vulnerable. I wasn't mates with them, obviously, what with being a really mature, basically adult sixteen-year-old, but my parents were friends with their parents. Connor caught my eye, waved and bounced over like it was brilliant to see us. He was wearing his yellow and black striped Gilpin Hornets football shirt. He has this puppyish thing going on which is quite sweet except for when it's really irritating. Ruby followed reluctantly. Nothing puppyish about her.

'Hey,' Connor said, with a grin that showed most of his teeth. 'Whatcha doing?'

Ruby answered. 'What's it look like they're doing? Can I have some coffee?'

She was going for my cup. I put my palm over it and her fingers brushed the back of my hand.

'There's hardly any left,' I said.

She sneered at me, which was not surprising, because a sneer was pretty much her default expression. She was wearing a black T-shirt and jeans, and a lot of black eyeliner. Long, straight hair that tended to swing in front of her face. It was a bit of a mystery how you could get twins so different from each other.

Asha's voice was clipped and impatient. 'Bye, then.'

Ruby sneered at her too, but Connor's grin hardly faltered. 'See ya round,' he said, like Asha had said something nice to him, and then they were heading off, him still with a bounce in his step, her slouching like Josh on a bad day.

Asha ignored them. She reached over, snatched my phone

out of my hands, and spoke as if we hadn't been interrupted.

'You're coming with us this time, you twink.'

I reached over and grabbed my phone back again. 'Right,' I said. 'How about everyone just calms down? The egg's been in Gilpin twice. Once four hundred years ago, and once last year. So we shouldn't expect it for another four hundred years. That's solid logic. You can't argue with it.'

Grace had her hands clasped in front of her and was looking at me steadily, like she was interviewing me.

'Except,' she said, 'the first time it turned up it got destroyed, whereas last year it hatched. Which is why maybe it'll think Gilpin's a good nest. And you've been having those nightmares, which must mean something, and it's the Anniversary and, Hector, we really want to do this together. Because, maybe you've forgotten this, but we haven't: you're our friend. So please, come with us?'

It wasn't just the word *Please*, although that helped. And it wasn't just Grace's argument, and the nightmares, and the Anniversary, although obviously all of that was important. It was the combined force of my friends all banding together, the history involved. Maybe it was a psychic bond, I don't know. Or it was just easier in the end to let them drag me along with them. I promised myself I'd retreat back to my room afterwards, my computer screen, my mugs of tea and my uncomfortable beanbag, and whatever happened I'd basically stay there till school started.

And even while I was doing that, solemnly promising myself that I was going to stay out of trouble, I sort of somehow sensed that it wasn't going to happen. Because I had a feeling, like inside me everything was tensing and clenching, I had a feeling that it was all starting again.

Which was rubbish, obviously. Just nerves.

Unless it wasn't.


I hadn't been to Max's house for a year, but I could probably have done the walk blindfolded. Along Horngate, down Crook Lane. We'd been back and forth to each other's houses so often, all the years we were growing up. I walked stiffly, not saying much. Tense and clenched. Blue sky, clear, cool light, a sense of summer fading. Grace and Asha in front, talking about something irrelevant, Josh next to me, going on pointlessly about some film I hadn't seen. All three of them chatting away like there was something they were trying not to think about, which there totally was.

And then I suddenly stopped.

And they stopped too, even though they'd been here loads of times in the last year. The irrelevant stuff and the pointless stuff stuttered and faded like someone was gradually turning the volume down and we all just stopped and stood there and stared. Because there it was.

The house where the creepy, flickering alien creature had emerged from its egg.

The house where Max died.

His family had never moved back in, they'd put it on the market and moved away, and it had been empty for a year. The grass on the lawn was long and thick like an untidy head of hair. Weeds wriggled out of the crazy-paving path, dangling dandelions and pink buds that smelt sweet and looked poisonous. The door and the window frames were still a cheerful red, but most of the windows were cracked or broken.

There was a lump of sadness in my stomach. I was thinking about my best mate, Max, about how he'd turned into a ghost, and had probably saved my life, and had slowly vanished as if his molecules had simply drifted apart and dispersed into the air.

We all stood there a moment, silent, staring at the house, probably thinking similar thoughts.

And then Asha clapped her hands.

'River,' she said. 'Last one there's a pussy.'

We ran, and although it felt a bit like we were running away from Max's house, it felt good to run. We slid down from the path on to the pebbly little beach and argued about who came last, loitering there, wasting time. It was almost like we didn't actually want to go on, across the river and into the woods.

Josh picked up a stone.

'So you reckon it's there?' Words coughed out of him suddenly, as if he couldn't contain them any longer. 'You reckon there's another egg in the woods? I reckon there is. Probably won't be, but there could be, right? Because of your nightmares. Because it's the Anniversary.'

He picked up a flat pebble, crouched, and his bent arm swung backwards. His body was still for a moment but there was a fierce, wound-up quality to it. He was like an archer taking aim. Two seconds, and then arm, elbow and wrist all snapped forwards in a blur, and the stone skimmed over the water also in a blur, bouncing too many times to count.

He did a little fist pump. 'I'm like a black belt at skimming stones. I should go professional.'

'So what exactly happens in your scary nightmares?' Asha said. 'I read about them in your lame blog, but have you got any detail? Am I in them?'

Great. Didn't want to talk about them or think about them at all. Not even a little bit. But Asha, Grace and Josh were all staring at me. 'It's just what you've read,' I said. 'Nothing actually happens. It's a presence.'

Asha shrugged. 'So what? Say I have a dream about Taylor Swift, doesn't mean I'm going to bump into her the next day.'

Josh stared at her. 'You have dreams about Taylor Swift?'

Asha was going to respond to that, but Grace got in first. 'Maybe they're actually communicating with you,' she said.

I looked at her. This was exactly what I'd been thinking but not saying, not even properly articulating to myself. The alien we saw last year had Matt's face, and Max's face, and then my face. There was a connection there. So was it sort of waving at me in my subconscious? Saying 'Hi, we're on our way, see you soon'?

'So what d'you think?' I said to her. 'D'you think ... we're going to find another egg?'

Asha shrugged. 'Maybe this year there'll be like fifty of them.'

That hadn't even occurred to me. It had always seemed logical to me that if the creature was going to lay another egg it might choose the same time of year as the last two times, and the same place. But the idea that it might lay a whole litter of eggs, or bring along some friends – that was new.

Grace did a small, nervous smile. 'Let's find out.'

She glanced at Josh and he joined her, back up to the path and along the riverbank, towards the stepping-stones. Asha and I followed them.

Josh hadn't changed his style in the last year. Still the dark hoodies and the bangles, still the mood skidding between a jangly sort of enthusiasm and a gloom that was hard to penetrate. He had issues with his mum but I didn't know much about it because he didn't like to talk about it. And maybe because I'm a rubbish friend who prefers staying in his room to actually interacting with people. Grace had had a bit of a makeover around last Christmas – that was when she'd had her brown bob cut short and dyed blonde, and started dying her fringe a different colour on a regular basis. She was still self-contained, still that sense that you didn't know what she was really thinking, but she seemed OK.

I wasn't sure if she was Josh's ex-girlfriend. They might have been going out for a bit, but I didn't know. I asked Josh around Christmas, I said, 'Are you and Grace a thing?' He said something or grunted something I didn't quite catch, I didn't get if it meant Yes or No, so I left it at that. Never found out. I can tell you in detail about how he skims stones, but his love life is a mystery.

We all walked along the riverbank. A year ago, Max had found a strange stone in the woods near his house, and he'd brought it home. It was shiny, it was a really black black, and it had a silver swirl rippling over its surface. Turned out it wasn't a stone, it was an egg. Turned out the egg did strange, mutant, disturbing things to the DNA of every teenager in Gilpin. And when it finally hatched, something alien came out, which was snatched away by its alien mum. Everyone who'd changed went back to normal when it left. But Matt was dead, and Max was dead, and the whole entire town was traumatised.

But now, instead of running away, instead of putting as much distance between us and Gilpin as possible, we were off to see if there was another egg in the woods.

The stepping-stones were boulders with jagged edges and wet, sloping surfaces. One of them had cracked a while ago and most of it had crumbled away. And the river was high, we'd had a whole lot of late summer rain, so it was bulging like it was muscly, and it was tumbling and rushing between its banks as if it had to be somewhere and it was late.

'OK,' said Josh. 'I'll go first, yeah? And if anyone falls in, I'm a great swimmer, so I'll rescue you.'

He was sort of joking, but he was mostly showing off for Grace. He stepped out on to the first stone tentatively, stepped over to the next one, obviously found his confidence building and skipped over the rest, including the broken one, without any trouble. He stood on the far bank and raised both arms above his head. Bangles slid down his thin wrists.

'Winner!' he yelled.

Asha looked at Grace. 'He's so sexy right now.'

Grace laughed, and set off across the stones. Asha

followed. They both paused at the broken one, sort of stutter-jumped over it, and leapt from the last stone to the bank.

'What'choo waiting for?' Asha shouted, pointing an index finger over the river at me.

She hadn't changed at all. She was still the biggest personality in any room she walked into. Her shiny black hair was loose around her face, and she was flushed with the pleasure of getting over the river and leaving me behind.

She'd dumped me because, she said, I needed 'to get something resembling a life'. Last autumn, when we first got together, she'd keep telling me there's a party, there's a film, we're hanging at Grace's house. Sometimes I'd turn up, but I'd be bent over my phone or staring out the window and basically not really there. And more and more I didn't turn up at all. I was like, 'Yeah, no, sorry, bit busy.' I knew I was pushing her away, and I didn't want to push her away, it was like I was deliberately trying to ruin my own life, but I couldn't help myself.

So she dumped me by text on January 1st, after I hadn't shown up at Freddie Butcher's party the night before. I was angry with her and upset with her and I totally couldn't blame her.

'What's the matter?' she shouted again. 'You scared?'

And right now I found her really annoying, and I really wished she was still my girlfriend.

'Yeah, yeah,' I muttered. 'Coming.'

I took a step on to the first stone. Looked down at the water flowing swiftly beneath me. *This isn't a problem.* Took another step. Josh in his dark hoodie, Asha in a red sweater,

Grace in a pale green denim jacket, all lined up watching me. We were here because if there was going to be another Event this year, another crisis, then we wanted to stop it before it properly started. We were also here because Gilpin was a laughing stock. The papers said there'd been some pranks, practical jokes which people took seriously, things had escalated, they'd got out of control, and the town had basically had a collective nervous breakdown. There'd been papers written about it, articles about 'the mass psychogenic illness in Gilpin'.

Most of the world seemed to accept that. Most of the world, apparently, wanted to be reassured, wanted to be told that reality was continuing in a normal, realistic way. Which is why the comments on my blog were vicious, bullying and relentless. I was an idiot, a liar, I was suffering from mental health problems. I got threatened with violence on a regular basis. I kept going in spite of all the abuse, because I wanted to write about important stuff, I didn't want to write about cardboard. But it was hard. I got why people didn't believe me. The idea that there was an elaborate government cover-up was ridiculous. And the idea that what they were covering up was some sort of alien intrusion, that was beyond ridiculous, that was the kind of thing that belonged on the far fringes of the internet, with the weirdoes and the wicky-wacky people with hats made of tin foil.

So apart from the whole nip-it-in-the-bud aspect of what we were doing, we also all wanted to prove that Gilpin hadn't lost its mind. And even though I was there reluctantly, dragged along by my friends, I wanted to prove that I personally was right and all the nasty, spiteful, bullying trolls were wrong.

I wanted to be able to say, *Told you so.*

So that's why I was balancing on a small stone in the middle of the river, with my friends lined up watching, laughing at me. It all made sense.

Josh was impatient. 'You coming or what?'

Asha was amused. 'Scared of getting wet?'

I'd reached the broken stone.

How exactly had they got over it? Was it best to jump right over it or put all my weight briefly on this narrow and probably unstable rock? The river sounded like a badly tuned radio and a breeze had suddenly appeared from nowhere, smelling of Himalayan Balsam and humiliation.

Every kid in Gilpin crosses these stones around the age of six. It's what passes for a coming-of-age ritual in my town. I'd crossed them myself more than once. But the stone was broken, and the river was high, and my state of mind wasn't exactly ideal.

So that's how it happened. That's how come I was balancing on a small stepping-stone in the middle of the river, swaying, wondering how the hell I was going to get over the next stone which had mostly crumbled away.

I got ready to hop over it.

Lifted my foot.

A sudden, loud hum buzzed in my ears.

I wobbled. Regained control.

Then a *Boom!* echoed down the river, making the air seem to vibrate.

I more than wobbled, I shook and swayed. Tried to regain control. My arms were out like a tightrope walker's, but they were windmilling and flapping both at once and I couldn't stay upright, I couldn't stay upright, I slipped and toppled and fell and the water waited beneath me, so fat and glossy that I thought I might bounce off its surface.

I didn't.

**2.27 p.m.**

#Anniversary **What hums, and then goes Boom?**

It was a full-on, star-jump style belly-flop, a face-first crash into the water. Which was icy cold, and seriously wet. The wetness of the water shouldn't have been surprising but it was – to go from dry to so utterly totally drenched in half a second just felt wrong.

It was only about three feet deep and although the current

was strong, it wasn't sweeping me towards a precipice or a waterfall or anything, but I did get a lungful of water and I was dazed and shocked by the suddenness of it. I was face down, floating fast, fingers scrabbling for the river bed, trying to get my feet down, trying to find some purchase, trying to lift my eyes out of the water, worried that the river was hurtling me towards a rock or a spiky branch.

I managed a blurry, swift glimpse and I angled myself, angled my whole body, and was swept in the shallow water, feeling like the river was gripping me, like it had me in its fist and was yanking me, I was swept, thrashing, towards the bank, towards the bank, towards the bank.

I grabbed at a bush, missed, grabbed at another, flailed at its twigs and leaves, clutched it, jerked my arm and shoulder as I half stopped, feeling its roots straining at the earth, managed to dig my feet toes first into the river bed, then bent my legs and launched myself right into the air, up and out of the water, and finally flopped down on to the earth like a big floppy seal, half on the bank, half in the water, panting.

'Whoa! That was brilliant. Nine out of ten for style.' Josh had run up, he was standing over me.

Asha's face was split by a huge grin. 'You just made my day,' she said. 'Look at you – half man, half fish. Can you do it again? I only caught the last bit.' She was waving her phone. 'We're going to put it on your blog, right?'

'Are you OK?' Grace sounded more curious than worried, but at least she was showing some concern.

I lifted myself on to my elbows, coughed and spat,

shook my head like a dog.

'What was that noise?' I said.

Part of me wanted to go straight home, strip off, get in a hot bath, and not leave the house till school started. But the water had woken me up, shocked me and sort of slapped me in the face just like Asha had wanted to earlier. A bigger part of me wanted to find the egg.

I got on to my hands and knees, coughed and spat some more. Stood up, unsteady.

There was no way I was going home now. The high-pitched whine was still there. The tension like a stretched rubber band, about to snap right in front of my face. It was as if that unsettling, cold presence I felt in my nightmares had actually leaked out of my nightmares and was right here with me in the ordinary, wide-awake world. It was an uneasy, nagging sensation, like the air wasn't quite right. Either I was being paranoid, which was entirely possible, or I was sensing something wrong.

Something that didn't belong.

I thought there was another egg in Gilpin.

Josh pulled off his hoodie and handed it to me. I used it to dry my face and hair. I peeled off my T-shirt, wrung it out and tried to dry myself from the waist up.

Grace looked at Asha. She only murmured but I could hear her. 'He's so sexy right now.'

Asha laughed.

'Right,' said Josh. 'I'm just gonna say it, because we're all thinking it. Was that noise a UFO? Was it an alien spaceship? It hums, as it comes down to earth, then something comes out and slams the door shut behind it. Hum, boom — spaceship. Yeah?'

'Get your T-shirt on, Fish Boy, the aliens don't want to see your perky little nipples,' said Asha. 'Let's go.'

There was some thin, cool sun by the river, but the temperature dropped as soon as we were under the trees. I had to hold my nose to prevent a sneeze, but I still spluttered a muffled, gasping sort of cough. They all glared at me, and I glared right back at them. We started following a track of sorts, but it was soon lost in long grass and bracken. A leaning yew trunk covered with furry moss blocked our way.

'Where did the sounds come from?' I whispered.

'This way,' hissed Josh, pointing left, as Asha simultaneously said, 'Over there,' pointing straight ahead.

'Let's stand still a minute,' said Grace. 'And listen.'

We stood still under the yew, listening. Wet, leathery smells. A snot-green ear of lichen was growing out of a moulding stump next to me. I edged away from it. Nothing to hear, except the breeze stirring the leaves, something rustling in a bush nearby, the sudden squeaky call of a bird. Dappled leaf-light.

I'd edged closer to Asha, and was tempted to hold her hand. Which would be a dumb move, obviously.

And then the humming again, suddenly. It didn't slowly get louder, it snapped on at full volume. It was harsh, suggesting machinery or an engine, and it was nearby.

'Not gonna lie,' Josh breathed. 'That's freaking me out a bit.'

But we still approached the noise. I was pretty sure at this point that round the next clump of trees was a great big massive humming spaceship, and if that didn't convince the world that I'd been right all along and Gilpin was being visited by aliens, then what would?

*Told you so.*

We crept closer. Grass, drooping ferns and the fat trunk of an oak tree stood between us and whatever was making that noise. My skin felt too tight. I was shivering and I could barely breathe, but I was still creeping closer.

And then I saw movement. Off to the left. What was that? A dark shape.

'Wait.'

I whispered that one syllable, holding up a shaking finger. We all stood still. And I heard a rustle. I jerked my head to the right. There was a shape over there as well. Whoever, or whatever, they were, they were moving around us, surrounding us.

Grace was biting her lip, Josh was restlessly moving his weight from foot to foot, I was trembling all over. Asha's hand moved into mine. Squeezed it. Grace nodded, indicated that we should move forwards. It was the only way left for us to go.

There was a clearing ahead, and there was something in the clearing, something bulky and metallic. I couldn't believe it. This was it, this was really it. A spaceship.

I took a step forwards, moved a leafy branch out of my way. It was a machine of some sort. Not a spaceship, not a UFO, just a big shiny machine with a golf-ball attachment on top and camouflage netting drooping in swags off the side.

'One of you kids want to run away, so I can shoot you? Cos I'm really bored right now.'

We whirled round and a guy in a black uniform, carrying a gun, appeared from behind a tree. We stared at him. He smiled lazily, sounding like we'd woken him from a nap.

It wasn't an ordinary gun. There were holes along the muzzle and a dark green light was bleeding from them.

'Got pretty clear rules of engagement,' the soldier continued. 'I see an alien, I zap it. Any of you kids aliens?'

His eyes, and his gun, pointed towards me. I was shivering and dripping and my hair was plastered to my face.

'Not too sure about you,' he said.

I sneezed.

## 2.44 p.m.

**#Anniversary Soldiers in black uniforms, weird guns, creepy machines, Colonel Doofus throwing his weight around. An ordinary day in Gilpin!**

I'd been given a green T-shirt that was a couple of sizes too big. I felt like a soldier. A thin, cold, damp soldier. We were ushered into a roomy tent where the air was still and stale, and a neat woman with a short ponytail was studying a large-scale map of the area. She didn't bother to turn round. We all looked at her back.

'What are you even doing here?' said Josh, after a moment.

No answer.

'You remind me of my geography teacher,' Asha told her. 'Are you her sister?'

Still no answer. There was a trestle table on the other side

26

of the tent with two cups of coffee, a laptop and a ring binder on it. The binder had the words GREEN FINGERS stamped on its cover in big, black letters. I was tempted to open it and have a look but before I could move, Colonel Douglas came in behind us, striding in like he was in a hurry, frowning as if we were an unpleasant distraction.

'Hector Coleman,' he snapped. 'If you were in my army you'd be out of my army. Court-martialled.'

Sandy hair, deep wrinkles on his face as if that frown was his only expression, pale, cold eyes. I'd last met him a year ago when he'd basically told me that everything that happened in Gilpin was my fault. I was defiant online, I called him Colonel Doofus. I wasn't quite so brave whenever I actually met him. There was something about his voice, his manner, the way he completely expected people to listen and obey, that made my insides feel like they were squeezing into a tight ball.

I nodded, tried to keep my voice steady. 'Hello. You remember me, then?'

'Oh, yes,' he grated. 'You're a red flag. All of you are.'

Asha had no problem with authority. She'd been giving teachers a hard time her entire school career. 'What's wrong with Map Girl?' she said. 'Doesn't she talk?'

Douglas looked at Asha, his eyes resting on her as if he was sizing her up.

Josh grinned. 'Give her detention,' he said. 'That works. Except it doesn't.'

Douglas finally sighed. 'What do you kids think you're doing?'

27

'We're not kids.' Grace didn't sound cocky like Asha, or nervous like me. She was simply stating facts. 'And we're doing the same as you are. Looking for an egg. Why are you here? D'you know something?'

Douglas hesitated a moment, as if searching for the right response. 'Come,' he snapped, and walked out.

We looked at each other. 'Think we should salute?' said Josh. We followed him.

There were two lorries parked in the clearing, beside a sagging awning that covered the machine we'd seen. It was a shiny, cream-coloured box with a chrome cylinder attachment on one side, the big golf ball on top, and a sloping side with a large panel on it. The panel intermittently glowed the same swampy green as the soldier's gun. Aerials stuck out around the golf ball like strands of hair.

Presumably it hummed intermittently, and occasionally went Boom!

'So what's that?' I said.

Asha was getting out her phone.

'Take a picture of it,' said Douglas, 'and I'll have your phone. You never saw this device. It doesn't exist.'

'But what does it do?' said Josh.

'Nothing,' said Douglas emphatically, as if he was explaining something to a stupid person. 'Because it doesn't exist.'

'Yeah, but it does, though, cos look,' said Josh, pointing at it.

Douglas ignored him. Four soldiers came out of the trees, looking at a tablet and talking animatedly. They were all in black uniforms, and all had the guns that glowed green.

'I want one of those!' said Josh. 'Can I have one? What's that green light, is it lasers? It's lasers, right? Can I just hold one?'

'OK,' I said, as Douglas's face went all pinched and angry, 'what's going on? Like Grace said, why are you even here?'

He looked surprised to be asked this question. 'Because of the timing. And because of you, of course,' he said. 'Because of your nightmares.'

I stared at him. I'd sort of known they'd be reading my blog, but I hadn't realised they'd actually care what I had to say.

'Four hundred years ago an egg was found in these woods, at this time of year, and it was destroyed. One year ago an egg was found, and it hatched,' Douglas continued, echoing what Grace had said in the square. 'We've been monitoring this location, and we decided the time was right to put boots on the ground.' You could almost feel the contempt radiating off him as his eyes swept over us. His voice was tight, as if he was only keeping his temper with difficulty. 'And this year,' he said, 'we're prepared. We're tracking fluctuations across the entire electromagnetic spectrum. The Coordinating Committee stands ready to shut down this town at the first sign of alien activity. We will immediately evacuate twelve- to twenty-year-olds to a safe location. Would you like to see that location now? Would you like to get to know it extremely well?'

We stared at him.

'Is it Ibiza?' Josh said. 'Cos if so, I'm up for it.'

Douglas didn't even look at him. 'This is your only warning,' he said. 'Get out of my sight.'

He stood there glaring at us, tall and straight and quivering like a stick of bamboo in his smart uniform.

We got out of his sight.


'All right,' I said, 'there's a good side to this.'

'Oh, excellent,' said Asha. 'Hector's going to hectorsplain it to us.'

We were on our way back, over the stepping-stones, past Max's house, along Crook Lane and down Horngate.

'I know,' said Josh. 'If we get chucked in teenage prison, then we miss school.'

I sneezed, rubbed my hands up and down my arms. I was thinking about a deep warm bath. I was also thinking about the nightmare not starting again, everything being fine.

'If they're all looking for the egg,' I said, 'if there's a full-on government agency searching for it with special secret machines and stuff, and they haven't found it, then . . .'

I hesitated, and Grace finished the sentence. 'Then maybe it's not there,' she said.

I nodded. 'It's not going to show up this year, is it?'

No one answered. I looked at them and saw in their faces that they were hoping, like I was hoping, that everything was going to be fine. The Anniversary would come and go and there'd be nothing extraordinary visiting Gilpin this year.

No one would have to die.

# DAY TWO

**3.16 a.m.**

*#Anniversary What if your dreams aren't dreams?*

I had a dream, but it wasn't a dream. Or it was more than a dream. It had the texture and depth of real life.

*Ruby came into Connor's room. He was sitting up in bed, awake, holding his stomach. The green numbers on the radio alarm said it was three in the morning. Ruby came into his bedroom and turned on his bedside light. He didn't ask her what she was doing there, he just whispered, 'I feel sick.'*

*She sat on his bed, thin and angular. She made very little impression on the mattress. Her eyes were red, like she'd been crying.*

*'Mum hates me,' she said.*

*Connor looked shocked. 'No, she doesn't.'*

*'I used to be her perfect little girl,' Ruby said. 'And now look at me.'*

*She was wearing a torn grey T-shirt with a smirking evil clown on it. Her long, straggly hair half covered her face and brushed her shoulders. She looked round Connor's room. There were a couple of weights in the corner. She sat up straight suddenly, like she'd been jolted by a small electric shock. She flexed her shoulders, looking a bit puzzled, then stood up and picked up the dumbbells.*

31

'They're too heavy,' Connor said. 'I never use them.'

Ruby tossed them both into the air and caught them, one in each hand.

She grinned at Connor. I could see his surprise. He wasn't used to that. Ruby grinning. That never happened. He was staring at her, properly awake now, and properly confused.

Ruby stared back at him. 'I know,' she said, looking a bit confused too, but still grinning, like she'd just opened the best present ever. 'Get me.'

She dropped one of the weights on to the floor. 'You know what this is?' she said.

Connor nodded slowly.

'We missed out last year,' she continued. 'Last year we were invisible. Not this time.'

He stared at her. She seemed to be unable to stop grinning.

'It's happening again, Connor, but this year it's all about us.'

I opened my eyes and gasped, not even sure where I was. Stared at the ceiling for a few seconds, moved my hands over the duvet. I half expected to be in Connor's bedroom with him and Ruby, but I wasn't, I was where I should be. I was in bed at home.

So what had just happened?

## 1.04 p.m.

#Anniversary **Nothing to report. Everything's OK. I'm completely relaxed, not tense at all.**

Sunday. It was about twelve hours since I'd fallen in the river. I'd dug out an old phone to replace the one that got wet, and it was working fine. I didn't have a cold, which was good, or

32

Weil's disease, which I'm not even going to describe because it's revolting. And there was still no sign of anything egg-related going on in Gilpin. So on the whole I was feeling OK.

There was that dream. That sort of 3D hi-res immersive film clip of Connor's bedroom that didn't feel like a dream, but must have been a dream, because what else could it have been if it wasn't a dream? I'd decided to forget about it. Shove it into a dark corner of my brain, slam the door on it. God knows I'd been tense enough, wound up enough. It was just some weird anxiety thing, best ignored.

'Hector! Lunch!'

And talking of ignoring things, that was Mum. She didn't actually mean lunch was ready, she meant come down and lay the table.

'Coming!'

I didn't move. Brown corduroy chair by the window, tea in a Cyberman mug on the radiator, feet on a pile of clothes in front of me, laptop on my lap. I was reassessing. I'd realised I needed to think a bit about the way I lived my life.

I was thinking if I was going to be a war correspondent I'd probably have to leave my bedroom.

I had this blog, *The Secret Diary of H*, and this Twitter account, and I was on Instagram, Snapchat and WhatsApp, and for a while I'd had crazy numbers of followers, and I still had quite a few, because Gilpin was the place where, for a short time, science fiction became fact. I wrote constantly, you could probably say obsessively in fact, about what happened last year. At first I interviewed my mates, and also my acquaintances, basically anyone I knew, about what had happened to them. Posted those reports, plus photos, personal testimonies, stuff like that. When I got slightly more hermit-like I went extensively into the four hundred-year-old history of what happened the first time. And I gave constant updates about what was going on from week to week in Gilpin. One time, when there was a flu bug and half the school got ill, I thought it was all starting again and yes, I admit, I overreacted. I wouldn't use the word 'hysterical' but it was definitely in that ballpark.

Maybe I would use the word 'hysterical'.

The thing is, rightly or wrongly, I always felt sure the egg was coming back. So I felt like it was my job to be vigilant, to log everything, to make a record.

And now, all of a sudden, I was thinking I could just drop it all. Just walk away and basically get out more.

It was tempting. What was the point in going on about eggs and aliens, now it seemed like there was a good chance – a fairly good chance – that they weren't coming back?

'Hector!'

That was my dad, with impatience vibrating in his voice. Time to go downstairs.

I clicked on a new tab, and checked out the latest post on a blog called *Gilpin Ha Ha Ha*. This blog, all on its own, was a very good reason for giving up going online.

There's a lot of material about Gilpin on the net, a big festering pile of it, but one of the main people who posts stuff is this guy, Dr Lazarus. If you imagine everyone who hates Gilpin as a gang, then he's the gang leader, the

Troll-in-Chief, the one they all suck up to and copy and try to be mates with. He has an avatar of Alan Rickman in *Galaxy Quest* looking disgusted. That's his thing – disgust. He's not just amused that me and people like me say an alien came to town, and he's not just sneering either. He's properly disgusted. He's all over the place on social media and commenting on articles below the line, but his main thing is this blog *Gilpin Ha Ha Ha* in which he basically rips the piss out of Gilpin non-stop.

I'm one of the main voices in Gilpin saying it's all true, it all really happened, so he's had a go at me personally lots of times. He's never threatened violence, like some of them do, but he's pretty effective. You try to take him on, and he steamrollers over you. You try to ignore him, and he mocks you. It gets tiring.

I shut my laptop, went downstairs.


Lasagne. I'm not a big fan, bit sloppy for me, plus Dad had followed Mum's recipe so it had chunky bits of red pepper in it. What was pepper even doing there? And even though he'd followed her recipe it was lacking something, it was lacking the sort of rich, herby flavour she gives a meat sauce.

'Mmm,' I said. 'Great. Thanks, Dad.'

Got to encourage him. He was sitting there looking a bit tired, with his hair going grey at the sides, grey stubble too, and the skin of his face a bit, sort of, slack. He's the kind of dad who usually has a bad mood simmering away just beneath the surface. I think he probably hates his job, and that feels to me like a big fat warning, like he has the word

*Cardboard* tattooed on his forehead. I love him, obviously, but I don't want to turn into him.

He took a big swig of red wine and nodded an acknowledgement at me because he likes gratitude, even if it's patronising. Then there was nothing but chewing for a while, and the scrape and tink of cutlery. Until Mum dropped some words into the quietness, all casual.

'Nice that your friends came round,' she said.

Mum likes to put her hands on my cheeks and look at me a bit sadly, like she's wishing I was still five years old. She's got a round, open, motherly sort of face, but it goes with eyes that seem to see right inside my head.

I didn't respond straightaway, I took a moment to analyse. Because conversations with my parents aren't really about the words, they're about what's underneath the words. It's a whole unspoken language that you become fluent in, if you're paying attention. When Mum said that about my friends, what she really meant was: *Nice that you left your room, nice that you actually saw daylight for once.*

I nodded.

'So.' Now Dad was joining in. 'The Anniversary. You've been worrying about it, haven't you?'

What he meant by that was: *But are you going to go back in your room now and not come out till school, and possibly not even then?*

Him and Mum both looking at me. We have a square kitchen table and since my brother left, one side of it is empty. There's no one else for my parents to look at, just me. I'm the point of their triangle. Sometimes I feel like I'm being interrogated.

I've barely mentioned my brother, have I? Jason. He was meant to be doing retakes last year and be at university this year, but none of that happened because first he got depressed and then, when it all kicked off, he stabbed himself in the shoulder with a rusty knife. Why? Because the egg that most of the world says never existed was turning him into a giant insect. I'm not even going to try to explain that. He went back to normal like everyone else but I wouldn't say he actually properly recovered. Any more than I did.

He's at my uncle Pete's now.

'We were thinking we could all go away,' Mum said.

But her tone was saying that it wasn't going to happen.

'School's starting next week,' I told her, as if she didn't know.

Dad nodded. 'And work's crazy at the moment.'

'And anyway,' Mum finished. 'All that. It's a year ago. It's over and done with.'

*All that.* That's how they referred to what happened. *All that.* They didn't know what had actually gone on and the truth is they didn't really want to know. They came back from holiday to find one son in hospital and both sons traumatised, and they just wanted *all that* behind them. They wanted, understandably, to move on.

I gave them a big, fake smile, one between them, which said, *I'm totally fine, what's for pudding?*

Mum stood up. 'I got some ice cream.' It's amazing what you can do without words. 'It's got a peanut-butter swirl,' she continued. 'I'm honestly surprised by how excited I am.'

And then, over the peanut-butter ice cream, things got worrying. Mum and Dad had finally stopped focusing on me, which was great, but now they were talking about their friends, the Walkers, parents of Ruby and Connor.

'I text him,' Dad said, 'then I wait half an hour drinking my pint, and finally I call him. Nothing. No answer. I'm sitting there, like Billy No-Mates. At some point he must have realised he was meant to be meeting me, so why didn't he get in touch?'

'I was trying to get hold of Anna,' Mum said. 'We had a loose arrangement to see a film. Same thing, no answer. They must've gone away.'

'But I saw Ruby and Connor yesterday,' I said.

'And the car's outside their house.' Dad gestured with a spoonful of ice cream, as if pointing at it. 'I don't think they're away. So what's going on?'

Ten minutes later, me, Josh, Asha and Grace were all pinging messages back and forth on WhatsApp, and all the messages were basically asking that same question: *What's going on?*

**Asha: They're on holiday. So what?**
**Me: Probably. But what if they're not?**
**Grace: What are you thinking, Hector?**
**Josh: He's thinking this all kicked off last year when Max's family disappeared.**
**Me: Right. And now the whole Walker family's disappeared.**

I didn't mention the dream that was more than a dream because I was still in denial, and anyway it was too big to squeeze into a message. But no one had seen Connor and Ruby since they'd turned up in the square yesterday. Had something terrible happened? Had they found the egg and now they were all hiding in their house because Connor had grown an extra head and Ruby was juggling dumbbells?

Grace finally got bored with us all avoiding the issue.

**Grace: We better go and knock on the door.**
**Asha: Knew you'd say that.**
**Hector: All of us?**
**Asha: No just you, idiot. Of course all of us.**
**Josh: Worth a try.**

I switched off my phone. I'd managed about twelve hours of feeling reassured, but now I had a twisty, sick feeling in my stomach because I was terrified that what Mum referred to as *all that* – changes, weirdness, soldiers on the streets, deaths – was all about to start again.

**3.00 p.m.**

#Anniversary **Turns out there's a feeling in the air, that there's a possibility, that perhaps everything might maybe not be OK after all.**

I walked past *Shake!*, thinking I might see Connor and Ruby inside. No luck. I looked around the square when I got there, hoping to see them outside *Love Bites* drinking lattes or hot

39

chocolates. They'd say their parents got called away because of a sick relative. Connor would be grinning, pleased to have the attention. He'd be like, 'What's the problem?' Ruby would sneer. I didn't know her at all, I was way too old to care about Year 8s, but when I saw her at school she was always alone, which is never a good sign.

They weren't in the square.

Josh was slouching towards me.

'How you doing?' I said.

Hands in pockets, eyes on the ground, he shrugged.

Josh was the only person I knew who'd enjoyed last year's events, had relished being kicked out of normality and made to live in a nightmarish version of ordinary life.

'Things all right at home?' I said.

This was a sort of code. It meant, *How's your mum?*

He sighed, shrugged.

I'd basically gathered that Josh's mum was trying to stay off the booze, and he was trying to help her. The feeling I got, from the outside, was that she maybe leant on him too much. But, given I'd been off in my own little world for a year, what did I know?

He kicked a stone across the square. Something had obviously happened to change his mood, and now he'd apparently decided that going to the Walkers' house was a waste of time. Nothing was going to happen. Life was going to stay beige and boring and actually hard work. I was all ready to try and talk him out of his bad mood, tell him that a) he might be wrong and b) I really hoped he wasn't, because beige and boring was fine with me, but then Grace showed up.

40

'You're all smiley,' she said to me, 'and you're not smiley at all,' she said to Josh. 'Maybe that's why you're a good double act.'

I stared at her. 'We're a double act?' I said.

Josh perked up a bit, like he always did when Grace was around, and then Asha was there, full of energy and mobile, like a boxer before a fight. She was up and down on her toes, she actually clapped her hands.

'All right, losers,' she said. 'Let's bounce.'

I told them about the dream that wasn't a dream on the way. 'It's probably nothing,' I said.

'Unless it's something,' said Josh, perking up a bit more.

My own mood was jagged too, like Josh's. I was getting increasingly nervous that it might all be starting to happen again, which could mean people dying, like Max died and Matt died. But I didn't say anything, kept quiet, squashed my feelings down. I was probably in full-on denial.

'File it under *Who Cares?* for now,' said Asha. 'Let's see if anyone's home.'

Ruby and Connor lived on Blakey Lane, a narrow, cobbled street with a massive hillside behind it like a lump of dropped dough. Sunlight had trouble finding its way around the hill, between the terraced houses, so it stayed cool here even when the rest of Gilpin was warm. And as we approached, the sun slid behind a cloud. Everything went grey.

We walked towards the house, hands in pockets. Josh was silent. Grace was quiet too, looking around cautiously, like there might be snipers behind the net curtains. Even Asha seemed a bit subdued by the dark street.

Josh looked up at the porridge-coloured sky. 'Did we take a wrong turning?' he said. 'Are we accidentally in Mordor?'

Wanting to change the mood, I told them about GREEN FINGERS, on the cover of the binder in Douglas's tent.

'What's that about?' I said.

'Aliens,' said Josh. 'Obviously. Aliens have green fingers, right?'

'There's a garden centre a couple of miles away,' Grace mused, 'called Green Fingers.'

Asha snorted. 'What, because Doofus wants courgettes for his allotment? No, it'll be a code name. Operation Green Fingers.'

Josh nodded, pleased. 'Nice.'

We were outside number 27. No one else was moving, so I walked up to the door and paused. My hand was actually hovering over the knocker, but it froze. I was about to find out if the Walkers were harbouring an alien egg. I was inviting them to open the door to a whole new world of confusion and pain.

So I hesitated.

There was a moment and then, as if he understood that we needed to take a minute, that none of us were quite ready, Josh spoke.

'You ever thought we should be in a band?' he said.

It was the kind of thing we might talk about over lunch at school, pushing pasta around the plate. Maybe Josh was nervous too, in spite of his jittery good mood, maybe he was stalling.

I lowered my hand. We stared at him.

'It just hit me. Look at us, we'd make a great indie band.

42

I'm the drummer. Asha, lead singer, because, obviously. Grace, keyboards? Or guitar?'

She smiled. 'I've got Grade Two piano.'

'Perfect. Hector on guitar, then. We'd be The Mutants.' Josh was getting into his idea.

Asha snorted. 'No way am I in any band called The Mutants. How about, I don't know, wait a minute ... The Winners?'

I sighed.

'Don't hassle me with your sighs,' she said. 'What? Too on the nose?'

Grace was still smiling. 'I think Hector wants us to focus.'

Asha looked at me like I was an idiot. It was a look she'd given me quite a lot in the last year. 'You're the one stood in front of the door, too scared to knock.' She reached past me impatiently, grabbed the knocker, and rapped on the door three times.

'And I'm not an indie kid,' she said. 'I'm a pop sensation.'

I didn't think it was even worth pointing out that she couldn't sing, as far as I knew, and I definitely couldn't play guitar, and Josh had never been near a drum-kit. I was busy listening. Nervously trying to hear if anyone was coming to the door, or moving anywhere in the house.

Nothing. Not a sound.

'Now what?' I was still nervous. My voice came out a bit high-pitched. I coughed, which probably only drew attention to it.

Grace was gazing up at the house, like she could see through the walls. (And if there was an egg in there, soon she might be able to see through the walls.)

'Round the back,' she said.

We went down a narrow snicket along the side of number 31, doubled back to number 27. We stood for a moment at a low wall looking at a yard and a kitchen window, then filed through the gate and knocked on the back door. Nothing.

'So,' I said. 'Where does this leave us?'

Josh's mood had dipped again. 'Nowhere,' he grunted.

And that's when the kitchen window shattered.

It didn't just break, it shattered outwards in a blizzard of glass shards and fragments. We all screamed or shouted or swore, staggering back, stumbling and falling, covering our faces.

I parted my fingers, which were over my eyes, and saw Ruby. She was in the space where the window used to be, leaning out. Her dyed black hair, which usually curtained and mostly hid her thin face, had been chopped back to chin length. And she wasn't sneering like she always did, she was grinning like she was in my dream that wasn't a dream. She was grinning like the sun was shining, which it wasn't, and it was the beginning of the summer holidays, which it wasn't, and everything in life was just peachy and perfect, which it definitely wasn't.

'Oops,' she said.

**3.21 p.m.**

#Anniversary **Here's the plan: stop it all before it even starts.**

'I know!'

Ruby almost sang the words. She was being way more expressive than usual, her thin, bare arms waving in front of her. Nails painted glossy black. Still grinning, like she was in on a joke we were all excluded from.

'Weird! The whole window just suddenly exploded. What's that about?'

We were at the kitchen table, although it felt like we were sitting outdoors because there was no glass in the window, apart from a few jagged triangles round the edge. We all had tiny little cuts on our hands and foreheads from when it had exploded in our faces.

Connor was quiet. Usually he was the chatty one, still a kid really, bouncy and full of himself. Not today. Today he was staring at his sister as if he didn't know her, and as if he couldn't quite understand the words coming out of her mouth. I think we were all staring at her the same way. There was something wrong. She was enjoying herself way too much.

'Are your parents around?' I said.

I was trying to stop my voice shaking and in fact I was trying to stop my whole body shaking. I'd been dreading this for an entire year, trying to tell myself that it wasn't going to happen again. But it was. It was happening.

Ruby's hair was cut unevenly, as if she'd done it herself with a few snips of the kitchen scissors. She was pale as always, with the thick black eyeliner and the mascara, and she was wearing a sleeveless black T-shirt with little white creepy-crawlies printed on it. She looked pretty intense, but she hadn't stopped smiling like today was the best day ever. It was disturbing.

'They've gone away for a bit,' she said, waving a vague hand off to one side. 'They have this whole big issue with me being me and they just couldn't take any more, so they're out of the picture.'

'Ruby,' said Grace, quiet and even. 'Are you OK?'

Ruby put her hands out in a big, theatrical, completely un-Rubyish gesture. 'Better than OK,' she said. 'Thanks for asking.'

'Because we could talk,' Grace continued. 'If you like.'

'What?' sneered Ruby. 'Two victims have a little support group? Hmm, let's see. Nah, don't think so.'

What did she mean by that? Grace wasn't a victim. Before I could say anything, Connor finally stopped staring at his sister and turned to us. 'D'you want juice or something? We've got no biscuits. But how come you're all here?'

A pause. None of us knew what to say. Connor was being nice, because that's who he is, he's a nice, friendly kid, but there was a little nervous edge in his voice.

'Yeah,' said Ruby. 'Good point, Con. Not about the juice and the biscuits, the other thing – what are you even doing here?'

The pause continued. I heard a drip of water from the tap in the sink, and then: 'We're starting a band,' Grace blurted. She looked at Connor. 'We want you to join.'

Asha made a surprised sound, which she tried to turn into a cough. I tried not to look startled. Josh nodded solemnly, like he'd totally been expecting her to come out with this. But we all knew why Grace had said what she'd said. There was something about Ruby, a thrum of hostility and violence in her voice, which was stopping us from just telling her why we were in her house.

'I've seen the future of rock music,' Josh said solemnly, wagging a finger so his bangles jangled. 'And it's us.'

'Except we're not rock,' Asha snapped.

'The Future,' said Grace quickly. 'That's our name. Want to sign up?'

Connor played trumpet in the school band, it was almost plausible, it was an inspired idea from Grace.

He looked puzzled. 'Didn't know you had a band.'

Josh was full-on grinning now, matching Ruby. 'You heard it here first, mate, we're The Future! We're going to practise at . . . at . . .'

He trailed off, looking a bit panicky.

'The Ruin,' I said. 'On the allotments.'

Connor stared at us for a minute, like he was having trouble taking this in, then he glanced at Ruby, looked back at us, and shook his head. 'No. No, thanks. Thanks anyway. Too much going on. Would have been great, though.'

Ruby's sunshiny, manic grin had faded to a smile that wasn't all that far from her usual sneer. It seemed to say she saw right through us. She was drumming an impatient tune on the table with her fingernails. Her hands turned into fists and she gently, rhythmically thumped the table, which rattled.

'Bye, then,' she chanted. 'Thanks for coming, bye.'

Usually, when anyone met Ruby's eye, she'd scowl and look away. You could guess she was shy and lonely and generally miserable, but it was all hidden behind a brittle, spiky exterior. Today was different. I looked at her and she stared straight back at me, eyes wide, challenging me to question her.

So I did.

'You're looking fit, Ruby,' I said. 'Been working out?'

Her smile changed all the way into a proper sneer. Her small, tight fists kept banging the tabletop. I started to feel nervous, like she might do something, like she might do anything.

She said three more words, banging the table between each one. 'Better.' *Bang*. 'Go.' *Bang*. 'Now.'

'OK,' I said hurriedly, 'we're going. Bye.'

We were all on our feet and Ruby was sort of ushering us out. Her bare arm brushed mine and it reminded me of something, that touch, that skin on skin. We left, we got the hell out of there, and when I walked out of the door I felt myself unwinding, untensing, as if I'd been holding my breath the whole time.

'Is anyone else a little bit freaked out?' I said.

No one answered. We headed for the park. Down Lee Road, across Arden Street, past *Shake!*, over the canal. I think we all wanted to put some distance between ourselves and Ruby.

We sat on the grass. Some kids were kicking a football around but they were too far away to overhear. Three of us sat,

Asha stayed on her feet. I leant back on my elbows, tense and scared and not sure why. Grace was cross-legged, Josh was on his back, looking at the grey sky. A few drops of rain fell.

'What the hell just happened?' I said.

Grace was nodding slowly. 'Ruby has a hard time at school. She gets bullied. I heard things aren't great at home either.' Her voice was calm, thoughtful. 'Don't think I've ever seen her smile before.'

There was a whole different conversation to have here, about victims, but now wasn't the time. 'Right,' I said, 'and I'll tell you who she reminded me of.' I pointed at Josh, who was lying on the ground like a dead man. My finger aimed straight for his chest. 'You. A year ago. Being so happy that you had the night sky splashed on your stomach because your life had suddenly got interesting. One day all miserable and angsty, next day – *boom* – someone's turned the lights on.'

They were all looking at me.

'I reckon the reason Ruby's smiling,' I said, 'is because she's changed.' I tallied off my points on my fingers. 'Their parents have disappeared, Connor looked scared, Ruby looked like she's won the lottery. I think they've got an egg, in their house, right now.'

Silence, while we all took that in. Sitting on the playing field with the big grey sky overhead, drops of rain spattering us, and the world changing around us. Again.

Asha finally answered. 'No.' She was shaking her head. 'No way,' she said, like it was down to her. 'Absolutely not. Don't even start, because I'm not having it, I'm not doing that again.'

Josh sat up. 'If you're right,' he said, 'what's going to happen to us this time? That dream you had, is that part of it?' Unlike Asha, he didn't sound worried. There was some tension in his voice, but there was a thread of excitement too.

I didn't speak. Too much going on, too much to try to understand. It was Grace, as usual, who got straight to the point.

'We went to their house because we thought the egg might be there,' she said. 'Then we got a pretty good idea that the egg was probably there. And then we ran away.'

No one said anything.

'That's not exactly nipping it in the bud,' she finished.

She was right, obviously. We were basically completely useless. But we had a good excuse – things were getting terrifying.

Silence again, like no words could really do justice to this situation. We'd been to the woods and looked for the egg and found nothing. We'd met Colonel Doofus, and he'd found nothing too. So we'd decided it absolutely wasn't going to happen again. And now it looked like we were wrong. It was difficult to adjust. I wanted to go home and pretend everything was fine and normal but I couldn't admit that's what I wanted, even if I suspected that Asha and Grace probably felt the same way. I was shaking again. I didn't want this. I wanted to go back to when they'd all invaded my room and push them out and somehow persuade my mum to drive me a very long way from Gilpin.

But it was too late for that.

I stood up, trying to sort of tense my whole body so I didn't shake. It made my voice a bit strained and throaty. 'You're right,' I told Grace. 'We have to go back, right now. We have to talk to Connor and Ruby, get them to hand over the egg before anyone else is affected. Damage limitation.'

Asha was shifting from foot to foot, restless. 'Yeah, all right. We go back and confront her. If she's got the egg we get it off her, we take pics to put online, we hand it over to the army. We finish this before it starts.'

I knew a few pictures weren't going to convince anyone of anything, but I kept my mouth shut. Asha stared at Josh, who was the only one still on the grass. She jerked both hands into the air, palms upwards, urgent suddenly, jittery.

'Let's boogie.'

**4.27 p.m.**

#Anniversary **The return of Professor Patronising! So we're all here. Now . . . where's the egg?**

We retraced our steps over the canal, past *Shake!*, across Arden Street and up Lee Road. We pushed rudely past a cluster of women outside the greengrocer's, sidestepped a bloke with a pushchair – in a hurry, just wanting to get there, wanting to get there, and at the same time not actually wanting to get there at all.

At the end of Blakey Lane we stopped. We didn't have any choice because an army jeep was parked across the road and two soldiers in black were barring our way.

One of the soldiers stopped stretching yellow tape across the road and looked over us like we were something unpleasant.

'You live here?' he grunted.

'We're seeing a mate,' I said, at exactly the same time as Asha said, 'What's it to you?' and Josh said, 'Yes.'

He nodded, like this made it perfectly clear. 'Get lost,' he snapped.

At that moment, behind him, Ruby and Connor's parents were ushered out of their house, towards another jeep. They were a mess. They were dishevelled, they seemed confused, and was that a bruise on Mr Walker's face? Mrs Walker looked up and down the road, as if she wasn't sure where she was. She spotted us watching her, and she pulled away from the soldier with her and started towards us. She did something for the council and she usually wore grey suits and smart shirts, but today her hair was scraggy and her pale blue shirt, which might have been smart once, was torn. I could see a bit of her bra and I was embarrassed for her. She looked like she'd been in a fight.

She stared straight at us, pointed a wavering hand towards us. 'Where are my children?' she wailed.

I'd never heard an adult use a voice like that before. It was vibrating with barely controlled hysteria, not far off a scream. The soldier with her got his hands on her shoulders, physically turned her away from us, moved her towards the jeep.

There was a humming behind us. We turned to find a black car pulling up. No engine noise, just that hum. Dark windows. The door opened and we waited. What now? I expected Douglas but it wasn't him, it was Professor Kirby. Red bun, narrow glasses, tight lips.

She stood by the car and looked over us, taking her time. Her eyes finally rested on me.

'Hector,' she said. 'Turning up like a bad penny.'

Professor Kirby and Colonel Douglas had been a double act last year. Whereas Douglas, the soldier, was obsessed with national security, Professor Kirby, the xenobiologist, was ruthlessly ambitious. It didn't make a lot of difference – both of them were happy to sacrifice teenagers for what they considered the greater good.

Last year, Kirby had had an unreliable smile that vanished when I refused to cooperate with her. She'd patronised us, lied to us and put our lives in danger. Still, she hadn't entirely got away with it – I'd called her Professor Patronising on Twitter.

No smile this year. Her tight lips were a thin, straight line. She came right up to the yellow tape, glanced at the others, then looked at me again. 'Now.' She made a tutting sound, like she was impatient before we'd even started talking. 'Tell me everything.'

I was rubbing my scarred finger anxiously, remembering what Doofus had told us in the woods. They'd been reading my blog. I guessed they'd also been monitoring our phones. 'We led you here, didn't we?' I said.

Her lips twitched towards a frown. 'Of course. We read your messages, and we came straight here. We're not entirely naïve, Hector, we know how deeply involved you all were last year. Ever since then we've been monitoring you, mapping social media, neutralising threats, controlling the narrative by using, shall we say, alternative facts.'

I shook my head slowly. Yesterday I'd wondered if the government was spying on my computer and I'd decided that was stupid and paranoid. Turned out it might be both of those things, but it was also true.

'If you get the egg,' I said, 'what are you going to do with it?'

I'd done some research last year. I'd discovered that when the egg had been found four hundred years ago it was damaged, and all the teenagers affected by it had died. It turned out the government were already aware of this, and they didn't really care. Examining the egg was priority number one. Anything else was basically not important.

'We've developed technology that may be useful.' Kirby looked pleased with herself, like she expected us to congratulate her.

'Green guns and a machine that goes *Boom!*' Josh muttered, excited.

'It's difficult to draw any firm conclusions given the limited facts that we have,' she continued, ignoring Josh, 'but one hypothesis is that we're being auditioned as a nursery for the aliens' young. Clearly we need to discourage that notion, or else next year, or sooner than that, there may be millions of eggs all over the planet. We refer to that scenario as a soft invasion.'

Her tone was calm and even, mine wasn't. I was thinking of the phrase I'd used earlier. Damage limitation. 'So if you want to "discourage" them,' I said, 'you'll destroy the egg, right? And you'll be like, *Oops they killed Ruby and Connor. Never mind.* You'll just cover it up and carry on.'

Kirby squashed her lips. I realised she was attempting to look sad. 'We'll do our best to save lives,' she said, 'but the stakes are high. These decisions are made at very senior levels.'

I had a vision of presidents, prime ministers and intelligence agencies having secret meetings, making decisions that would affect us all.

'What about Green Fingers,' I said. 'What's that about?'

She definitely looked surprised. The trouble was, I couldn't tell if she was surprised that I knew something, or she was surprised that I was talking gibberish. 'I've said enough,' she snapped. 'You fail to understand how little a bunch of obnoxious, self-obsessed teenagers matter in these circumstances. Why did you come here?'

Grace answered. 'We heard the Walkers had disappeared. We wanted to see if they were all right.'

She nodded as if she'd expected this. 'They were not all right. Mr and Mrs Walker were in their bedroom upstairs. They weren't locked in but they were told not to leave.'

Josh asked the question, even though we all knew the answer already: 'Who told them?'

Professor Kirby's eyes flicked to him, then back to me. 'Their daughter. We believe both Ruby and Connor have been affected by an egg.'

One of the things you notice about Grace is the intentness

of her gaze. She was looking steadily at Professor Kirby. 'And the twins have disappeared, with the egg?'

Kirby turned to Grace. Her steely eyes met Grace's intent gaze. 'Yes,' she said. 'And if we don't find them very quickly, Gilpin will be shut down. So now we're left with the same question that poor Mrs Walker asked: where are Ruby and Connor?'

# DAY THREE

#Anniversary **So Professor Patronising says they plan to destroy the egg. And if teens die? Tough.**

It was hard to sleep that night, knowing that unless Ruby and Connor had managed to leave town, the egg was out there, pulsing with the radiation that poisoned teenagers. I seemed to feel it creeping over my skin like cold, damp fingers; I seemed to feel it creeping under my skin like some slithering parasitical creature that intended to feast on me, eat me from the inside out.

Ruby couldn't be trusted. Ruby was obviously loving it. She apparently didn't care that the egg didn't just change your body. It also, sometimes, messed with your mind. And it also, sometimes, killed you.

I punched my pillow and yanked my duvet and rolled this way and that on my rumpled sheet, imagining the radiation coming through my window, tangling itself up with my brain and my blood, my metabolic pathway, whatever the hell that was. We thought it interacted somehow with personality. It had found Ruby's resentment, unhappiness and anger, and it had moulded them into something dangerous. So if it latched on to aspects of our characters, what was it going to do to the rest of us? Once it had finished delving inside my head, what was it going to do to me this time?

I thought Old Hector might come back, knocking at the door, all-knowing and even more patronising than Professor Patronising, and basically completely useless. Or maybe I'd get something different this year, something fatal, like Matt who coughed fire till his blood boiled, or Max who faded away completely, like wisps of smoke disappearing into the air. Max and I used to have a game where we tried to make each other laugh. He always won. Straight-faced, he'd just say teachers' names, like a register, only with odd little additions and changes. I'd last about five seconds, my mouth all scrunched up, trying to think about sad things, and then the laughter would splutter out. I'd be crying sometimes.

This is what happened whenever I thought about Max. I got distracted. Ended up circling around memories, regrets and useless speculations.

How scared must he have been in that week it took him to die? How lonely?

Might be different this year. This year I might die. Maybe Josh would be remembering me when the next anniversary came round, wondering if he could have done anything to save me. That so-called dream I'd had, the vision, of Ruby with the dumbbells, that had to be something the egg was doing to me. It felt like I was standing in front of Grace's mum, Dr Thompson, waiting for a diagnosis. She'd look serious, she'd sigh and shake her head.

*Hector, I'm sorry to have to tell you this . . .*

The pillow was too hard and the mattress was lumpy and I twisted on to one side and then the other. I was too hot (perhaps my blood was boiling), and it seemed pretty certain I was never going to get to sleep (perhaps the egg was going to give me terminal insomnia).

And then I was somewhere else. I must have been sleeping, because I was dreaming. Except it didn't feel like a dream. Flashes jumped into my head like a badly edited film, different images in proper immersive 3D.

*Ruby was sitting up in bed. Grey, evil-clown T-shirt, long hair around her shoulders. She looked puzzled, she felt her face, felt her arms and hands.*

*Ruby was in Connor's bedroom. 'This year,' she said, 'it's all about us.'*

*Ruby was slamming a door so hard that it shook. She had tears in her eyes, but she battered her fists on the door and wood splintered. 'You come out of there,' she screamed, 'and I'll kill you!'*

I tried to doze for a while after that, but I couldn't because the dreams/not dreams were way too disturbing. This was definitely the egg. Somehow I was seeing what Ruby had been doing. The changes were beginning, I was sure of it.

I sat up in bed eventually, checked Twitter on my phone. Dr Lazarus had replied to my Professor Patronising tweet.

**So over this now. Just for God's sake shut up about it. If you're scared, leave town.**

It had been two days since I'd blogged about the Anniversary. I'd been busy since then, and right off the whole idea of social media, but it was time to have a look at the comments. I sat at my desk in my boxers, cleared the socks and the old cups of tea away, fired up the laptop.

All the usual stuff. Some people told me about the aliens they'd met, some people sounded sorry for me, most people seemed to be competing to come up with the nastiest, most inventive, most threatening insults. I skimmed over all of them, wanting to know what Dr Lazarus had to say about my blog.

I found him. He was unusually restrained. *Give it up*, he said. *It's been a year. Let it go, dude. No one cares. Seriously — walk away.*

I clicked over to his own blog, *Gilpin Ha Ha Ha*. Same thing. *Gilpin*, he said, *we've had enough. You carry on if you must, but here in the real world, the world of grown-ups with grown-up issues — we don't care any more. To anyone there still fretting, here's a thought — get out of Gilpin.*

It was like he'd run out of disgust. Now he was just weary. But he was wrong about everything, as ever. I pushed the chair away from my desk and picked up my phone. Stared at it. Pulled on my dressing-gown, went into Jason's room and rummaged around in the drawer of his bedside table. I found an old family photo — all four of us in front of some Welsh castle. I found a birthday card I'd hand-drawn for him when I was twelve. Snoopy on his kennel saying Happy Birthday!

It gave me a little sweet-sad pang to know that he'd kept it, even though he'd probably forgotten that it existed. I found two condoms, four loose cigarettes, an old bus pass, various coiling wires and finally what I was searching for. An old phone.

I picked it up, along with its charger. Doofus and Patronising weren't monitoring this phone.

Downstairs, Mum came in as I was pouring milk on my Maple Crunch. 'Have some fruit,' she said, like she always did. I kept my head down over my bowl. Just an ordinary morning. Dad was already at work, Mum would be going soon.

She didn't go. She sat down. That was a bad sign. She put a finger under my chin and raised my head so that I was looking at her.

'What's up, Hector?'

'Nothing,' I said. 'Didn't sleep so well.'

She gave me that Mum look, right inside my skull.

'Try again,' she said.

I took a slow breath, looking at her concerned face looking into mine. Hesitated, then whispered, as if these were words that shouldn't be said out loud:

'What if it's happening again?'

She took a slow breath too. 'I've never known what to think about last year,' she said finally. Her tone was slow and careful, like even now she was thinking about it, trying to work it out. 'What's worse? You and Jason and half the town having some sort of breakdown or ... or government conspiracies and aliens and things I can't even comprehend?'

I didn't answer. If she wanted to shove me in the car and take me to stay at Uncle Pete's with Jason, then so be it. I'd be far away, and whatever was going to happen could happen without me. I waited. A long second went by. Two. Three. The future out of my hands.

And then: 'We'll talk about it tonight,' she said. 'With Dad. Maybe all three of us will get away for a while, maybe just you and me. Is that OK? Can you wait that long?'

I nodded, not sure I trusted my voice.

'And in the meantime – I can't believe I'm saying this – just stay indoors. Stay out of the way of . . . everything. OK?'

'OK.'

She stood up, held my face in both hands and kissed my forehead like I was eight years old and had fallen over. Then she left for work and I put my dish in the sink, cleaned my teeth and had a look at myself in the mirror, as if I expected to see something different today. Short brown hair, pale skin from too much time spent in my bedroom, worried brown eyes, bitten lips. I don't know if I even like my face. I pushed my cheeks around, wondering what Asha saw when she looked at me. There's nothing much wrong with my nose. I flared my nostrils, trying to look dramatic. Bad idea.

I took off my dressing-gown and put on a T-shirt with a robot on it, hoping it would magically lift my mood. I checked myself out again, wondered if I should start dressing a bit older, and then, about ten minutes after Mum told me to stay indoors and I agreed that I would, I left the house. It was almost as if I wanted terrible things to happen, almost as if I was opening my arms and saying, 'Bring it on.'

We met in the park again. We sat in a circle on the football field and I tugged at white-painted blades of grass. Josh was bouncing a little, restless, Grace was sketching something. It was a picture of a girl in our year. Eden James. Bit random. Asha looked annoyed, like there was somewhere cooler she'd rather be, which was probably true.

'They're most likely watching us,' I whispered.

Josh looked up and jabbed a finger in the air. 'Look, it's a drone! No, wait. Blackbird.'

I sighed. 'I'm serious. You heard what Kirby said.'

'Let 'em watch,' said Asha. 'Perverts.'

No one spoke. A cool breeze slipped between us. There was an odd, prickly tension between the four of us, like we all had secrets to reveal.

I started. 'I had another dream last night.' I looked round my friends' faces. 'Except it didn't feel anything like a dream.'

They looked back at me. Asha snorted. 'We supposed to be impressed? What did it feel like?'

'It was like I was there,' I said. 'In Ruby and Connor's house, with them, while stuff was actually going on in front of me.' I described the three images that had flashed into my head: Ruby sitting up in bed; Ruby in Connor's bedroom; Ruby slamming the door on (presumably) her parents.

'She touched my hand, the other day in the square, when she was after my coffee. And then again yesterday when she was getting us out of the house. I think that must be relevant.' They were looking at me blankly. 'Don't you get it?' I said. 'She touched me, and then I saw stuff that really happened to her. I think that's my thing this time.'

Grace put away her sketch pad. She was looking puzzled. 'But you saw stuff that's already happened.'

I nodded.

Asha snorted. 'You're saying your power is that you can see into the past? Not the future, the past? Are you serious?'

I shrugged. 'I didn't choose it.'

Josh sighed. 'Speaking of,' he said. He took a small box out of his pocket. It was an oily, intense black, with a silver ripple running through it.

'Jesus!' I was on my feet, backing away. Asha and Grace were both scrambling back too.

'Is that it?' Grace's voice was squeaky and scared. 'Is that the egg?'

Josh tossed it from one hand to another. 'Ever seen a square egg?' he said.

I sat down again, still keeping a bit of distance between me and the box. 'All right,' I said. 'Then what is it?'

'I'll tell you,' said Josh. 'I'll tell you what it is. It's everything bad I've ever felt or thought, all squashed together and squeezed into this box. It was there on my bed when I woke up this morning, like the worst Christmas stocking in the world, ever.'

We all stared at him. 'Don't ask me how I know,' he said. 'I just know.'

'Well,' I said, 'that's new.'

'Wait,' said Asha, 'does that mean you're like all skippy, good feelings inside, because everything bad is stashed away in there? Cos that would be nice.'

'Yeah,' said Josh. 'No. Everything's normal in here.' He

tapped his head. 'It's just everything bad is super-concentrated in here.' He tapped the box. 'So,' he sighed and waved a finger between Asha and Grace. 'You two?'

'Nothing,' said Asha. 'Nothing yet. Nothing that I've noticed.'

Josh did a disappointed pout. 'With no power comes no responsibility,' he said. 'So there's that.'

And then we were all looking at Grace. She sighed, put her fingers up into her blue fringe and pushed it off her forehead. There was a lump there, right in the middle. It was the shape and roughly the size of an almond lying on its side.

Asha made an impressed noise. 'Is it going to be a horn?' she said.

Josh laughed, delighted. 'You're turning into a unicorn! One for the kiddies. Reckon you'll be able to fart rainbows?'

Grace didn't answer, just let her fringe flop back over her forehead. No one said anything for a minute. That cool breeze still snaking around us, that prickly tension still in the air. Then Asha sighed.

'So, summing up.' She jabbed her index finger at me. She was wearing gold nail polish. 'You can see the past. Not the future, the past which, as I've already said, is rubbish.' She nodded at Josh. 'You're carrying a little box of sadness around with you. Nice.' Another nod, at Grace. 'You're a unicorn. That's brilliant, just brilliant. Why can't one of you fly, or run at super-speed? Is that too much to ask? Worst. Powers. Ever.'

Josh shrugged. 'Least none of these feel like they're going to be fatal,' he said.

'Oh yeah,' I snapped. 'Tell that to Matt and Max. Just cos things are OK at first doesn't mean they'll stay that way.' I looked at Asha. 'But you're not even affected this time, so I guess that's a plus.'

Asha glared at me. 'Hector,' she sighed, 'you are as stupid as that tree. Something's going to happen to me cos something happens to everyone. Last year I start off with a nice healthy glow and I finish up like a walking bomb. What's it going to be this time?'

I started to say something, but she raised her hand. 'Not looking for an answer, you spoon.'

'Also,' said Josh, looking at the box, turning it over, 'I've got a bit of an urge to open this, to be honest. But at the same time, I think it would be a very bad idea.'

Grace squeezed his hand, and he put the box in his pocket. 'What do we do then?' she said. 'Wait for Colonel Douglas to round us up?'

I was rolling three blades of grass in my hand. I looked down at them as I spoke. 'My mum said she'd take me away. Maybe we should all do that – we should just leave while we still can.'

Grace looked at me. 'Too late,' she said. 'We're all affected.' She looked at Asha. 'Except possibly you. And that means if they destroy the egg, we die.'

Josh seemed to be ignoring us. He was still playing with his little black box, turning it over, examining it, squeezing it, smelling it. 'Maybe if I point it at someone,' he said, 'a big black fist will come out and hit them. D'you think?'

I sighed. 'Not helping, Josh.'

He shrugged. 'Teenage Mutant Detectives aren't working out so well this year.'

Another silence. Teenage Mutant Detectives. That's what we'd called ourselves last year, when we had a mystery to solve. There was no mystery this year – we knew exactly what was happening. The only problem was we had no idea what to do about it. I felt completely powerless. And fear was bubbling away inside me like I was a kettle about to boil.

Asha, Grace and Josh's phones buzzed. It was a WhatsApp message, sent out by Suzie May to basically everyone she knew.

**Anything strange or weird or just wrong happened? Meet in the square, 11 a.m.**

She'd remembered the wording I'd used a year ago, when I was gathering teenagers in the park. It was confirmation if we needed it – the egg was changing every teenager in Gilpin. We were the people best equipped to stop it, and we'd completely failed to stop it.

This was too big and too sudden to cope with. The town should probably have been evacuated before any of this started, but the government couldn't do that because they were still pretending nothing had actually happened last year. And maybe in fact they secretly wanted another egg to arrive, so they could first examine it, and then destroy it, to send a message to our alien visitors.

So here we were, back in the middle of it, trying to work out how to deal with a situation that was skidding way out of control. Mum and Dad were at work, expecting me to be there when they got back, expecting to take me away. Jason was already at Uncle Pete's, refusing to be anywhere near Gilpin around the Anniversary, even though he was too old to be affected. The army was out searching for Ruby and Connor, and the egg. And I was twisting blades of grass in my fingers, thinking about not going home, thinking about getting into trouble, just like last year.

'There's nothing we can do this time,' Asha said. 'Option One, we leave Gilpin and Kirby sooner or later finds the egg; Option Two, we stay in Gilpin, get put in a camp, which is basically a prison, and Kirby still gets the egg.'

Grace had that intent look again. On her forehead, behind strands of hair, something moved inside that almond-shaped lump. I didn't think it was going to be a horn.

'Option Three, we find Connor and Ruby,' she whispered.

I nodded slowly. 'We find them,' I agreed, 'we get the egg off them, we get it the hell out of Gilpin. We dump it in the middle of nowhere, then maybe no one's condition will get any worse, and no one else will get infected.'

Now Asha was smiling, like someone had finally said something worth hearing. 'OK,' she said, 'that could work. Maybe I'll take a sweet little selfie with the egg in my hand to prove it's the real deal, and then we'll leave it to hatch halfway up a mountain or something. The alien shows up, the alien goes home, and everyone goes back to normal. Job done.'

'Until it comes back next year,' Grace muttered.

'That's long-term,' I sighed. 'All we can deal with is getting rid of it now, and stopping everyone from dying.'

Josh was biting a thumbnail, although it looked like there wasn't much left to bite. 'Yeah,' he said, 'that all sounds fine except it doesn't, cos I can't go on a little outing halfway up a mountain with you. It's a bad time to leave my mum on her own.'

'We can do this without you,' I said. 'But we're a team, aren't we?'

Grace put a hand on his hand, moved it gently away from his mouth. 'It won't be for long,' she said. If I'd tried to reassure him I'd probably have come across as insensitive or just stupid. When Grace did it, she somehow got the tone right. 'We'll get rid of the egg, we'll come straight back.'

He sighed, and their eyes met for a slowed-down moment.

'All right.' He nodded finally. 'All right, then. Surgical strike. Get out of Gilpin, dump the egg somewhere it can't do any harm, come back.'

He shoved the black box into his pocket. 'I know where we get transport.' And now a slow smile was forming on his face. 'It's gonna be a road movie. Sweet.'

**10.46 a.m.**

#Anniversary **To our parents, who didn't ask for this any more than we did – sorry. Really really sorry.**

I went home and wrote a note. Or tried to write a note. I picked the post up off the floor, found a bit of junk mail, got a biro, then stared at the back of the envelope. Checked my

69

phone after a couple of minutes, realised I was running out of time. I had to write something or I'd end up writing nothing.

Hi Mum and Dad,

Sorry. You know you said about 'All That' being behind us, Mum? It's not. It's here and now. Again. And it's not a hoax, it's nothing to do with anyone having a breakdown, it really is about aliens and government conspiracies. So the point is, I'm going to be gone for a few days and I won't be able to contact you. Colonel Douglas and Professor Kirby might come round. You can tell them whatever you like because you don't actually know anything.

See you soon, I hope.

Love,

Hector xx

I left the note on the kitchen table, ran upstairs, packed pants, socks, a spare T-shirt, toothpaste and toothbrush into a small rucksack, pulled on a sweater. I was about to run back downstairs but I paused on the landing. Went into Jason's room. Don't know why. No one there, obviously. There'd been no one there for a year. We'd visited him in hospital, and at Uncle Pete's, but he hadn't wanted to come back to Gilpin. Understandably. Most of us had had friends and family to help us through the experience. He'd been on his own, sunk in anger and depression while his body went through horrifying changes. 'Everyone has their own way of coping,' Grace had said. Jason's way was to leave town, to put it all behind him. I stood in his empty room looking at a stripped bed and bare shelves, smelling a neutral, dusty smell, which was the smell of absence. My brother. I wondered what he was doing right now, what he was thinking. I swallowed, worrying about him, worrying about my parents too. They'd feel like they were losing another son.

Then I ran back down the stairs and out of the house, moving fast and not thinking, not giving myself a chance to change my mind.

I was planning to run all the way, because lingering in Jason's room had made me late, but when I got to the square I had to stop. I'd forgotten about Suzie's message. The square was full of teenagers.

Zahra Khan was sitting next to Sam Carver on a bench. Zahra's clothes were wet, there was a puddle of water around her feet, and water appeared to be dripping from her fingertips. Sam was holding his hands up in front of his face, watching bright sparks arc back and forth between his palms. There was Suzie herself, checking her phone, and looking pale, like the colour was leaching out of her. Livvy Read was talking to Freddie Butcher. She looked sort of weary and old, the skin of her face was drawn, and actually wrinkled, which might just have been anxiety, or might have been something else. Freddie waved at me, and I saw fierce little claws curling out from his knuckles.

'Hey, Hector!' he said.

I didn't stop. I waved back, but I kept going. I was thinking of what Doofus had said.

*We stand ready to shut down this town. We immediately evacuate twelve-to twenty-year-olds to a safe location.*

We didn't have much time.

Beyond Blakey Lane, Gilpin starts fading into countryside. You go down a wide, dusty road with new redbrick houses on one side and an abandoned mill on the other, over an old stone bridge, and from there it's mostly green. I met Asha and Grace by the bridge, told them about the teenagers in the square.

'Think we can rely on Josh?' said Asha.

There was a bit of a worrying silence after that.

'Let's hope so,' I said.

'So we think Ruby's strong.' Grace had clearly decided to change the subject. 'And we know she's not friendly. Supposing we actually find them, how are we going to deal with her?'

I shrugged, spoke without thinking. 'We dealt with Naveen,' I said. Then looked at Asha quickly, embarrassed. 'Sorry.'

There was an awkward moment, before Grace broke the silence. 'How is—' she began.

'He's down south, with my dad.' Asha interrupted abruptly, like we were having an argument. 'Haven't seen him for a year, and that's fine with me.'

A year ago the egg had changed Asha's brother into a horned psychopath. If the egg amplified what was already inside you, then it had found some pretty nasty stuff inside Naveen. He'd hit Asha, and he'd tried to kill me. None of us wanted to talk about him.

We kept walking, no one speaking now. Me in my thin red sweater, Grace in her green denim, Asha in a black V-necked top, like a commando, all of us carrying small backpacks. We were heading for the allotments. I'd mentioned the Ruin when we were at Connor and Ruby's house, it was quiet and secluded, we thought it was a decent place to start looking for them. Once over the bridge we turned right and walked along the river, past the field where they do archery. It was the same river that would lead eventually to Max's house.

'Wonder what's happened to Connor,' I said, because I wanted to end the silence.

'Maybe this year, maybe the egg's not affecting everyone. Maybe nothing will happen to him or ...' Grace looked at Asha. Her last words came out like a question. 'Or to you?'

'Bollocks,' Asha snapped, and her anger didn't hide her nerves. 'Something's going to happen.'

So we stopped speaking again. The path was too narrow for us to walk together. Me and Grace were walking side by side behind Asha. I was looking at the curve of Asha's neck, glossy black hair bouncing a little with each step, her shoulder blades moving under her top. I wouldn't usually stare but she was right in front of me and she couldn't see me staring so I thought it was all right. I wanted to hold her hand, like we'd briefly held hands in the woods. I wanted to run my fingertip along the curve of her neck.

I felt Grace's eyes on me. She was watching me staring at Asha. She made a little tch sound, and looked away. I'd got a bit confused last year about my feelings: being around Asha and Grace, liking them both, being unaware that Josh liked Grace, finding out that Grace once liked me, not knowing if she still did. It was a whole big thing, and when Asha called me all kinds of stupid it was definitely one of the kinds she was thinking of.

Now I just felt like I wanted to get to know Grace better. And I was wondering about the way she'd looked at Josh, when she'd reassured him that we wouldn't be gone for long.

'So,' I said. 'You and Josh. Are you actually . . .'

I trailed off, because of the way she was staring at me.

She rolled her eyes. 'Unbelievable,' she said, and she sped up and walked beside Asha.

OK, I was totally missing something there. I filed it in my head along with Ruby's use of the word 'victim'. I'd not really communicated much with anyone for a year, and I obviously had some catching up to do.

So here we were, three of us, anyway, by the river, on an egg-hunt again, Teenage Mutant Detectives again, and not speaking to each other. We'd all been a bit scratchy and uncomfortable with each other ever since they'd forced me to leave my bedroom. Partly because we were still getting used to the idea that this creepy and bizarre situation was settling over our town again, like a toxic cloud. Partly because, I don't know, feelings.

The river I'd fallen into the day before shrugged and tumbled past us on our right. On our left were four pockmarked targets, tilted like easels, waiting for the archers.

We followed a bend around the archery field as a crag

rose up beside us, and then the bank bulged out into a scrubby patch of land. The allotments might have been allotments once, but they weren't any more. It was a small, wild area covered in brambles and nettles with here and there surprising clumps of gooseberry bushes, redcurrants and rhubarb. If you looked closely you could see bricks under the green chaos which had once shown the boundary between different plots.

And squatting near the back, up against the crag, was the Ruin. It was a small house with half a roof and no windows, and a wall that looked like someone had taken a bite out of it.

'If I was in a band,' Asha said, 'I'd never in a million years rehearse here.'

'But maybe you'd hide here?' I said.

We pushed open the old gate and waded through undergrowth. A nettle stung my left arm and a bramble scratched a red line down my right. There was a musty, dead flower smell. Insects buzzed. Kids went to the Ruin to drink and smoke and possibly have sex and smoke spliffs, but it didn't look like any of that had happened recently. It had been a place to hang out for a while, but people had found somewhere else. I didn't even know where because I wasn't old enough, or cool enough, or both. There were charred sticks outside, two disposable barbecues, fag ends and beer cans, but they all looked ancient, like the last remains of some lost tribe.

There was still a door, which had been green once, and it was ajar. Darkness behind it. We stopped. Grace and Asha were both looking at me, which obviously seemed completely unfair. Girl power, anyone? Equality of the sexes?

Asha raised her eyebrows.

'Hello?' I shouted. 'Anyone there?'

No answer.

'All right, all right, OK,' I said, as if they'd been nagging me.

Without actually pushing the door open at all, I put my head inside, into the darkness. I was half expecting Ruby's fist to connect with my face. How strong was she? I'd seen her tossing dumbbells around, but that didn't tell me much. Was she as strong as a big bloke, or was she like the Hulk? If she hit me would I fly back and land in the river, unconscious, and drown?

My eyes adjusted to the half-dark. I took a step inside. No one here. Tin cans everywhere, a plastic bag and a mouldy rug shoved under the window, something slimy I didn't want to look at too closely against the back wall, something small and dark scurrying into a corner. Nothing.

I turned my head back towards the door. 'Don't think there's anyone here,' I said.

And then there was a loud, sudden noise, a harsh cry, and a black shape sprang into the air in front of me. Something sharp scraped across my head as I ducked and screamed, panicking.

*Oh my God, can she fly? Can Ruby fly?*

I cowered, almost on my knees, holding my head, then rose slowly, hands still on my scalp, still half crouching, trying to see what was happening before I made myself too tall, too vulnerable.

Asha was laughing. 'Whoa, Fish Boy, that was almost as good as falling in the river.'

Why was she laughing? I'd just been attacked, hadn't I?

'What happened?' I said. 'What was that?'

'It was a crow,' Grace said.

'OK.' My breath was still fluttery. I pointed at Asha. 'OK, next time you go first.'

'Good scream, though,' Asha said. 'You model it on a six-year-old girl?'

At least her mood had improved. I groped in my pocket, wanting to change the subject. Found my mobile and Josh's. 'Here's as good as anywhere,' I said.

Grace got hers out. Asha's face fell. 'Do we really have to?'

I had a plastic bag. Josh's and Grace's mobiles went in. 'Colonel Doofus can use these to find out where we are,' I said. 'Cos, I don't know, satellites. We'll get them back if nothing happens.'

Asha was glaring at me. 'What about you?'

I got out three phones. 'This is the phone that went in the river.' I dropped it in the bag. 'This is an old phone that I've been using since then.' I dropped that in the bag too. 'This is an even older one of Jason's I found. I think maybe, if I'm careful, I can keep using it.'

She looked sceptical, but she got her phone out. 'Bye, little friend,' she said. She placed it carefully in the bag, looked at me, looked at Grace. 'Now what?'

I tucked the bag into a dark corner of the Ruin under a rotting bit of wood, and we made our way back out of the allotments. Stood there, by the gate, looking upriver and downriver.

'Right,' said Asha, 'you'd better have one of your' – she made air quotation marks – 'visions. See if you can give us a clue.'

'I can't just have one,' I said, 'just like that. That's not how it works.'

'Do you know how it works?' said Grace.

I opened my mouth. Closed it again.

'Close your eyes,' Asha instructed, 'and think about Ruby touching you. But not, please God, in a sexy way.'

I glared at her, started to say something, didn't.

I closed my eyes. Squashed my hands over my eyes. Took a long, slow breath in and out.

I put my palm over my coffee cup and Ruby's fingers brushed the back of my hand.

Ruby ushered us out of her house and her bare arm brushed mine.

Skin on skin.

I felt, or imagined I felt, a tingle on the back of my hand. On my arm. A prickling.

*Ruby was right in front of me.*

I stumbled back because for a moment I thought I'd opened my eyes and I was looking at her, but that wasn't it. She was right in front of me, but this wasn't the 3D high definition I'd seen before, she was blurred and dim and standing in some place I didn't recognise.

Daylight falling through a long, dirty window, threadbare carpet, a couple of old chairs, a counter with a small kitchen behind it. It was all out of focus, it was swimming a bit, as if it needed tuning in. I heard the sound of the river but that might have been the blood in my skull. Connor was there, clutching his stomach, looking ill. Ruby wasn't grinning now, she was angry and unhappy, ranting about something. I tried to hear what she was saying, but the harder I tried the more it seemed to fade.

I opened my eyes. Asha clapped her hands like she was waking me out of a trance, and it helped, it shocked me back into the moment. So did the fact she was right up in my face.

'What've you got, Mystic Boy? You got anything? What've you got?'

I told them what I'd seen. We all thought about it, tried to think about it, wondered where it could be.

'Wooden walls?' said Grace.

I nodded. 'Think so.'

'But bigger than a shed. It had a kitchen, carpet?'

I nodded again. We were walking further along the river, past the allotments, past a clump of trees to where the bank widened out again, this time to include an overgrown bowling green and its clubhouse. Its long, low, wooden clubhouse.

We stopped. We all stopped.

'Think we've found them,' said Asha.

**11.51 a.m.**

We retreated to the clump of trees and waited there, staring at the clubhouse. I think we were all hoping something

79

would happen so we wouldn't have to walk right up and knock on the door.

I took a moment to open a new Twitter account, under the name Kurt Wagner.

'Oh good,' said Asha. 'Glad you've got your priorities right.'

I ignored her. No way was I going to let Doofus and Patronising spread their fake news without being challenged. There were a lot of people tweeting about Gilpin, there was a proper Twitter storm, and I was hoping a new account on an unknown phone wouldn't get noticed. I wanted to stay in the conversation without effectively jumping up and down and waving to tell Colonel Doofus where I was. I used a different, but popular hashtag.

#WeirdandProud **You can't hide the truth for ever. It'll come out. Maybe sooner than you think.**

I put the phone away, looked at the clubhouse again, looked at my friends. We weren't sure that Ruby and Connor would still be there. If what I'd just seen was the past, they might have left by now.

'Let's do it,' said Asha.

She didn't sound confident, Grace was biting her lip, and I had a queasy feeling in my stomach. What if Ruby went full-on Naveen on us? She could actually kill us, possibly without even meaning to. Still, we left our little clump of trees, walked cautiously along the bank, sort of half crouching behind bushes, then crept towards the clubhouse.

The voice came clearly through the open door.

'We hitchhike,' she snapped. 'We go to Leeds, Manchester. How sweet would that be? A whole city would totally lose its mind.'

*How are we going to deal with Ruby?* The question had never been answered but here she was, super-strong and planning to bring basically a Weapon of Mass Destruction into a city. We looked at each other, and our faces all said the same thing: *What the hell do we do?*

'I think we need to get the army,' Grace whispered. 'This is beyond us.'

In my mind I was picturing Ruby and Connor sitting in Piccadilly Gardens in Manchester, or Millennium Square in Leeds. Ruby had the egg in her lap and it was throbbing with evil radiation, mutating tens of thousands of teenagers, creating the frenzy of fear and horror that it seemed to feed on. I was thinking Grace was right, we should get Douglas and Kirby involved immediately and just hope they could deal with it.

But then Ruby and Connor came out of the clubhouse. No warning, no time for us to hide, they just walked out and saw us standing there.

'Um,' I said. 'Hi.'

Ruby in her sleeveless black T-shirt, Connor in his stripy football shirt, like he was just off to training. Except he had a hand on his stomach and he looked a bit queasy. He managed an uncertain smile.

No smile from Ruby. 'What the hell are you doing here?'

None of us was sure how to answer that.

'We want to help,' Grace said finally, in a small voice.

I looked at Connor, tried a nervous smile back at him. 'You all right, mate?'

Ruby stepped in front of him protectively, which meant she stepped towards us aggressively. 'He's not your mate.'

'Right.' Asha was suddenly in most-popular-girl-in-school mode. Her tone said, *Of course you'll listen to me, why wouldn't you? Everyone listens to me.* She lifted her index finger and waggled it in Ruby's face. 'You need to back off, Rubes. I mean it, take a moment.'

She did, she took a moment. A long, tense couple of seconds. I was actually holding my breath. Asha was using the full force of her personality to try to make Ruby back down; Ruby was staring at her, cheeks sucked in, lips pursed like she was having trouble containing herself. What was going on behind her face?

And then she smiled.

There was a large tub full of earth on the paving outside the clubhouse. It had a plant in it that looked like a small tree. Ruby picked it up without any apparent effort at all.

'Look at me!' she said. 'All of a sudden you've noticed me, right?' Her eyes were shining. I was trying to think of a good answer to that, something reasonable and soothing, but it turned out she wasn't looking for an answer.

She threw the tub at us.

We scattered and stumbled out of the way and she laughed. Asha was nearest to her. Ruby walked right up and drew back her fist. And now her lips pulled back in a twisted, angry smirk.

Ruby's punch could snap Asha's neck back and kill her. It could fracture her skull. It could knock her on to the ground where she could smack her head on a stone and die. If Ruby was aware of these possibilities, they didn't seem to bother her at all. I was going to do something, maybe throw myself at Ruby, but before I or Grace or maybe Connor could act, before Ruby could move, Asha roared, 'DON'T!'

And that single syllable echoed around all five of us. Asha's voice had a depth and a resonance I'd never heard before. It was like her own voice, the one that said, *Of course you'll listen to me*, but it was multiplied by at least a hundred. It reverberated in my head as if she was harmonising with herself.

And Ruby staggered back.

Asha's face went from scared to puzzled to a big, delighted grin. She shimmied her shoulders and chanted, 'Oh yeah,' and then as Ruby straightened up she pointed at her again and roared, 'STAY BACK!'

It made Ruby pause but it wasn't quite as good the second time, the command didn't have the same dense, layered quality as the first syllable she'd yelled, which had erupted out of desperation and urgency.

'Connor,' I said. 'Who's got the egg?'

He looked confused for a moment. Then he said, 'Me.'

'Come with us!' I shouted, trying to shock him out of his indecision.

He wavered. Looked at me, looked at his sister.

'You can't let her take the egg to a city,' I said. 'It hurts people. It kills people.'

'Please, Connor,' said Grace. 'There's something wrong with Ruby. We can help you.'

He was still wavering, but Ruby went to grab him and that did it, because she was snarling and strong and properly scary. He dodged and twisted and ran towards us.

She wheeled round, facing him and me and Grace and Asha.

'Connor,' she yelled. 'Don't you dare!'

Maybe if she'd been gentler, maybe if she'd asked him to stay with her, told him she needed him, everything would have been different. But she yelled at him, furious, spit-flecked, quite possibly murderous, and he shrank away from her.

So she took a step towards us, fists clenched.

'Asha,' I screeched, 'you have to really mean it!'

Her grin vanished. Ruby was advancing on her like a predator turning on its prey and she was scared and angry and desperate again. All those emotions were tightly twisted into two furious syllables as she yelled, 'STAY THERE!' right into Ruby's face. She really meant it.

We ran. I glanced back over my shoulder and saw Ruby rooted to the spot, furious, shaking and quivering as she struggled to move. We carried on the way we'd been going, upriver, over the new bridge, past the weir, and up the long flight of steep, uneven steps with gardens on either side. Ruby would be following soon. As soon as she shook off the effects of Asha's amazing Voice she'd be sprinting after us. I looked over my shoulder again when I was at the top of the steps. There she was, at the bottom, bounding up the steps three at a time.

We veered left. It was half a mile to the National Trust car park and I didn't think we were going to make it. I was panting already, so were Grace, Connor and Asha. She probably wouldn't have the breath to do the Voice. We had to run, we had to run.

Ruby leapt up from the steps as if she'd been catapulted, looked right, looked left and sprinted after us.

My legs were heavy, I stumbled and nearly fell, I had a stitch. 'Oh, God,' I panted. 'Oh, God.'

I glanced over my shoulder a third time. She was gaining on us. But there was the van, just where we'd agreed. I waved, Grace and Asha waved too, and shouted. We could see Josh sat in the driver's seat. He was parked in a narrow slot between a grey Scenic and a black BMW, and he was reading a comic. He was slumped in his mum's bright red campervan like he was on some boring holiday somewhere and was refusing to get out.

'Josh!' I screamed. I was screaming again.

'Josh!' Grace and Asha were screaming too.

I don't know if he heard us, but he looked up. He stared, apparently taking a long moment to work out what was happening. Why? Why would it take a long moment? Me, Grace, Asha and Connor were running for our lives, Ruby was right behind us – which part of that was hard to understand? And then I could see him fumbling with something, the key presumably, and there was an even longer moment. Again, why? Why wasn't the key already in the ignition? Had he dropped it? Had he lost it?

And then finally the engine coughed.

And turned over briefly, and died.

He tried again.

Same thing happened again.

'Oh, God,' I gasped. 'Oh, God.'

He tried a third time. The engine coughed and strained and nearly caught and then he stamped the accelerator and suddenly it was roaring. He started to carefully, slowly, back out of his parking place. Why had he parked so awkwardly? He was the worst getaway driver ever.

And then there was a loud scrape as he hit one of the cars next to him. He corrected his steering and seemed to get himself diagonally stuck between the Scenic and the BMW.

I stopped running. Couldn't manage another step. Turned my back on Josh and his mum's campervan, and faced Ruby. Sort of faced her – I had my hands on my knees, my chest was heaving, and I was mostly looking at the road. Grace, Asha and Connor kept going. I was doing the whole *Go-on-without-me-I'll-hold-them-off* thing. Not because I was brave, I wasn't, I was terrified, but I was also knackered.

I looked up. Ruby stopped about five paces away from me. I held up a hand which was shaking, only partly because I was still out of breath.

'Ruby,' I panted. 'Come on. No need for this.'

'No need?' she said, like she couldn't believe what she was hearing. 'Do you have any idea what it's like to be me?'

I didn't even try to answer that. I felt like if I said the wrong word she might actually break my neck.

'Course you don't, you and golden Asha and your stupid, smug mates. You don't even notice me.' She shoved me in the

87

chest. I stumbled back. 'Or you take the piss.' She shoved me again, a little harder. She was only using her fingertips, but it hurt. 'Or you feel sorry for me.' There was a concentrated force in the word sorry, and there was a concentrated force in the shove too. She used her palm this time, and although there didn't seem to be much effort in it, I was thrown back on to my bum in the road. 'Even my own parents sigh when I come in the room.'

I looked up at her. Black T-shirt, black hair, dark eyeshadow, thin face. Purple lips drawn back into a growl which revealed her teeth. She looked pretty good, actually, and I wondered if I should tell her, but I was too busy sort of shrinking into a ball because I was afraid she was about to start kicking me. A year ago, Asha's older brother Naveen knocked me down outside the Health Centre and started kicking me like he was intending to break ribs. This year it was thirteen-year-old Ruby. I really needed to take a look at some of my choices.

'Want to know how I feel now?' she said.

I got to my feet. Carefully, in a non-threatening way. Not that there was any way I actually could threaten her. I was pretty sure I had a bruise on my chest where she'd been shoving me. I had a feeling that if the kids at school who bullied her were here she might have broken them into pieces by now.

'Sure,' I nodded, my voice a bit fluttery, thinking conversation was good, much better than kicking.

She nodded. Paused, with a sense of dramatic timing.

'I feel important,' she said.

She was about to hit me, I could see it coming, it was the perfect punctuation to what she'd just said. She'd been stopped from punching Asha – now she was even angrier, even more lethal.

'Your mum doesn't hate you,' I stammered, desperate. 'I saw her outside your house, she's worried sick.'

It stopped her. I could see her confusion. It stopped her for just long enough, because then she looked over my shoulder and her face changed, so I looked over my shoulder too, and we both saw Josh's mum's campervan hurtling towards us. Josh was at the wheel looking scared, yelling something and making frantic *Get out of the way!* motions with one hand.

We got out of the way. She dived left and I dived right, which was just as well because that was the side the door was on. I jumped up, grazed and bruised, and ran along beside the van, which had slowed down a little but was still moving, as Asha slid open the door.

'Jump in!' she yelled.

I jumped halfway in, and then my knees and feet were dragging along the road and I yelled in pain, but Asha and Grace dragged me properly into the van, hurting my bruised chest, and Josh stamped on the accelerator just as Ruby hammered on the other side and we screeched away. Asha slammed the door shut with a cheer from Josh and a hoarse snarl from the engine and a wail of pain from me.

For a few minutes we just drove. Out of the National Trust woods, down the lane to the main road and then up the hill to Oxley moor. Me still on the floor, clutching my bleeding knees, all of us panting, trying to compose ourselves.

Finally Josh looked over his shoulder at us. 'Meet Vinny the Van,' he said. 'He just saved your life.'

I didn't know how to answer that, so I just said, 'You all right driving?'

He was looking at the road now, which was a relief. He shrugged. 'So far so good. How'd you get away from her?'

'Asha's got this Voice,' Grace said. 'It kind of makes you do what she says.'

Josh looked over his shoulder again, and we swerved. He was laughing. 'Oh my God, you're a Jedi.'

'Watch the road!' I shouted.

Asha was laughing too. 'Yes! Winner! I've got the best power. I'm a legitimate superhero.'

Connor was quiet. I was bruised and grazed and still feeling the aftermath of full-on terror, but I could see he could do with a friendly word. I gingerly picked myself up off the floor, sat down on the bench seat next to him.

'Hey, Con,' I said. 'You all right?'

He shrugged.

Grace and Asha were on the bench seat opposite. Grace was giving him one of her intent looks. 'It wasn't your sister's fault, Connor,' she said, finally. 'She's not herself.' Asha snorted, but Grace ignored her. 'Last year the egg seemed to choose Naveen to protect it,' she continued. 'This year I think it's chosen her.'

'Then we have to help her!' Connor said.

Grace nodded. 'We will,' she said. 'If she'll let us.'

There was a bit of a silence after that, because obviously she wasn't going to let us. If she got anywhere near us she was more likely to murder us.

'So anyway,' Josh eventually shouted from the front, 'what's happened to you, Connor? Are you super-strong, like Ruby?'

He shook his head.

Asha was studying him. 'You've got big hands,' she said finally.

'I've always had big hands,' he murmured.

I was starting to get worried. 'Also, where's the egg?' I said. 'You told us you've got it. You have got it, right?'

A pause. All of us looking at him now except Josh, who cast a glance back over his shoulder now and then, making the van swerve every time.

'Connor?' said Grace.

'Tell us!' Asha barked.

It wasn't the Voice, but it did the trick. Connor flinched and looked at her, looked at all of us.

'I think it might be . . .' he began. He started again. 'I know this sounds unlikely but . . .' He hesitated again, as if it was hard to get these words out. 'I think it's inside me.'

**12.22 p.m.**

#WeirdandProud **My genius plan. Stage One – tick. Stage Two – wait, what was Stage Two again?**

Josh got a big orange waterproof coat out of the back of the van. He slammed the door and then patted it. He actually patted it.

'Had this van since I was three years old,' he said. 'Went on holidays to Scarborough with Mum and Dad. And I named it Vinny.'

'Nice,' I said.

Asha sighed. 'Don't encourage him.'

Josh flapped the orange coat and laid it on the grass. It had a grubby stain the shape of Australia on it, and damp streaks criss-crossed it.

'I'm not eating off that,' Asha said.

'OK,' he said. 'Don't eat.'

I didn't care what the coat looked like, I was hungry and Josh had volunteered to bring the food. He got a Morrisons bag and tipped it out on the coat. A box of chocolate cereal, two pints of milk, a slab of mild Cheddar that was the same orange as the coat, and a packet of digestives.

'Ta-da!' he said. 'Lunch.' He stretched out his hands like he'd just put a feast in front of us.

We stared at him.

'What?' he said.

We were on the moor, and we were all not talking about the big, obvious thing that needed talking about. Because in a world full of impossibilities this particular thing was just too impossible. Maybe Connor was just wrong? Life was very confusing lately, and he was only thirteen, and maybe he was just mistaken.

So we didn't talk about it. We had lunch instead. It was like an ordinary picnic, except the food was ridiculous, and we'd never had an ordinary picnic together, or any kind of picnic, and if we ever did we wouldn't choose to sit out on the moor, especially when it was cold and raining. It was that irritating rain which feels like someone's persistently flicking water in your face. When I leant back wet grass was flattened under my palms. My bum was damp and there was rain on the back of my neck. Everything was moist.

I hate that word. Moist.

We sat there in a circle under the high grey sky, heads bowed, cold and wet, not talking about the thing that needed talking about. It might have looked like we were praying, but we weren't praying. I think we were slowly taking it in: what we'd done, what it meant.

Josh had brought two dishes but no spoons. He slurped his Coco Pops straight out of the bowl then passed it to Asha. She made a disgusted face and passed it on to me.

'I hate picnics,' she grunted.

'OK,' said Josh. 'Important questions. Can you use your magic Voice on more than one person at a time?'

Asha shrugged. 'Don't know.'

'Can you use it on animals?'

She rolled her eyes. 'Don't be stupid.'

'Can you move things with your mind?'

She sighed. 'Stop talking to me.'

'All right.' Josh was unabashed. 'Another important question: Ruby's the Big Bad, she's the new Naveen. How do we kill her?'

Connor looked up from his own bowl of cereal. 'What?'

'I mean we won't kill her, obviously,' Josh said, lifting both hands in the air. 'We might. But we won't. But we might.'

'We definitely won't,' Grace told Connor.

'Of course we won't,' I said. 'We just stay away from her.' I took a deep breath. The notion of the egg being inside Connor wasn't just more impossible than usual, it was also more weird than usual. And it was gross. But someone had to ask him about it.

'Thing is,' I continued, 'our whole plan was to leave the egg somewhere where it could hatch without hurting anyone and now you're saying . . .' I was looking at Connor. And then we were all looking at Connor, because this was the big, unexpected thing. 'You're saying it's inside you?'

He was tipping the chocolate cereal directly into his mouth from the bowl. He lowered it, wiped his lips, realised we were all staring at him.

He nodded. 'I know,' he said. He put his fingertips on his stomach like he was feeling something in there. 'Crazy, isn't it?' He blew air through his lips, tried a smile. It quivered.

No one said anything. I was wondering, and I'd guess we were all wondering, how on earth we were supposed to deal with this.

'You're sure though?' I said.

He nodded. 'Oh yeah.' His fingertips pressed into his football shirt. 'Definitely something there.'

Now we were all looking at his stomach.

'Last time, I was too young,' he continued. There was a definite edge of It's so unfair in his voice now. 'I know Matt Spencer died and that was horrible, but me and Ruby were both too young and we had to be on the edge of everything and watch everyone else. Ruby felt left out, like she always does, and I wanted to fly or be telekinetic!' He shrugged. 'So this time, Ruby gets strong, Asha gets a magic Voice, you all get whatever you've got, and me . . . I'm sort of pregnant. It's rubbish.'

Asha jumped in before anyone else could speak. 'Last year wasn't a game,' she snapped. 'Yes, Matt died. Max died too.' She jerked her head at me. 'His brother ended up in hospital, my brother lost his mind and I bloody hate him.'

Awkward silence. Asha looked a bit taken aback by those last four words, like she'd said more than she intended to. We'd never actually discussed Naveen, who'd been such a huge part of our lives a year ago. Which, thinking about it, was a bit ridiculous.

She got to her feet and walked a couple of steps away as if she couldn't bear to sit with us any more. It was like she wanted to storm off but there was nowhere to storm off to so she just stayed there, two steps away, with the wind spitting rain into her face.

The awkward silence became a tense silence. Connor had lost his quivery smile. Everything Asha had said was true, and it was fair enough to be angry, but none of it was his fault. He was only a kid and he was scared, and his sister had basically turned into Naveen, which meant she was influenced or maybe to some extent controlled by the egg, and was definitely possibly trying to kill us, and he still hadn't explained what he was even talking about when he said the egg was inside him.

I didn't know what to say to him.

Fortunately, Josh did.

'I know exactly what you mean,' he announced. 'I loved what happened to me. I got like this moving tattoo of the universe growing all over me.' He moved his hand over his stomach and chest like he could feel it. 'And for the first time in my life I was in a tight little clique. Teenage Mutant Detectives, that's what we called ourselves.'

Connor's smile returned. 'Brilliant.'

'So I get it,' Josh continued. 'People died, people's heads were messed up, it was the scariest thing that ever happened to me, and I still wouldn't have wanted to be on the outside, looking in. But you're totally one of us this time, mate. Teenage Mutant . . .' He paused.

'Fugitives,' I said.

'Perfect.' Josh nodded enthusiastically. 'Teenage Mutant Fugitives. Now tell us what's happening, Con. What d'you actually mean the egg's inside you? What's that all about?'

'It's not an egg this time,' Connor said. 'The thing, the creature, the thing itself is inside me.' He pointed his fingertips at his stomach. 'It's really in there, I can feel it.' He put a hand on his stomach again. 'It was achy at first but it's settled down. It's a fuzzy feeling.'

'How did it get inside you?' Grace asked.

Connor smiled and shrugged, sheepish, like a teacher was asking him a tricky question. 'Dunno. Ruby came in my room two nights ago, and woke me up. All of a sudden, she was strong and the thing was just there, inside me. And she said, "This year it's all about us."'

Another silence. It wasn't awkward or tense this time, it was more like a pause while we tried to process what we'd just heard. We were all staring at him, probably all thinking the same thing. But only Asha actually said it.

'OK, in *Alien* it bursts out of his chest, right? So . . . don't want to worry you, Con, but is that in fact what we're looking at here?'

Connor laughed. It was surprise rather than amusement but still, I don't know anyone else who would have laughed at that question. He laughed and shook his head. 'No! I mean, I don't think so. I s'pose I don't know, but it doesn't feel like that.'

Silence again. This was like a conversation in slow motion, where everything that was said needed thinking about. The problem was there was no solid ground, no foundation that we could all understand. Instead, we were starting from an impossible place and it was just getting more impossible.

'Remember how it flickered?' Grace said, finally.

A year ago, we'd all stood in Max's garden and watched the egg crack open. We'd all seen what came out. None of us actually remembered it very well because it had a slippery quality, it was hard to retain a clear memory of the creature. But it definitely flickered.

'Like it was here,' she said, 'and not here. In its own dimension, but in ours at the same time.'

'So, what?' said Asha. 'You think it's going to flicker out of Connor's stomach?'

Grace nodded. 'Maybe. Like he's an incubator.'

Josh gave Connor a thumbs-up. 'So, good news, mate. We get you to some godforsaken spot in the middle of nowhere, stand well back while Fuzzy, the little baby alien, pops out without hurting you, then we all lose our so-called powers, same as last year, and we go straight back home.' He looked at the rest of us. 'Right?'

I nodded. 'I guess that's the plan. Thing is, last year, from when me and Jason went to Max's house, to when the egg hatched, it was about seven days. So I guess, maybe, it'll be the same this year. And if this happened two nights ago, then we're only on day three right now.'

That brought the mood down a bit. We were going to be spending three or four days on the run. Josh looked like he was about to say something, but he didn't. He chewed the inside of his cheek instead.

'We stay on quiet roads away from towns,' I continued, 'so no one else gets the effects of the egg that isn't actually an egg this time.' I looked round at everyone. 'I think we have to do this,' I said. 'Cos if we don't, if Doofus and Patronising get the egg, we'll probably all die. Anyone disagree?'

Silence for a moment, while no one disagreed.

'OK,' Josh said finally, his voice tight, like his chest was constricted, 'I'm getting, like I said, a bit of an urge to open my little black box of sadness, but aside from that, none of us looks like we've got a terminal condition this year. I mean you probably can't die from having a magic Voice, or from seeing the past or having a unicorn horn, right? So, in summary – yay.'

Grace made a sound.

She opened her mouth and closed it again, and her lips or her tongue made a small sound. A 'tch'.

We looked at her.

She lifted the blue hair off her forehead, and ran her fingers gently over the almond-shaped lump that was revealed.

'It's not a horn,' she said.

We looked at the lump, stared at it. Something moved underneath it. And then she closed her ordinary, conventional, side-by-side eyes and she opened her third eye. It was a greenish blue, like the sea, and it looked at each of us. When it was focused on me I felt a cold shiver pass over me.

'It sees the future,' she said. 'Sort of.' Her voice was strained, like a thin bit of material pulled tight. 'And I've seen one of us die.'

## 1.09 p.m.

**#WeirdandProud How many kids have to die before the government admits this thing is really happening?**

We all stared at Grace. All of us too shocked, too scared, to ask the next question.

She shook her head anyway, as if one of us had asked it.

'I don't know,' she said, still in that strained, tight voice. 'I don't know who.'

'OK,' said Josh, 'OK, nobody panic. We can deal with that because of Hector's finger, right? We just need to try and work out which of us is going to die, and how, and what we do to stop it. Right?'

Grace's third eye was closed again and she'd pulled her fringe back over her forehead. She had her hands on her cheeks and she was crying out of at least two eyes. Asha was back in the circle, crouching with an arm round her.

'I don't know,' Grace stuttered again, 'I don't know the answers to any of those questions. I didn't see anything, not exactly, I felt it, this horrible sense of loss, like a great empty pit, and I knew someone we cared about was gone. And it's one of us sitting here, I'm sure it's one of us.'

I didn't want to be there any more. Sitting on the moor talking about death with a wet bum and a mutant, possibly murderous, teenager after us. I wanted to wind back time and be safe in my room. I wanted Mum to have said to my friends when they came round a couple of days ago, *Sorry, he's not up for seeing anyone at the moment.* Better to be a weird, friendless loner and alive, than back out in the world and dead.

But I was here, and Grace — Grace, of all people — was weeping, so I held up my right hand in front of her, showing her the long scar on my index finger.

'Josh is right,' I announced, trying to sound more confident than I felt. 'No one has to die, this is proof.'

Connor was looking at me like I'd lost my mind. 'Wait, what? How is that proof?'

'He met his older self last year,' Josh said, like he was talking about me meeting some cousin I'd lost track of. 'It was a whole big thing. Old Hector had his finger cut off by Asha's brother, but young Hector only got that scar. So you can definitely change the future, and we're all going to live happily ever after. Maybe. Probably not.'

Connor suddenly had his fingertips on his forehead, like he had a headache. 'Sorry, I don't understand that at all.' He smiled at us, looking embarrassed, like he was having a problem in a maths lesson. 'But it doesn't matter,' he continued. 'Ruby's coming.'

We all stared at him, but no one actually moved. Someone was going to die and Connor had a fuzzy alien baby inside him and now apparently super-strong, super-unhappy, super-angry Ruby was coming after us. And no one moved. There was a definite, unspoken sense of *For God's sake let's just give up now. This is too much.* It wasn't just me, it was shimmering around all five of us, sat there on the wet grass under the high grey sky in the cold and the spattering rain. It was so tempting to continue not moving and just wait for Ruby, or get back in Vinny the Van and drive back to Gilpin, find Colonel Doofus and Professor Patronising and let them take over.

Behind me, Mum and Dad and lasagne. Ahead of me pain, probably, and fear, definitely, and a whole pile of weirdness.

I stood up. I didn't stand up urgently, I stood up slowly, reluctantly. 'We better go then,' I said.

Asha stood up next to me. 'Fish Boy's right.'

Connor got up next. 'Fish Boy?'

Grace was a bit slower, but she stood and stretched with a sigh. 'He fell in the river.'

Josh jumped to his feet. 'Asha's got it on her phone, she'll show you some time, it's epic.'

**#Weird&Proud My Brilliant Plan. Stage Two, sorted. OK, 'brilliant' might be an exaggeration.**

Josh drove again. The campervan was an automatic, and he'd assured us he was fine at the wheel because his mum had let him have a go in Morrisons' car park, he'd watched a How To Drive video on YouTube, and anyway it was like driving a dodgem car. None of that was reassuring. I was on the passenger seat next to him and behind us the others were on the two cushioned benches facing each other, their knees knocking together.

I was torn between keeping a wary eye on the way Josh was driving and leaning back to take part in the conversation.

Asha was questioning Connor. 'How d'you know she's coming?'

Connor started to answer then stopped, as if unsure how to put it into words. He shrugged. 'I can feel it,' he said, finally.

'Maybe it's a twin thing?' I said.

'Or an alien thing. Maybe she can sense where Fuzzy is.' Josh had twisted round to speak to us and the van swerved across the road. We all shouted at him. 'All right, all right,' he said, getting us back on a straight line, staring straight ahead.

'So she's right behind us.' Grace was looking through the back window.

Josh nodded, still watching the road but raising his voice to make sure he was heard. 'It's a twin-telepathy, alien-finding, super-tracker thing. So basically, wherever we go, whatever we do, she's going to keep following us. We could switch horses and run through water and split up, but it won't make any difference.'

'She must have hitched a lift,' I said. 'And now maybe she's forcing the driver to do what she wants.'

'She can't be reasoned with.' Josh was using a deep, American voice. 'She doesn't feel pity, or fear. And she absolutely won't stop, ever, until we're dead!'

Josh was trying to be funny, because that's what Josh does, but it felt like someone had sucked half the air out of the van. I had an image in my head of Ruby standing in front of Asha, her face twisted with rage, her fist pulled back; Ruby snarling, 'I feel important,' about to hit me, loving her new power.

Asha sounded impatient, because that's what Asha does. 'Great,' she snapped. 'That means we can't just go somewhere quiet and wait for Fuzzy to pop out of Connor's stomach so we can all go back to normal. We have to keep moving, because if we don't keep moving your sister's going to find us and kill us and drag you to a city.'

'She won't kill you!' Connor squeaked.

No one answered. I could actually hear my short, shuddery breaths.

'Also,' said Josh, finally, 'don't want to ruin this great vibe we've got going, but we have slight issues with petrol and a small problem with food. And when I say "slight" I mean "major", and when I say "a small problem" I mean there basically isn't any. So there's that.'

I sighed. I stopped twisting round towards the others

behind me. Tipped my head back against my seat and closed my eyes. How had this even happened? I was on the run, and I was completely unprepared for being on the run, and I didn't know what to do.

My phone buzzed. Someone had replied to my tweet. In fact, Dr Lazarus, the uber-troll with the Gilpin Ha Ha Ha blog had replied to my tweet.

**Bit of free advice, Kurt – whatever's going on, stay out of it.**

I read it, and then reread it. First I tried to work out if he knew that Kurt Wagner was actually Hector Coleman. I thought probably not, so that was good news. Then I tried to work out what he was up to. I'd always assumed that Dr Lazarus was a government plant, or a whole big team of nerdy government agents typing away furiously, doing their best to make Gilpin look stupid. But lately he'd told me to leave town, to walk away, to get out of Gilpin, which was all actually good advice. And now this. Weird. I stared at the phone for a few more seconds, then clicked it off, because I wanted to save the battery and there were more important things to think about.

I looked at Josh.

'You got a road atlas?' I said.

Grace got the map out of a drawer under her bench and I climbed over the back of my seat and joined her, Asha and Connor. We pooled our cash. We'd all grabbed what we could when we'd left, but we'd been in a hurry. We had fifty-seven pounds and twelve pence. We also had some cheese, milk and Coco Pops left. We really should have prepared better for this. We could have had a full tank of gas, a couple of rucksacks full of food, a few bottles of water and maybe a hundred quid between us. Instead we were short of petrol, short of cash, hungry and thirsty. We couldn't use cards because Douglas and Kirby would be able to trace them and find us. And Ruby was on our tail.

'OK.' I looked at Connor. 'Ruby can't drive, right?'

He smiled. 'Obviously not.'

'Then let's assume she can't force someone to keep following us for ever. They'll get away, she'll have to find another lift, she won't want the police chasing her – it'll all slow her down.'

I studied the map. We needed a destination. We couldn't just drive aimlessly. We needed a destination and a plan. I turned a couple of pages looking, basically, for nothing, for no houses, no sign of life.

I put my finger on a village. 'Burrage.'

'Bless you,' said Josh.

'It's a tiny village,' I said, ignoring him, 'in Northumberland. I had a family holiday in a cottage near there when I was ten or eleven and it was rubbish. There was nothing there. Me and Jason thought it was the worst place in the world. We should go back to that cottage.'

'What?' said Asha. Her voice was a bit high-pitched, like she couldn't altogether control it. 'Go there and wait for Ruby to turn up and grab Connor and slaughter us? Brilliant idea.'

'If Ruby turns up we can snatch her car key, or disable her car somehow, and then that's it, game over. She's in the middle of nowhere with no way to get to a city. And anyway, maybe Fuzzy will arrive before Ruby does.' I shrugged. I didn't especially like the idea myself, but I couldn't think of anything better. 'What d'you think?'

'I think who died and put you in charge?' said Asha.

'Still got a small issue over no petrol and no food,' said Josh.

'We get petrol wherever we can, then we find some little village where we can buy some food. In and out, then we get moving again. Head for Burrage.'

No one said anything. I didn't know if that meant they all agreed with me or not.

'It's about a hundred and fifty miles,' I said. 'We're going on small roads and we'll probably get lost, so we'll need to stop somewhere overnight.'

Still no answer.

'So,' I said, 'are we all agreed?'

No one looked happy, but no one actually said anything.

'What am I doing, then?' Josh shouted from the front.

I climbed back into the seat beside him, with the road atlas. 'You're driving,' I said. 'To the worst place in the world.'

**1.34 p.m.**

#WeirdandProud **It's like telepathy, only completely different. And sort of horrible.**

Josh didn't like the idea of driving on a motorway, and none of us much liked the idea of being driven by him on a motorway, and anyway we wanted to be away from people as much as possible, so I tried to direct him on A roads and then B roads and then little windy roads that didn't even have a letter. I was also hoping this might make it harder for Ruby to follow us or for Colonel Doofus to find us.

Connor tried to chat to Asha and Grace but neither of them were saying much, so he knelt on his seat and talked to me and Josh. 'You're like our mum and dad sitting up there in front.'

Asha snorted. 'Who's Mum and who's Dad?'

'Bagsy Dad!' Josh shouted.

Asha made an approving sound. 'That makes you Mum, Hector. Sounds about right.'

I sighed. 'I'm stopping your pocket money,' I said.

It was tricky to navigate because I wasn't used to maps, I was used to my phone or the satnav telling us where to go. In fact I was mostly used to my mum telling my dad where to go. Our route zigzagged, lurching first one way and then another, without making much progress northwards. And we didn't see a petrol station. The needle on the gauge was nudging red.

'OK,' I said, 'new plan. We need a bigger road. One with a petrol station on it.' I stared at the map. It was starting to look like a piece of abstract art.

'Give it to me,' Asha demanded.

I passed it back to her and she leant over the front seats barking directions, making Josh speed up and slow down, reverse and at one point turn back the way we'd come. The needle on the petrol gauge was now firmly in the red.

'Stop,' said Grace, eventually. 'Look.'

She was pointing at a sagging wooden sign which said Heaton was two and a half miles away. 'Let's go there,' she said. We followed a narrow road all the way to Heaton where we saw a bigger sign towards Kittredge, and outside Kittredge we finally found a blue sign which mentioned York and Harrogate. There was more traffic around now and I was anxious, because any teenagers in the area might be affected, and if Doofus had worked out we were in Josh's mum's red campervan he might have the police and CCTV searching for it. And also Josh's driving got more erratic when there were other cars on the road. But we badly needed petrol.

So we moved on to an A road and after a couple more miles we saw a forecourt up ahead.

'Right,' I said. 'What d'you think? Twenty quid on gas, save the rest for food?'

'I'll do it,' said Asha. 'Cos I've got the Voice.' She almost sang the last five words, giving her shoulders a little shimmy as she did so. So far, she was enjoying her power too much to worry about any way it might get out of control or go wrong. It was like she was on stage in her sleek black outfit, impressing some reality show judge. Although to be fair, she also acted that way before she got the Voice.

'No,' I said. 'We can't use that, we need to keep a low profile.'

Josh jerked to a stop at the first pump with the van at an unhelpful angle. There was a beep behind him.

'What?' he barked, to no one in particular.

'Go up to the next pump,' said Grace. 'You're blocking the way.'

Josh was scowling into his wing mirror. 'Getting a serious case of road rage,' he snarled.

'Low profile,' I murmured. 'Remember?'

Connor had a totally inappropriate smirk on his face. 'You aren't really used to being on the run, are you?' he said.

Josh moved the van jerkily along to the next pump, and I got out. Where was the petrol cap? I tried to look like I knew what I was doing, found it on the wrong side. Great. I pressed the right buttons and pulled the pump round the back of the van. It only just stretched. I unscrewed the cap and started pumping. Of course from here I couldn't see how much it was going to cost. Asha had gone in to pay. I waited a while as petrol pulsed into the tank, then thought I'd better stop pumping.

I was wishing the van wasn't bright red, wishing it and we were less conspicuous, and I was just about to pull out the pump, when someone grabbed my wrist. His hand closed all the way around it, like a manacle.

'Hey, buddy.' I jumped. It was a big unshaven bloke in a green bomber jacket. His nostrils were flaring and his free hand was bunched into a fist. 'Were you swearing at me?'

I stared at him. 'What?'

'Saw you giving it that in your mirror.' He was jabbing two fingers at my eyes with his free hand.

'No,' I stammered. 'No, I'm not even driving, but . . . my mate was talking to me, not you.'

His face looked heavy. It looked bigger than it needed to be. He moved his tongue over his teeth. He obviously didn't believe me. But then he said something that completely surprised me. 'Do I know you?'

I shook my head. 'No.'

He was going to snarl another question at me, and I was going to take my hand off the trigger on the pump because I was aware Asha was signalling to me from inside the little shop, but something else happened.

He didn't speak, and I didn't move my hand, because a flood of memories was suddenly filling my head.

They weren't my memories.

The big man's mouth dropped open, his eyes went glassy and bright flashes jumped into my head.

*I was a little kid hugging a puppy and feeling a rush of pure pleasure; a woman towered over me, bent down to pick me up, but she was yelling at a man; I was older and I kissed someone, it was a bloke and he touched my cheek and there was that rush of pleasure again; but now he was walking away, he was leaving and sadness welled up inside me . . .*

The man in the bomber jacket snatched his hand off my wrist like it was burnt, letting out a furious gasp of pain and shock.

'What did you do?' His voice was squeezed as if his throat was closing. 'What did you do, you little bastard?'

I'd let go of the pump, finally, and we were staggering away from each other. He was staring at me in horror like I'd just made his teeth disappear.

'Sorry . . .'

His horror was turning to anger, he was snarling at me and he took a step towards me, but then Asha was suddenly between us, and she was in my face, furious. 'What happened to twenty quid? You've just spent all our cash, genius! Hey, I'm talking to you!'

I focused. I saw her squashed, angry face and her fiery eyes about three inches away from mine. I screwed the cap back on and grabbed her – holding her sleeve not her bare flesh – and pushed her, actually pushed her, into the van. I jumped in beside Josh.

'We have to go,' I said.

Josh started the engine. It spluttered and died. I watched green bomber jacket in the mirror. He had a hand on his forehead, like he was dazed, but he was staring at us. Josh tried again, and this time it caught. We left, we got the hell out of there. I saw green bomber jacket fumble for his phone.

We pulled back on to the main road.

'We have to get out of here,' I said. 'On the small roads again. We have to get going.'

'Well, on the bright side,' Asha said, her voice vibrating with anger, 'we can probably drive all the way to Aberdeen now, cos you filled the tank, didn't you, Fish Boy? You know how much cash we've got left? Two pounds forty. We can buy a couple of Mars bars.'

I watched the petrol dial climb up to show a full tank.

'And what the hell were you pushing me for?'

'Sorry,' I muttered.

Grace leant forward. 'What happened?'

I told them about the man's hand on my wrist, the flood of memories. 'Ruby barely touched me,' I said, my voice still low and shaky, 'and I got these vivid pictures of what she'd been doing. This guy held on to my wrist and I saw all these super-bright moments all at once, like his memories were my memories and I was more or less living them.'

'Ew,' said Asha.

'Whoa,' said Josh. 'What did you see?'

'This is what I mean!' said Connor. 'You guys get the fun stuff, I get Fuzzy inside me. It's so unfair.'

'Connor,' I snapped. 'It wasn't fun.'

Josh had confidently said nothing bad could happen with our powers. I wasn't so sure. Last year Matt and Max both died, Grace nearly stopped speaking, and Asha might have exploded, taking all of Gilpin with her. Something was probably going to go wrong with at least one of us. It was just a question of which one. And how?

Grace, as usual, was keeping her eye on the important question. 'So if we're broke, how are we going to get food?' she said.

Josh yanked the wheel and we screeched off the A road. We drove between high hedges with fields on either side, and then we were under a green canopy with trees crowding in around us and meeting over our heads like fingers interlocking. I felt better here. I was thinking about that guy, watching us, getting out his phone. *Do I know you?* What did he mean? Why did he think he might know us?

It was definitely better to be on the quiet roads, a long way from civilisation.

We drove in stuttery stops and starts, reaching a signpost to a village, checking its location on the map, driving around it, trying to keep heading north, towards Burrage, away from Gilpin, away from home, away, we hoped, from Colonel Doofus and Professor Patronising.

No one had much to say. Josh was worrying about his mum, but we were all worrying about our parents, about everything we were leaving behind. We didn't actually want to be getting further away from home, from everything we knew. We didn't want to be chased by Ruby, and probably Doofus, didn't want unpredictable powers that might somehow spiral out of control and kill us, didn't want any part of this situation that had suddenly taken over our lives. It's just we didn't seem to have any choice.

'I could eat beetroot,' said Josh, finally. 'With Marmite. On cream crackers. And I really, really hate beetroot and Marmite and cream crackers.'

We'd only made about fifteen miles towards Burrage, but a signpost in front of us told us we were a mile from somewhere called Middlemiss.

'Stop the van,' Asha said.

Josh did as he was told.

'Gotta get food,' Asha announced. She glared at me. 'Somehow.'

I looked at Connor. 'Any sense of where Ruby is?'

He didn't say anything, but his eyes went distant and his face sort of relaxed and went vacant. He had no expression at all. His chin dropped towards his chest. Nothing for a few moments, just an eerie hush as we all watched him and waited. It was as if he wasn't even there. Then he looked up, and the smile was back as if nothing had happened.

'Not close,' he said. 'I reckon. Could be wrong, don't think so. Can you get fish and chips? I love fish and chips.'

'Good call.' Josh was kneeling on the driver's seat, looking into the back. 'Salt and vinegar, no mushy peas, extra chips. Imagine more chips than you can imagine, that's how many I want.'

We found a shady lay-by for Josh to park Vinny in, next to a crossroads. We agreed that Grace would wait with Connor.

Asha put her hands on Grace's shoulders. Looked into her eyes. 'So how do the big scary prophecies work? D'you need to open your magic Eye to see them?'

Grace nodded.

Asha gave her a small, tight smile. 'Open it then. Before we go. Cos if this is where one of us dies, we should probably know.'

Grace sighed and pushed her fringe off her forehead. There was the lump behind its thin eyelid, moving back and forth as if seeking a way out of the darkness. Grace closed her ordinary hazel eyes and opened her extraordinary greenish-blue Eye, the colour of the sea on a sunny day.

The Eye moved over us, and again I shivered as I felt it pass over me. What did that mean? Did it mean I was the one who was going to die?

'What do you see?' I whispered, rubbing my scarred finger.

'Is it like a trippy light show?' said Josh. 'Swirls and fireworks and melting clocks and a caterpillar on a mushroom smoking a pipe?'

She shook her head. 'I see anger,' she said. Her voice was strained and fast, as if she wanted to get it over with. 'There's anger like a storm at sea and there's a jagged stab of guilt through it.'

'OK,' said Asha. 'We didn't ask for poetry.'

Grace closed the Eye quickly, let her fringe fall back over her forehead. 'It's what it looks like,' she said. 'What it feels like.' She opened her ordinary eyes again slowly, as if she was expecting a bright light to be shining at her. 'Sorry.'

I let out a long sigh. 'Well,' I said. 'We need food. We up for this?'

Josh shrugged. 'Anger and guilt? Story of my life. Let's do it.'

Grace had found a pack of cards in one of the drawers in the back of the van. She said she was going to teach Connor trumps. Josh and Asha and I left, heading down the road. One mile to Middlemiss. Get food, which probably meant steal food, and leave. In and out, and then get moving again.

Simple.

## 4.37 p.m.

#WeirdandProud **I don't care if I am a mutant, where's my fish and chips?**

Asha was stamping down the road, hands in the pockets of her leather jacket, hair bouncing on her neck. 'Can't believe you spent all our money.'

'It wasn't my fault!'

'Oh, right, my mistake, so that wasn't you at the pump wasting fifty quid.'

Josh interrupted, before I could answer. He got in front of us and walked backwards, pointing his finger at us. 'You two ever noticed that you're always bickering? You know what that means, don't you?'

Asha pushed his finger away. 'Means he gets on my tits.'

Josh shook his head, with a big grin on his face. 'Means you lurrve each other.'

I laughed, more at his stupidity than anything else. I thought Asha's lips might have tweaked into a brief smile, but I wasn't sure. She sighed. 'Why am I walking down a road in this big green puddle of nowhere with the two lamest guys in Gilpin? What's gone wrong with my life?'

'Maybe we should all break into song,' said Josh. 'Lift the mood a bit. Cos we are The Future, right? Who wants to start?'

Asha didn't answer. I didn't answer either. I just gave him a look, like *For God's sake, get a grip*. We kept walking. Trees gave way to spiky bright yellow gorse, we passed a couple of detached houses and then a pond and a terrace of cottages, and finally we approached the village green. There was a church, a closed post office and a small Spar.

Josh groaned. 'No fish and chips. Unbelievable. What kind of a village is this?'

'OK,' I said. 'What's the plan?' I wanted to get moving, I wanted to get in, get out, get back to the van. I felt exposed. Could I hear something? Could I hear a helicopter?

116

'Gotta shoplift,' said Asha. 'No choice. We can send them the money later. I'll distract, I'm good at that, you two shove some sandwiches up your jumpers. Let's go.'

We went.

A little bell rang over the door as we entered, and Asha went straight to the counter, where a middle-aged woman with stiff yellow hair was waiting. That was a shame, I was pretty sure Asha would have a better chance of distracting a young bloke. She looked brilliant all in black and she had possibly, just for a second, almost smiled when Josh said that stupid thing about us being in love. Maybe not. Probably just wishful thinking.

We picked up a basket so it would look like we were doing some proper, ordinary shopping. Then we filled our pockets with prawn mayonnaise and beef and English mustard sandwiches. I found a tub of hummus, a box of Laughing Cow cheese and a packet of salami. I put them all under my sweater with a couple of bottles of water and then tucked it in. Josh dropped some apples into the hood of his hoodie. I went for a box of cakes.

Josh protested in an angry whisper, 'I don't like Country Slices, they're not even cakes, they're more like bread with sugar on. I want French Fancies.'

I stared at him and whispered angrily back, 'I don't like French Fancies. Too sweet.'

He stared right back at me. 'There is literally no such thing as too sweet!'

I snorted. 'Don't you even know sugar's bad for you?'

He ignored me, grabbed a box of French Fancies.

We weren't natural shoplifters.

At the counter, Asha was talking to the woman about the best route from here to York. There was some pointing going on and mention of the A something or other and the roadworks on the bypass.

'Let's go,' I hissed.

'This is rubbish food,' Josh whispered back at me, loudly, looking at the shelves, looking for something appetising.

I picked up a cucumber, just as a man came out from the back to help with the directions. I nodded, smiled nervously, looked at the cucumber as if considering whether to buy it. Where was I going to put it, up my sleeve? The man wore a quilted green anorak which made him look like he should be carrying a shotgun over his shoulder.

I replaced the cucumber. 'Come on!' I insisted.

We headed for the door, our pockets bulging and our stomachs looking lumpy and angular.

'Wait! Excuse me, wait!' That was the woman.

'Hey, you two, stop!' That was the man.

I hesitated, my foot was literally in the air and I was swaying a bit, trying to decide whether to go forwards or backwards. It was a bit like when I was on the stepping-stones over the river. I had that same strong sense of precariousness, that feeling that I'd really like to be somewhere else.

The woman with the stiff hair and the man in the green anorak came round the counter and marched towards us.

'What?' said Josh, turning to face them. 'What's the problem?'

And then a box of French Fancies and a bottle of water slid out from under his hoodie and landed on the floor.

I'd lowered my foot by this time. We were standing in the doorway. I don't know about Josh but I was trying not to look guilty, trying not to physically shrink away from the man and the woman in front of us. I was failing at both these things. Green anorak didn't have a gun but he was a big bloke, probably a farmer. He looked like he threw hay bales and possibly sheep around in his spare time. He jabbed a big fat finger into Josh's chest.

'You're the problem, sonny.'

Josh opened his mouth, like he was astonished. 'Wait, oh my God, are you my daddy?'

Green anorak's lips drew back from his teeth in a proper snarl. 'Funny boy,' he gritted. He grabbed a fistful of Josh's hoodie. I could see the dark, curling hairs on his fingers.

'DON'T!'

Asha's Voice reverberated around the shop, like a bell chiming in a clock tower. The man's snarl froze, turned gradually to a look of confusion. He was still holding Josh's hoodie, but he didn't look threatening any more.

The woman looked worried. She touched his shoulder. 'Ian?'

And then Asha tried something else. 'WE'RE LEAVING,' she said. There was no urgency in the Voice this time, just a layered, persuasive resonance that seemed to tug you towards agreeing with her. 'WE'LL PAY LATER,' she said, in the same tone. Her fingers were on her temple, and she was wincing a bit. What was that about? Ian let go of Josh's hoodie. He and the woman with the stiff hair both stepped away from me and Josh. Asha was nodding urgently towards the door, so we backed through it. 'That's fine, isn't it?' She smiled at the man and the woman as she squeezed past them. She picked up the French Fancies and the water off the floor, and then she left with us.

We stood outside the shop, staring at her.

'I've got serious skills,' she said, palms out, fingers splayed, like she'd just done a magic trick. Which she had. 'They were all up in your face, and I was like *Back off!* and they totally backed off.'

'We know,' said Josh, grinning, 'we were there.'

I hugged her. Couldn't help myself. I made sure not to actually touch her skin to skin, because I didn't want to be snooping inside her memories. And she didn't push me away, she let it happen for a good couple of seconds before she stepped back.

'This is where you tell me I'm fantastic,' she said.

I nodded, no hesitation. 'You're fantastic. But did it hurt? You were rubbing your head.'

She shrugged. 'Bit achy, no big deal.'

We headed back to the van with Asha in a brilliant mood – 'I totally saved you, you two were like damsels in distress' – and Josh also in a brilliant mood – 'Asha Ben Kenobi, you are actually honestly my hero.' I was enjoying them being happy, and I was thinking about getting something half-decent to eat, but I was also worrying about Asha's headache. She clearly didn't want to talk about it, but it was new and it was disturbing. Maybe she wouldn't even need to use her power again, so it wouldn't matter, but it definitely bothered me. And it probably bothered her too, somewhere underneath all the smiles and the bragging.

And I still had what Grace had said on my mind. Anger like a storm at sea. A jagged stab of guilt. Ian and his wife hadn't exactly been happy with us but I wouldn't call it a storm at sea. So was that still to come?

Cottages, pond, houses, bright yellow gorse, trees. We walked quickly, carrying our plunder awkwardly, and we found the shady layby ten minutes later. Josh hammered on the side of Vinny the Van.

'Honey, we're home!'

No answer.

I opened the door of the van. Grace and Connor weren't there. We looked around in the trees at the side of the road. No sign of them, they were definitely gone. Where? Where the hell had they gone? Overhead, all of a sudden, I heard the chop-chop-chop of a helicopter.

It was Doofus, I was sure of it. He'd found us, and Grace and Connor were missing.

**5.38 p.m.**

#Weird&Proud **Kids can be monsters, can't they? I mean, literally, they can be monsters.**

We dived under the trees, and I had a memory of doing this a year ago, with Asha, while a helicopter's searchlight pierced the darkness just outside Gilpin, hunting for us. Now here we were a year later, in exactly the same situation.

How had I allowed this to happen again?

Doofus told us a couple of days ago that he was going to round up teenagers 'at the first sign of alien activity'. He'd definitely know by now that the four kids who tormented him last year had left Gilpin at the same moment that Connor and Ruby had disappeared. He'd be searching for us, no question. If he found us we'd get locked up, and we'd probably be safe from Ruby. But the minute they had Connor they'd start their experiments. And the minute they harmed Fuzzy, we'd all die.

We hugged the trunk of a large oak, peering up through branches and leaves at the insect-like thing battering at the air above us.

'They can't see us,' I shouted. 'We're OK, we're under cover.'

'What about Vinny?' Asha shouted.

I looked at the dirty red van in the layby and didn't answer. There was no way of knowing.

The helicopter suddenly lifted away, as if an invisible hand had plucked it out of the sky. We watched it go.

'Right,' I said, 'whether that thing saw us or not, those two in the shop are going to report what happened. We have to get out of here.'

'Wow,' said Asha. 'You work that out all by yourself? The point is, Megamind, we can't go anywhere till we find Grace and Connor.'

Josh had climbed into the van. He came out holding a piece of paper. 'I mean it, you two,' he said, 'get a room. Also,' he waved the paper at us, 'this might help.'

It was a note, written in a quickly scribbled version of Grace's neat handwriting.

*Heard helicopter coming, thought we should go. Farmer stopped to ask if we were OK. Gone with him. Clay Royd Farm, one mile west.*

Josh turned in a slow circle, his index finger pointing vaguely at nothing in particular.

'Which way's west?' he said.

I kind of liked using Jason's old phone, because it was a connection between me and my brother. I got it out and found the compass. We took the left-hand road at the crossroads, and set off. They'd gone because Grace had seen the helicopter coming. I guessed that made sense. But they'd gone off with some stranger, putting their trust in him. Surely that was risky? I wanted to discuss it with Asha and Josh but what was the point? It was done, we had to find them and then get away again as quick as we could. Also, it was no use talking to Asha, because her mouth was full of beef and mustard sandwich. Josh was shoving a pink, too-sweet French Fancy into his mouth. I pulled the cellophane off a prawn mayo sandwich.

We kept walking. Chewing, not speaking, worrying.

I had a stitch by the time we reached the turn-off. A neat, white cast-iron sign with black lettering told us Clay Royd Farm was down the lane on our right. We headed for a thatched house, and I tried not to think of something else that had happened this time last year. I'd been searching for my brother and had ended up along with my older self at Jim Byron's farm, being threatened with a shotgun. Meanwhile Jason was in one of Byron's barns planning to use a rusty knife to cut off a pair of insecty wings that was growing out of his back. Strange times.

And now I had a horrible sense of history repeating itself. Not my older self turning up, and not the insect thing either, but the rest of it – we were running away from Gilpin, from Doofus and Patronising, and maybe some crazy redneck was about to charge out of the thatched farmhouse ahead pointing a shotgun at us.

I wished there was some way to make everything stop. That would be a really useful power. I'd lift up a hand and shout *Stop!* ... Fuzzy would disappear, Ruby and Doofus would back off, no one would be left damaged and traumatised, no one would die, no one would even look like they might die.

To be fair, the front door wasn't the kind of door you'd expect to see a crazy redneck coming out of. It was apple green and it had a stained-glass panel with a heron on it. It opened and I held my breath for a moment, but then a woman in jeans and a flower-printed shirt came out. She was large, she had a lot of reddish brown hair, and she had a big smile on her round, pink face. No shotgun.

'Now, don't tell me,' she said, 'don't tell me.' She pointed her index finger at Asha. 'Asha, obviously. Such a pretty thing.' She pointed at Josh. 'I'm going to say you're Josh, am I right?'

He nodded and she looked delighted with herself. 'Grace said he wears a hoodie and he'll look hungry. Two out of two! So you must be Hector.' She gave me a big smile, and I wondered how Grace had described me. 'Welcome, all. My name's Maureen. Now, I know you're probably in a hurry, Grace and Connor said you would be, but what would you say to a bowl of stew?'

She had big pink arms to go with her big pink face and she looked like an old-fashioned sort of woman who thought being a mum and providing for kids was the best job in the world. No sign of any anger or guilt here, but still I didn't think we should be saying yes to stew.

'Right now, I would marry a bowl of stew,' said Josh, 'and have little stewie children.'

He and Asha walked in, so I followed.

We sat round an oak table in the kitchen. Maureen binned the remains of our sandwiches and Grace and Connor, who'd already eaten, sat there and watched us shovel food into our mouths. There were big, tender pieces of lamb in a thick gravy with carrots and potatoes and probably things like swedes which I don't even like, but in this case I did like them. There was home-made crusty bread to mop up the gravy from our steaming plates, and the steam smelt so good it almost felt like it was another lovely thing to eat. There was a pot of coffee on the table and I felt pretty certain that there would be home-made cake or biscuits to follow. I remembered the Famous Five books my mum used to read me when I was little. Four kids and a dog, rocking up at a farmhouse in the middle of an adventure, getting fed brilliant food by motherly farmers' wives. I hadn't actually held up my hand and shouted Stop! But, just for a minute, it felt like I had, like nothing bad could happen in this place.

'Isn't it great?' Connor said. 'Isn't it fantastic? Maureen, you're the best cook in the world, ever.'

She smiled and ruffled his hair. 'Aren't you the sweetest thing?' she said.

When Josh finished his portion, she ladled some more on to his plate before he could even speak.

My mouth was full and my stomach was getting full too, but I was still worrying, because we weren't actually the Famous Five. We were Teenage Mutant Fugitives, which was a whole different thing.

'Do you have children, Maureen?' I said, in a lamb-muffled voice.

'Grace asked me that.' Her tone was light, but for just a moment there was a sharpness in her eyes. 'They're at school. Kids at school, hubby back out in the fields. Will you have some more, Hector? I'm sure you will.' And the sharpness had vanished. Had I imagined it?

Grace was looking at me. And as she looked at me she gave a tiny shake of her head. I said, 'No thanks,' even though I could easily have eaten another plateful, and then Grace said, 'I'm just going to the loo.'

And again, she was looking at me. 'Me too,' I said. 'That was brilliant, thanks, Maureen.'

'You're most welcome.' She had a warm voice, a kind voice. What was Grace's problem? 'Toilet's on the left of the front door.'

Grace and I went out together. 'What?' I whispered, as soon as we were out of the kitchen. I nodded at her forehead. 'Have you seen something?'

'No,' she said. 'But something doesn't feel right. Her husband, he shot off as soon as he'd dropped us here, and him and Maureen, they looked at each other and just for a moment ... there was something going on between them.'

'We should go then,' I said. 'We should just get out.'

She was looking over my shoulder. Opposite the front door was an office. A desktop computer sat in front of a window with a view over fields. We glanced at each other, hesitated a moment, then nipped into the room. I checked over my shoulder then touched the keyboard. The screen lit up. Grace opened Explorer and it went straight to the BBC's homepage. She clicked on History, clicked on the most recent heading, and then we both gasped. Froze. Stared at the screen, silent.

We were looking at ourselves. Old photos, full-face, not particularly flattering but very clear. Me, Grace, Asha, Josh, Ruby and Connor. Along with our faces was the word **REWARD** in big, bold capitals. I remembered the guy in the petrol station. *Do I know you?* The smaller print said we were probably in a red campervan. It said we were dangerous, it said that in particular other teenagers should not come near us, and it gave a number that should be rung the moment we were seen.

'Let's go,' said Grace, her voice tense and high-pitched.

'What's this?' said Maureen. 'Leaving already?'

She was behind us, standing in the doorway. Blocking the doorway.

'Yes, sorry.' Grace was trying to sound casual, and failing.

'Thanks, but we've got to go.' My voice felt squeezed, it was hard to get the words out.

Maureen wasn't smiling any more. 'What have you done?' Her tone was hard. 'And how are you dangerous?'

I was contemplating grabbing her arm but I really didn't fancy that slippery rush of someone else's memories filling my head again. I was going to call Asha so she could use the Voice, even though I didn't want her to have another headache, but before I could do anything Grace lifted her fringe off her forehead, closed her ordinary eyes and opened her third Eye.

Maureen let out a small scream, an actual scream, as the Eye rested on her. It stared straight at her.

'Do you want to know something terrible?' said Grace in a weird, breathy voice with an edge of a tremor. 'Because I can see it. I am seeing it, right now. Grief like a fog, a fog you can't find your way out of.'

Maureen stammered something panicked, it wasn't a word it was just a sound, or a series of sounds, and she backed out of the doorway. I pushed past her.

'Asha, guys, we've got to go!'

Maureen was white, she was shaking. 'What . . . what . . .' she said. She couldn't seem to get any other words out.

Grace had dropped her fringe back over her forehead, opened her eyes. She looked mortified. 'I'm sorry,' she said. 'I'm so sorry.'

'Thank you,' I began. I nearly said *for having us*, but I stopped myself. 'Thank you for the meal.'

Maureen's round, pink face twisted and seemed to shrink. She found her voice. 'Get out of my house, you monster,' she spat at Grace. I wanted to say something else, to find some words to explain to her that Grace wasn't a monster, none of us were, that we might not actually be the Famous Five, but we weren't bad people at all, but she screamed at us: 'Get out!'

Anger, like a storm at sea.

Josh, Asha and Connor came out of the kitchen and we bundled out of the front door.

'We need to run,' I said.

And we ran, because her husband would be back any minute now with police cars, or a helicopter would be landing in a field or, I don't know, black-uniformed soldiers would be marching out of the treeline carrying guns with green light glowing out of the muzzles.

We ran off the lane and into the trees, but as we ran, jostling and panting and listening for car engines or the clatter of a helicopter above us, I was thinking of Maureen's face, the anger and the shock in it, and I was thinking of that word 'monster'. And I was thinking maybe we should forget about getting to the remote cottage in Northumberland, maybe we should just get ourselves caught instead. Maybe that would be best.

A jagged stab of guilt.

**#Weird&Proud Everything's going well! Couldn't be better! Just having a little break now. Wake me up if the world ends or anything.**

We were by the van. My face stung where it had been whipped by a twig, and I had a bruise on my knee where I'd stumbled over a root. It went with the grazes I'd got when we were escaping from Ruby back in Gilpin. Hard to believe that was only a few hours ago. I was taking long, shaky breaths and I had a stitch again. The others were the same, clutching their stomachs, limping. Josh had his hands on his knees, Asha was leaning against a tree.

'I bloody hate the countryside,' she panted.

'They should pave the whole lot,' said Josh.

The grey sky was darkening, gloom seemed to be creeping in from the trees around us.

'I liked Maureen.' Connor's voice had a bit of a whine in it. 'Why did we have to go?'

'Let's find somewhere to hide,' I said, 'where we can park for the night. Then we can talk.'

I meant talk about giving up, but I didn't say it. No point – we'd probably get caught in about ten minutes anyway. I was convinced Doofus would be setting up roadblocks and sending his troops in to saturate this area. We got in the van, Josh tried various buttons and knobs till he found the lights, then we drove off.

'How d'you hide a big red van?' he said. 'Sounds like a joke but it's not a joke.'

'Maybe we should walk?' Grace called from the back.

'I hate walking!' Asha shouted.

'That's not helpful,' I called back.

'You're not helpful,' she snapped.

'Nor's your face,' I said.

Josh laughed, but he didn't sound amused. 'This is going so well,' he murmured.

There was a bend coming up, and suddenly there were full-beam headlights shining on to it, evidence of a car about to come around the corner and face us.

Josh started to speak. 'What should we . . .?'

I grabbed the wheel and yanked it to the left. We swerved with a jarring tyre-screech into a narrow lane, scraped a hedge, and Vinny the Van rattled and shook as it bounced over ruts in the ground.

'Brake, Josh!' I shouted. 'And kill the lights!'

But he was panicking, and he did neither. There were screams from the back and the thump of someone falling off their seat as we sped straight for a wall of green. It was a dead end and this was the moment Josh chose to turn off the lights.

I shouted and put my hands in front of my face, convinced we were all about to die. There was a threshing noise like a thousand fingers and fingernails scraping and scratching our sides as we smashed through undergrowth, hedge, twigs and branches until finally Josh found the brake and stamped on it.

I was flung against my seat belt and there was a thump and clatter as bodies hit the floor behind me. We were a tin box filled with panic and screams.

We jolted to a sudden, final stop two inches from a fallen tree trunk that would have mashed the front of the van.

Silence, except for panting and whimpers.

Behind us the car with the full-beam lights sped by. There was no way of knowing whether it was the police.

More silence. Uneven breathing, groans. Asha swearing.

'OK,' Josh stuttered, eventually. 'Think I handled that pretty well.'

We stretched and flexed, checking to see if anything was broken. Connor had hit the floor first and Grace had fallen on top of him. He had a sore shoulder and a big bruise on his ankle, but he was OK. We were all OK.

'Sorry,' I said. My voice was shaking. 'But you saw that car, right? We had to hide.'

We all climbed out. There was barely room to move. Josh squeezed slowly all the way around the van, patting it again, feeling it, like that was going to make any difference.

'I think Vinny's all right,' he said.

There was an interlocking canopy of branches above us, the fallen tree was in front of us like a great spread hand, and a thick hedge had closed up behind us. We were in a small green cave, like a cell.

Prickly green walls up close all around. Thin, twiggy fingers stretched towards us on all sides. Evening light slanted in from the setting sun. There was a fresh smell like cut grass, and a dead smell like flowers that had wilted in a vase. Something rustled nearby.

'All right.' Josh was nodding now, his breathing almost even again, his tone calmer. 'Couple of joss sticks and a Dark Knight poster,' he said, 'and I could actually live here.'

Asha broke off a twig that was threatening to poke her in the eye. 'So now we're basically woodland animals?' she said. 'That's new.'

But she didn't sound annoyed, more sort of intrigued. Maybe because of the quiet, or the smell, or the sense after all that panic of being safely held in a textured green hand. I was feeling less anxious now. I was pretty sure we all were. Ruby was still on the way, Doofus was still searching, but we seemed to have found a hiding place. The van's engine cooled, making little tinks and clicks. Insects buzzed, a bird warbled a series of long, low notes. The evening light faded.

You could almost believe that time passed more slowly in this place, that when we finally emerged, years would have gone by. I pulled a pale leaf off a low branch and rubbed it under my nose, smelling it, getting a sappy green stain on my fingers. I felt like I had the last fragments of summer between my fingertips.

We got back in the van once it was properly dark. There were five too-sweet French Fancies left in the box. We had one each, and passed around a bottle of water.

Josh got a notepad and biro out of his bag. He peeled the pink icing off his cake with his teeth, staring at a blank page, tapping it with his pen.

I was completely confused. Josh wasn't a diary-keeper. He wasn't a writer of any sort, as far as I knew.

'What you doing?' I said. 'Homework?'

He ignored me. Meanwhile, Grace had taken her sketch pad out of her bag and was drawing something. She was working on the sketch of Eden James again, but when I looked more closely I saw she was doing something odd with it. It wasn't a caricature, but she'd made Eden's face thin and hard and there was something very clear there that was usually hidden. Malice. She'd made Eden look nasty.

So they were both acting weird, basically. I was going to say something to Grace, see if she actually bothered to answer, but my phone buzzed. It was Dr Lazarus. He was replying to the tweet about kids being monsters.

**Define monster, Kurt. How about someone who's so sure he's right he doesn't notice when he's being selfish and stupid?**

OK, Dr Lazarus was really bothering me now. He wasn't just trolling any more, hurling abuse, this was a whole new approach, he was sounding almost reasonable, like he was having a debate with me. It was like he knew I was going wrong and he wanted to help out, he wanted to set me straight. I read the text to the others.

'Maureen called Grace a monster,' I said. 'She was proper scared.'

Silence for a moment. Then Josh put away his notepad. 'So?'

I sighed. 'So . . . does anyone else feel like giving up?'

'No!' said Josh.

'Yes!' said Asha. 'Obviously. I thought I was the only one. Cos we'll get caught anyway, and Grace says someone's gonna die and, Connor, they won't cut you open they'll just put you somewhere safe where they can watch you till creepy little Fuzzy comes out of you. So what are we even doing here?'

I was nodding. I agreed with most of what Asha had just said. I didn't think they'd just sit back and watch Connor, but I thought maybe we should take that risk. Because I didn't want to be a monster. I wanted to be one of the good guys.

Grace lowered her pad. I was keeping my phone on, so we had a bit of greenish light to see each other by.

'We know from last time,' she began slowly, 'that if they harm the egg, or the foetus, or whatever it is, then people who've been changed by it will die. That means all of us will die, plus Ruby will die, and every teenager in Gilpin who was affected before we left will die. And we think Douglas and Kirby might want to deliberately harm it, don't we? To send a message, to say "Don't send any more of these things down here." So they'll harm it, and we'll all die.'

Grace usually preferred to listen, and put in the odd wise word, rather than make a speech and have everyone staring at her. She was a dark shape, looking at us, waiting for us to respond.

'We don't know all that for sure,' said Asha finally, 'because there's no egg this time.'

Josh shook his head. 'There is an egg,' he said, like it was obvious. 'The egg is Connor. Fuzzy's mum must have decided eggs aren't safe, humans are safer. And I absolutely want to get back,' he continued, not leaving a moment for anyone to argue, 'soon as possible. For reasons. But everything Grace said is totally on the money.'

Grace hadn't finished. 'I agree with that tweet,' she said. 'People who are sure they're right usually haven't thought very hard, and mostly they're horrible people. But that's not us, that's Douglas and Kirby. If I trusted them at all I'd say we should give up, let them take over. But I don't trust them.'

'Yeah,' said Josh. 'We're not sure we're right. We've got no idea what we're doing!'

I turned to Connor. 'What d'you think?'

He frowned, and I thought he wasn't going to say anything. I was looking away, not wanting to put him on the spot, when he blurted: 'It's too soon to give up, isn't it? We haven't even managed twenty-four hours yet.' He looked at us, like he was worried he'd said too much, then continued, more hesitant: 'And I don't really like the sound of Doofus and Professor Patronising. And anyway ...' He smiled nervously, a bit embarrassed. 'Anyway, it's good hanging with you.'

They all looked at me. I was the only one who hadn't given an opinion.

'We keep going then,' I said. 'You're right, it comes down to do we trust Doofus and Patronising. And we don't. Plus, I agree with Connor – turns out, I like spending time with my mates.'

Josh nodded. 'Right,' he said, 'no one wants to give up, stupid idea. But let's not head north any more, straight to this cottage. A friend of my mum's lives near Whitby. We could have a break there, maybe get some food and some money off him.'

I shone my phone on to the map. It was a great big detour, but maybe it made sense to set off in a new direction.

'I guess we're going to the seaside, then,' I said.

'Fine,' Asha sighed. 'Much more important question – anyone bring loo roll?'

Josh and I stayed in our seats in the front, the benches behind us made a double bed for Asha and Grace, then there was a sort of cramped shelf for Connor above them.

'Just like old times,' said Josh. 'Nice one, Vinny.' He patted the steering wheel. He sounded genuinely happy. He got his notepad out again and started writing, like he suddenly knew what he wanted to say.

So I tried asking him again. 'What you doing?'

He just shushed me, and didn't answer. Kept writing for a few minutes then put the pad away again.

None of us slept. We dozed. I spent a lot of time looking out of the window at blackness, listening to small animals moving outside, hearing at one stage a helicopter passing overhead.

I turned towards Josh at some point in the night, and blearily saw he had that little box out. He was turning it over, feeling every little bit of it. When he saw me looking, he put it on his palm and showed it to me. It was inky black, darker than the darkness around it, with a swirl of silver drifting around it like a fish.

'See this?' he whispered, pointing. 'See here? This little ridge? It's a lid. This box has a lid. I want to get my fingernails under it and pull it open and let whatever's in there get out.'

I stared at him. 'But you're not going to, right?'

'It's speaking to me,' he said. His face was just a blur of darkness but I could hear the tension in his tight, controlled voice. 'It's totally muttering in my ear all the time.'

'How about we leave it here when we go?' I said, trying to sound calm and constructive. 'Yeah? We'll bury it about ten feet deep and leave it here.'

He shook his head. 'Can't do it.' His hand quickly closed around the box as if he thought I was going to snatch it away from him. 'Can't let it go. It's a part of me.' He put it back in his pocket. His voice was slowing down, words coming more slowly, like he was getting sleepy. 'If I open it, like I want to open it, then I think I'd just fill up with sadness, and you know, that's probably not good, at all, is it? Even though there's a bit of me . . .' He stopped talking, turned towards the dark window, left his sentence trailing away in the gloom.

I must have slept for a while after that. Max drifted into my dreams, the way he often did. We were in Shake!, in Gilpin, and he was grinning at me, but then he started to fade, and I said his name and reached out, but there was nothing there. He was gone. I woke with a gasp and lay still for a moment, letting that familiar wave of sadness pass through me.

It wasn't exactly light, but it wasn't exactly dark either. I heard a big yawn behind me. Connor, on his shelf. Then a pause, and a thump as he got down.

'Hey,' he said. 'Anyone awake?'

He sounded worried. I twisted round in my seat. Asha and Grace were stirring, Connor was standing crouched behind them.

'She's coming,' he said. 'Ruby. She's close.'

# DAY FOUR

**6.20 a.m.**

#Weird&Proud **The big sky, the open road, and a great big horse with scary teeth. Because . . . why not?**

I stood in the middle of the road and looked left. Looked right. No cars, no sound except for birds getting overexcited. The sky was pink over the treeline. I shouted that it was all clear and waited, peering back down the lane at the hedge down at the end. It looked like a solid wall of green.

Nothing for a moment.

Then a coughing, throaty growl as Josh revved Vinny's engine.

Startled birds flapped away in a panic.

The growl turned into Vinny's best effort at a roar, and the red back of the van suddenly burst out of that green wall like a volcanic eruption. The wheels actually left the ground for a moment, and it raced backwards down the lane, bouncing and bumping over ruts and holes, sideswiping branches and twigs, hurtling towards me.

I jumped out of the way and Vinny screeched to a stop beside me. Josh leant out the window with a big, toothy, pleased-with-himself grin. He slapped the door.

'You've gotta respect this vehicle,' he said.

I smiled back at him. It felt like we were doing all right. We had a destination and a plan. We'd found, accidentally, a brilliant hiding place, and managed to avoid the police, Doofus and Professor Patronising. One of us was apparently going to die, our faces were online with a reward attached, we were thieves, Maureen and Dr Lazarus thought we were all monsters, and Ruby was right behind us, but those things could hopefully be sorted out. We were all more or less in agreement about what direction to take next. We'd soon lose Ruby.

So far, so good.

But then, as I got in the van next to Josh, Grace screamed. She pointed down the road and full-on screamed.

'She's here!'

A bright green Vauxhall Corsa had skidded round the bend ahead of us. It straightened up and paused a moment, like a bull eyeing up a matador. It revved and revved, there was a protesting screech from the tyres, then it jolted into motion and charged directly at us.

I glimpsed the scared face of a young man driving, and the snarling face of Ruby beside him. She had a hand gripping the wheel. Josh hit the accelerator and yanked the steering wheel at the same time and Vinny shook and jerked like a startled animal, lurching to the right, narrowly missing a head-on collision, raking along the side of the Corsa, then ricocheting off towards the hedge.

Josh hit the brake and we tipped sideways as a wheel slid into a ditch beside the road.

Twenty metres behind us the Corsa had swerved and stopped too.

'Josh,' I said, trying to keep my voice steady. Failing.

'I know!' he snapped.

He touched the accelerator. The wheels spun. The wheels spun and we didn't move. I twisted in my seat and looked back, trying to think what Ruby was thinking. If she got out of the car to come for us on foot the man would probably drive away immediately, and then Ruby would be stranded if we got the van moving again. The Corsa started to turn. Ruby was playing it safe, she was going to drive right up alongside us before she got out of the car, ripped the door off the van and jumped in.

'Come on!' Asha shouted.

Josh didn't answer, he just touched the accelerator gently, not overdoing it.

There was a complaining rattle from the engine, as the van slowly, so slowly, pulled itself out of the ditch. We had all four wheels on the road again.

'Go, go, go!' I yelled.

'I know!' he yelled back at me.

I twisted round again and watched the Corsa turning to follow us.

'Faster, Josh,' I pleaded.

He was staring ahead, concentrating. 'Shut up!' he barked. 'Captain Obvious.'

Vinny's tyres squealed as we skidded round the bend the Corsa had just come round, and slowly, slowly started to accelerate. The van was maybe twenty years old, it had five people and luggage in it, it definitely wasn't built for a car chase. We were approaching a T junction. I looked over my shoulder – still no sign of the Corsa.

'Turn before she sees us!' I said.

'You think?' he bellowed, an edge of hysteria in his voice. 'You think?'

I took a deep breath as we approached the junction, then pressed my lips together, trying to stay silent, not wanting to wind Josh up any further. Being driven at speed down narrow twisty lanes by a hysterical Josh was almost as frightening as being caught by Ruby. He was barely slowing down as he approached the blind corner, banking on the hope that there was nothing coming on this quiet road early in the morning. He bared his teeth as he veered on to the wrong side of the road to give himself room, then gave a small scream as he yanked the wheel abruptly in the other direction.

We all flew to our left as the tyres squealed and we turned. Vinny shuddered and tipped. Josh didn't pause, he straightened up and stamped the accelerator again.

'Oh, yeah!' he shouted, pumping both fists in the air. 'Smashed it!'

I grabbed the wheel with one hand. 'There!' I pointed with the other. There was a turning up ahead – if we took that road we could be out of sight before Ruby reached the junction.

Josh brushed my hand away and yanked the wheel again as I looked over my shoulder. No sign of Ruby.

'Nice one,' I breathed.

'Tyre tracks,' said Grace, looking out of the back window, 'we're leaving tyre tracks behind us because of the skidding. She'll see them.'

Nothing we could do about that. We kept driving. Connor, Asha and Grace all staring out of the back window, Josh checking the mirror almost as much as he was looking ahead, me mostly worrying about meeting a car coming the other way, because Josh was still driving like a madman.

'But maybe I should just talk to her?' Connor's voice was mild, tentative, as if we were in the middle of a conversation. 'She'll be lonely. I'm like, to be honest, her only friend.'

No one said anything until, predictably, Asha said something.

'Your ultra-violent, straight-out-of-a-horror-movie sister shoved your parents in a room and wouldn't let them out,' she snapped. 'She threw a small tree at us and was all set to punch me in the face with her super-strength. She wants you sat in the middle of Leeds or Manchester turning the whole place mutant.'

'All right . . .' I said.

'No, not all right!' Asha snarled. 'Keep up, Connor. That alien inside you has turned her completely mad, same as it did with my brother, who's a completely lost cause by the way. She's being controlled by that thing which, in case you haven't noticed, loves making teenagers freaks. It wants to be where people are, so we have to keep you away from her. Once it's out of you, once it's hatched, she might be OK again, maybe, but till then – we stay nowhere near her. Got it?'

Connor bit his lip and nodded. He was a frightened kid, worried about his twin sister, worried about, basically, everything.

Grace gave him a tentative smile, put a hand on his shoulder. 'You're our friend now, Connor, so Ruby can be too, when this is all over.'

Asha snorted, and I spoke quickly, before she could say anything. 'She'll be all right,' I said, trying to sound reassuring, like I knew what I was talking about. 'Once Fuzzy's out of you she'll be fine. We all will. That's what happened last year.'

Well, it sort of happened last year. Except Asha was

estranged from her brother, and mine had turned his back on his family, and I'd suffered, basically, post-traumatic stress for a year. But we were all still alive, that was something.

Connor didn't say anything. No one did. I wasn't surprised – I hadn't even convinced myself. We kept driving.

The tense silence continued for a while, all of us thinking dark thoughts. 'Everyone probably reckons we're still going north,' Josh said, finally. He sounded like he was trying to persuade himself. 'We'll lose them, definitely, we'll lose them.'

That was it for the next few miles. Josh muttering to himself, Asha seething, Connor possibly trying to hold back tears, Grace staying quiet, me with the map on my lap, pointing at turnings occasionally, hardly daring to speak in case Josh lost his temper again. It was like one of those family outings where the kids have been dragged along, the grown-ups have had an argument, the atmosphere's horrible and everyone's thinking of somewhere they'd rather be.

Another crossroads coming up, but we had priority, so Josh wasn't slowing down. Fair enough. I was looking at the road ahead, thinking about possible routes. I was aware of yellow gorse and a scatter of blue daisies on the verge, and the sky was brightening so I was starting to feel better. Time and sunshine were doing their work, and the bad feeling among us was slowly, slowly, starting to fade away.

There was a blur of movement in the corner of my right eye.

I started to turn towards it.

A green blur.

In a terrifying, heart-in-mouth sliver of a second I realised Ruby's Corsa was hurtling towards us.

And then there was a

CRASH!

The whole van rocked, and I thought it was going to tip over. Josh's head flew into my right shoulder and I flew into the side door, slamming my left shoulder against the glass. Screams, bangs, the van skidding towards the hedge.

I tried to reach over Josh, who was a dead weight on me. I scrabbled for the wheel but I could only brush it with my fingertips. The van jolted and reared up over the verge like an out-of-control beast, hurtled straight through the hedge, stumbled over a shallow ditch, and skidded into a field.

We stopped.

Somebody whimpered. Uneven, panicky breathing. A sob. Otherwise, it was eerily quiet. I sat up carefully, moved Josh, who was still a dead weight, reached over and switched off the engine. Looked into the back. They were all on the floor, in a tangle of limbs and heads. They were stirring, I was pretty sure they were all stirring.

Josh wasn't.

'Josh? Mate?'

Was he dead? Was this what Grace had seen?

*This horrible sense of loss, like a great empty pit.*

'Josh!'

He groaned. He definitely groaned. He was unconscious, but still alive.

I took off my seat belt, knelt up in my seat and looked out of the back window. The Corsa had skidded off to the right and was embedded in a hedge on the other side of the road. No movement there yet.

I took off Josh's seat belt, shouting over my shoulder. 'Someone give me a hand!' We needed him in the back, being looked after, while I drove. Assuming Vinny the Van would move, assuming it hadn't died, and also assuming I'd be able to drive it. My shoulder ached where it had hit the side window. 'Anyone?' I'd opened my door and I had my hands under Josh's armpits. I climbed out backwards, dragging him after me. He groaned again, which I hoped was a good sign.

The long grass was wet with dew. My ankles were getting damp. A horse that had galloped off when we arrived was now looking at me curiously, from a safe distance. The low sun dazzled me. Everything was too bright.

Grace and Connor got out.

Connor stroked the side of the van. 'Poor Vinny,' he said.

'Let's get Josh in the back,' I said, 'then I'll see if I can get us out of here. Is Asha OK?'

I didn't give them time to answer. I could see the road through a gate in the hedge, I could see the back half of the Corsa on the other side of the road, strangely skewed with its nose buried in the hedge. As I watched, there was a screech of tearing metal, and the door of the Corsa flew off its hinges, as if it had been kicked.

Ruby got out of the crumpled car with a sinuous twist and pulled herself free of the hedge. Black T-shirt, skinny jeans, short black hair. She still looked like a thin-limbed, gawky kid who couldn't intimidate a nervous kitten, but she also looked like a rock star. A short, angry rock star.

There was blood on her forehead. She touched it, looked at it on her fingers, then steadied herself a moment with a hand on the roof of the car.

And then she looked up and her eyes met mine. We looked at each other for a long, still moment. I found myself wondering what it must be like to be her. She probably didn't think she was the bad guy, she just wanted her brother back, and she was just following Fuzzy's prompts. Even while I was terrified, I was a little bit worried for her. Naveen seemed to have finished up pretty much an outcast. Supposing we all survived this, was Ruby going to end up the same way? She'd been sidelined all her life, and nothing she was doing was going to change that.

So I felt sympathetic, but right now, in the present, I was mostly worried about the whole full-on, super-villain strength thing.

'Get him in,' I shouted. 'We have to go!'

I didn't think I had time but I was about to run round to the driver's side when the engine turned over, wheezed and rattled, and then caught. It revved like a racing car.

'Jump in, Fish Boy!' Asha yelled.

I jumped in.

She grinned at me, a wild look in her eyes. 'Don't you know women are the best drivers? Let's boogie!'

Connor and Grace slammed the door, Asha stamped on the accelerator and thankfully, unexpectedly, incredibly, Vinny the brilliant, elderly, multiply dented and scratched red van bucked like it had been hit with a stick and set off across the field with a confused, dappled horse, sleek, big-toothed and horsey, cantering alongside it.

## 7.13 a.m.

### #Weird&Proud Tick, tick, tick. How long is this going to take?

We were back on the road. The Corsa, as far as I'd been able to tell, wasn't going anywhere. I took a long, shaky breath in, let a long, shaky breath out.

'This is where you tell me I saved your life,' said Asha.

I looked at her. She'd changed into a purple top with her black jeans, she had little gold stud earrings, and she was sitting there holding the big steering wheel, back straight to give her a bit more height, staring out at the road. She was grinning, but the grin was wobbling a bit as the shock of what had just happened bubbled away inside her, like it was bubbling away inside all of us.

I wanted to kiss her really badly.

'You totally saved my life,' I said.

She nodded. Glanced at me, then fixed her eyes back on the road. 'That's how I roll,' she said.

I looked back at Josh. He was awake, or half-awake, his eyelids were flickering. He was slumped on the bench back there, pale as a pillowcase, and Grace was stroking his forehead. He'd got the black box of sadness out of his pocket. He was clutching it in his fist.

'Don't let him open it!' I said.

Grace went to take it from him but he snatched his hand away. His knuckles, closed tightly around it, were white. He gritted his teeth and pressed it right up against his temple.

'What's happening, Josh?' I said. 'What are you doing?'

He let out a long, hoarse sigh.

'What the hell's up with him?' said Asha, looking in the mirror. 'Is he possessed?'

'No, he's not,' croaked Josh, in a demon voice.

'Oh my God!' Connor shrieked, delighted. 'Was that a joke, or are you actually possessed?'

Josh wiped a hand over his scalp and then sat up slowly. He closed his eyes and took a deep breath, then opened them. He'd got some colour back in his face. 'The box did something,' he said. 'Somehow I knew it would. It sucked up all the pain in my head.' He held it in front of his nose on the palm of his hand, studying it.

'Brilliant,' I said. 'That's something good it can do then.'

Josh nodded. 'Yeah. But that pain is another thing trapped inside here that I really don't want to let out.' He raised it even closer to his eyes. 'Except,' he said, flexing his fingers, 'I really do want to let it out.'

'Put it away, Josh,' I said.

He put it back in his pocket. 'Don't worry,' he said, 'I'm fine. I mean I'm not, obviously, but none of us is, right?'

No one answered. No one needed to.

And then, an hour and a half later, the sea.

Optimism arrived suddenly. The fresh, tingling, ozoney smell, along with the strip of deep, rich blue under the skyline, changed the mood. Connor actually briefly started singing about the seaside. It was like autumn and winter were already over, and it was the first warm, sunny day of spring, and I'd just kissed Asha and she'd kissed me back. It was like all those things at once, and I felt a great urge to actually do that, lean over and kiss Asha, and not even say anything, just let her understand that obviously, *obviously*, it was the right thing to do.

All that from suddenly seeing and smelling the sea.

'Where we actually going, then, Josh?' said Asha. 'You even know?'

'And does this man live in Whitby?' Grace said. 'Because we don't want to be in a town.'

And then we got lost and doubled back and tried again, and got lost again. Josh kept saying things like 'Wait, I recognise this bit!' And, 'Maybe we should have taken that left a few minutes ago.' And, 'It's exactly like this, but it's not this.' Asha got more and more irritated, and that good mood and optimism started draining away as fast as it had turned up.

Josh was leaning over the back of our seat, staring out of the windshield, with his chin on his crossed wrists. It meant his elbows were poking at our ears. 'This could be . . .' he began. He'd said that before so we didn't get excited. 'No, seriously, this might be . . .' Still nothing to get excited about. 'Yes!' He was shouting right in my ear now, and jabbing a finger at a little terrace of four houses looking out over small gardens and a couple of fields towards the sea. 'Found it! You're welcome!'

Asha stopped outside, pulling in under the inadequate cover of a tree, and stretched, waggling her arms. 'Totally nailed driving then,' she said. 'Don't know what all the fuss is about.'

I was looking behind me, at Josh. 'D'you know if there are any teens here?' I said.

He pointed at the first house: 'Old couple.' The second: 'Holiday home, probably empty.' The third: 'Don't know.' And the end one, which had a mountain bike in the garden and a garage with thin walls and a sagging roof leaning up against the side wall: 'That's where Simpson lives. Which is his name.'

'And who actually is he?' I said.

Josh paused, and I thought he wasn't going to answer at all. He glanced at me, glanced away. 'He was my mum's boyfriend after my dad and before she started properly drinking,' he mumbled. 'He's all right.'

Grace squeezed his hand. 'Let's hope he's there,' she said.

Surely there was something going on between those two? I'd totally missed it last year, but this year I could definitely see something. Almost definitely. I made a mental note to ask Asha. We got out, Asha sliding across to my side because her door wouldn't open. I didn't want to slam my door too hard because I thought the van might actually fall to pieces if I did. I stretched, took a deep breath of salty sea air, then walked around the van. The driver's side was crumpled as if a giant had punched it.

Josh shook his head, looking at Connor. 'See what Ruby did? See what she did to Vinny?'

Connor nodded.

Josh sighed. 'She's got anger issues, your sister.'

Grace was looking at Simpson's house. 'So we know we can trust him,' she said, looking at Josh. 'But still, shouldn't we talk about this first?'

'Yes. Like what are we even going to say to him?' said Asha.

And then, before anyone could answer that, the front door of the end house flew open. A barefoot, muscly, stubbled black guy in shorts and a grey T-shirt stepped out.

'Josh,' he bellowed. 'Is that you?'

'OK,' Asha muttered. 'Never mind.'

'Wonder if he's seen our faces online?' I whispered.

'Fugitives!' he said, approaching us, and answering my question at the same time. 'You know there's a price on your heads?'

'That's why I've brought them here,' said Josh. 'So you and me can split the reward.'

We all looked at Josh. He laughed. 'Your faces.'

Simpson put a large hand on Josh's shoulder. 'Good to see you, mate.' He looked at each of us. 'All right, no offence, but I'm not getting chills looking at you people.' He poked a finger in my chest. 'You dangerous?'

Connor put his hand up as if he was in a classroom. 'No, it's me,' he said. 'I'm dangerous.'

Simpson tipped back his head and laughed. 'Got it,' he said to Connor. 'Don't mess with the little one. You coming in then, or what?'

We hesitated, and he looked at us and nodded again,

like he understood. If I'd had the energy to explain it, I'd have told him we were all worried about what our parents might be thinking; we were tired because none of us had slept well; we were shocked, because we'd been in a car crash; we were paranoid, because a number of people were out to get us; we were anxious about the probably impossible quest ahead of us and, oh yeah, we were worried we were going to die.

'Depends whether you trust me, I suppose,' he said finally. 'Can't make that decision for you.' He sounded serious but I saw amusement in his brown eyes. 'What d'you think?' he said. 'Am I going to sell you out for the price of a new mountain bike?' He paused. 'Put it like that, it's tempting, to be fair.'

He stood there looking at us, and we stood there looking at him.

'Give me the keys, idiots,' he boomed suddenly. I jumped. 'I'll get this wreck out of sight. Get inside, get the kettle on.' We were still all staring at him, like we were frozen. He clapped his hands. 'How the hell did you losers get this far? Come on, move!'

I opened the front door and an enormous Alsatian barked at me. I jumped and staggered back.

It had a shaggy black and brown coat, its cold, black eyes were fixed on me, and it took a step towards me. It bared its sharp, wet teeth, and growled. The sound was low and threatening.

I tried to back up further but the others were coming in behind me.

'Don't mind Peaches!' Simpson shouted. 'She's a sweetheart.'

The sweetheart took another step forward. As I stumbled towards her, pushed by Asha, she started to bark ferociously. It was loud and throaty and seemed to echo right inside my head. Saliva dripped from her jaws and I was pretty sure I saw nothing but hate in her eyes.

'Peaches?' I stammered. 'He calls her Peaches?'

I thought for one moment that was equal parts terrifying and embarrassing that I might actually wet myself. Why would anyone have a pet like this? It was literally like having a wolf in your front room.

Josh pushed past me. 'Peachy!' he yelled. 'Remember me?'

He threw his arms round her neck and the barking stopped immediately, replaced by excited panting and wet, licking sounds (which was Peaches) and mutterings of 'Peachy, Peachy, Peachy,' (which was Josh) while he hugged her and tipped right over on to the carpet with her so that her tail, wagging frantically, beat the floor like a drum.

'Well, this is adorable,' said Asha. 'I'm getting a nice, warm feeling, but what about that kettle?'

The front door had taken us straight into a sitting room with a big window looking out at the sea and a whole lot of sky. A narrow staircase led upstairs, and the kitchen was a small room at the back. We all started to crowd in but that got ridiculous.

'Go and sit down,' Grace instructed us. 'I'll do it.'

We went and found seats, but Grace put her head out of

the door almost immediately. 'Do we still think it's going to be seven days altogether?' she said.

'Any longer and I'll need more knickers,' Asha muttered.

I looked at Connor, as if he might have the answer, but he just shrugged. 'I don't know what's going on inside me,' he said. He was watching the dog with a small smile, like he wanted to hug it too, but at the same time his hand was moving cautiously over his stomach.

So I thought about a year ago, which meant I thought about Matt, and Max, and my brother. I could picture me and Jason walking up Horngate, and down Crook Lane in a different, sunlit, more innocent world. I'd discovered over the last year that when you missed someone it wasn't just an emotion, it was a physical feeling, a heaviness, a sinking in your chest. 'We have to assume seven days,' I said.

Asha tutted. 'Which means three more days. We can't just stay here and wait, because Ruby will catch up with us, quite possibly go all serial killer on us, then probably head straight for a big town with Connor. But if we could be here for a night before we go to Northumberland, that would be good.'

I nodded. 'Let's decide now, before he comes back: are we going to tell him everything?'

Peaches stopped pressing her nose into Josh's stomach, she jumped up and swivelled towards the door, tongue out and panting, all expectation and contained delight.

'Oh yeah, you're going to tell me every little thing.' Simpson's deep voice didn't seem to have any doubt in it. He lowered one hand to stroke the dog's head as she came and rubbed against his legs. 'I want the whole story.'

## 9.13 a.m.

#Weird&Proud **The thing about strange scary powers is . . . handle with care. Cos it turns out they're strange and scary.**

So we told him everything. None of us, apart from Josh, were certain we could trust him, we could certainly have held some of it back, but there was something about his presence and his personality that encouraged us to spill it all out. He seemed reassuring, like someone who could cope with all this information. Maybe it was the muscles.

We told him about last year and he said, 'Wait, you serious? Aliens?' So we said, 'Yeah, aliens.' He shook his head, closed his eyes, and said, 'Give me a minute.' Then he just sat there for a bit. When he opened his eyes he let out a long whistle and said, 'All right. Heard the rumours, honestly never believed them. On you go.'

So we told him about this year, about Connor with the alien we were calling Fuzzy inside him; Ruby with the super-strength, and the rage mixed with misery, and the Terminator-style tracking ability; about what had happened to each of us; about Grace saying one of us was going to die; about Maureen, and monsters, and Burrage, and Vinny the amazing Van. I even mentioned Dr Lazarus and his blog *Gilpin Ha Ha Ha*, and the odd feeling that he'd started offering me advice.

'And there was a horse,' Connor added, right at the end, 'galloping along next to us. It was so cool!'

And Simpson listened, with his hands around a big mug

of coffee, while Peaches rested her head on his knee. She looked up at him, trusting and content. She was an old dog, with grey hair around her jowls, and she wasn't frightening any more, she was a reassuring presence, snuffling occasionally when Simpson scratched the back of her neck. He nodded and made mm-hmm noises, but he didn't interrupt, letting us get it all out.

Turned out it felt good to talk to an adult who wasn't one of our parents (who'd be worried sick), or Colonel Doofus (who'd basically arrest us), or Maureen (who thought we were scary monsters). It felt good, and I think we all felt a little bit less anxious when we'd finished. There was actually a temptation to ask Simpson to take over now, to tell us what to do, to take all the responsibility off our shoulders. But we didn't go quite that far.

When we'd finished he leant back, legs crossed at the ankle, and let out a long breath, making a sort of 'hooo' noise as he did so. 'Quite a story,' he said. 'Quite a time you've had. You've still got about a hundred miles before you get where you're going. Sounds to me like you better stay here a night, then head off early with some cash and supplies before Bad-Ass Ruby finds you. Anyone want breakfast?'

We all started thanking him at once.

He interrupted: 'I'll have a look at the van, see if it's roadworthy.' He looked at Grace. 'But, Bluey, why can't you open your magic Eye and just tell us all what's going to happen before it happens?'

Her fingertips brushed her forehead. Her mouth moved, like she was biting the inside of her lip. 'It doesn't work like that,' she said.

He was still looking at her. 'But you think someone's going to die?'

She nodded, looking like she didn't trust herself to speak.

He leant forward, his eyes were on her and his voice had the whole deep, reassuring thing going on, so it felt a little bit like Asha's special Voice.

'Not on my watch,' he said.

So it was decided. We were staying overnight with Simpson, then heading on to Burrage in the morning. 'One condition,' he said. 'There's a bathroom upstairs with a shower. All of you use it. Because . . .' He made a face. 'You're like a toxic event.' Then he gave Josh some money, and a bag of food. 'Put the bag in Vinny, and keep the cash on you,' he told him. 'That way if Dangerous Connor says his scary sister's coming, you can move fast.'

Connor grinned. 'Dangerous Connor,' he said, nodding. 'Can you all call me that from now on? Or just Dangerous, if you like.'

We showered and put our dirty clothes in the wash, then we had crispy bacon and fried eggs with really bright yolks and toast and juice and more coffee, and then we went out with the dog. We crossed the muddy field, opened a sagging wooden gate, and ran on to the beach. We were clean for the first time in four days, and we were well fed and by the seaside and it almost, just about, felt like we were on holiday.

Peaches led the way, looking at Josh now and then with adoring eyes, running over paw tracks she'd probably made herself a few hours earlier. We couldn't go too far away from the van, just in case, but it was still good to be out there, under the enormous sky. I went right up to the edge of the water, where foamy little waves hit the sand and hissed over the pebbles, and the smell of the sea made me feel like I was six years old. Asha was walking with Grace and the dog, Connor and Josh were scraping messages into the sand.

There was a cold breeze coming off the water, and I shoved my hands in my pockets and hunched my shoulders up around my neck, trying to keep warm. Turned my back on the sea and looked at my mates. Asha, Grace and Josh. They were pretty much my only mates since I'd gone all reclusive after Matt died, and Max died, and my older brother stabbed himself, and my older self told me I was destined for a life writing about cardboard. They were the ones who'd cared enough to come and find me and drag me out of my bedroom.

*This is an intervention. We're here to rescue you.*

It was a joke, but it was also true. They'd rescued me. They'd also put me into all kinds of danger but still, they'd definitely rescued me from the rubbish life I'd been living.

Why were they my mates? I'd actually given it some thought, because I do that, think about things, maybe too much, but I can't help that. I've always liked that they're themselves and not trying to be someone else. They never pretend, never try to put a different face on. Asha's always big and loud, whether she's at school, with her mum, or with us. Grace is always quiet and watchful wherever she is, and Josh is – well, whatever complicated, uncomfortable mash-up of

Tigger and an emo Charlie Brown he is, it doesn't change in different situations. It's not that they're shallow or stuck in their ways, it's the opposite really. They're honest. That's why they're my mates. Along with the fact Asha sort of radiates energy and is clever and gorgeous, obviously, and Grace is probably, secretly, the coolest person I know, and Josh cracks me up when he's not driving me mad.

Anyway I definitely, really desperately, didn't want any of them to die. Or Connor, obviously. I wanted us all to, somehow, get through this. Maybe Grace's whole prophecy thing wasn't even a hundred per cent accurate? After all it was more of a feeling, a general emotional sense, than anything specific.

The sea washed up behind me and flowed right over my feet, and I shouted and jumped away. Wet socks. That's one of the worst things ever. I was shaking my legs, as if that was going to make any difference, when Asha and Grace started coming back with Peaches and I saw Grace's face was screwed up as if she was in pain, or trying not to cry.

'What is it? What's wrong?'

Josh and Connor heard my tone, stopped scratching rude words in the sand and ran towards us.

'It's Peaches,' Grace moaned.

Asha had her arm round Grace's shoulders. 'Her Eye opened,' she said, 'her magic Eye. She was basically gone for a minute, then she suddenly looks at me and says she's feeling sadness like a great slow wave. And Peaches is going to die.'

Josh sank to his knees and put his arms round the dog's shaggy neck.

'But you don't know that,' I said. 'You can't be sure, right?'

'It's not as hazy as before,' she stuttered. 'Maybe because . . . because it's close.'

'How?' squeaked Connor, high-pitched and scared.

'I don't know!' Grace hardly ever got cross but there was a stab of anger and frustration in her voice.

'She's old,' said Josh. His face was buried in fur so his voice was a bit muffled, but I heard a crack in it. 'Maybe it's just because she's old. I'm going to tell Simpson.'

'Me too,' said Grace.

Josh took her hand, which was nice. Connor went with them and Peaches, potentially doomed Peaches, trotted along beside them, looking trustingly up at Josh, like everything was right in the world. Asha and I lingered. I sneezed. Asha was shivering a bit, because it was cold obviously, but also possibly because she'd just watched Grace look into the future and Peaches was maybe going to die, and one of us was apparently going to die too. I felt like I had a cold stone in my stomach because this adventure, this road movie as Josh had called it, was turning out to be pretty terrifying to be honest.

'I actually hate the seaside,' said Asha.

I didn't say anything.

'Last night,' she continued, 'you and me, we both wanted to give up. Why didn't we give up? Why did we let them persuade us?'

I'd been thinking the same thing but I didn't want to admit it. 'Grace had some pretty good reasons.' I scraped an H in the sand with my toes. And then I was thinking about the sketch she'd been doing in the van. 'What's she got against Eden James?' I said.

Asha looked at me like I was an idiot. 'Grace has major issues with Eden. Haven't you noticed this whole last year?'

She could tell from my face that I had no idea what she was talking about.

'You don't know anything about what's going on with her?'

'Is it something about her and Josh? Are they a thing or not?'

She shook her head, like she couldn't believe what she was hearing. Her How-Stupid-Are-You? face turned up a couple of notches. 'You remember how last year the egg made Grace talk only in questions and you didn't even spot what was up with her for ages?' she said finally.

I nodded.

Asha nodded too. 'Yeah,' she said.

So that was the end of that conversation.

I wondered what I looked like to Asha. Apart from stupid, obviously. Thin-legged and awkward probably, with my rubbish haircut and my old spider-web T-shirt and my mouth moving nervously, like I was chewing something. And my wet socks. Asha could have any bloke she wanted in Year Twelve, or Year Thirteen. Why would she even be interested in me? I'm just a bit rubbish with girls, that's the truth. But here we were, alone on the beach, and it felt like an opportunity.

'We haven't had a moment, have we?' I said. 'Just you and me.'

A bit of silence. Cold wind, the sea chuckling over the sand and pebbles. Wet feet. Plenty of time for me to replay what I'd just said and decide it was a bit dumb, a bit needy.

'You're a worrier,' Asha said eventually. 'That's actually the main thing about you – you worry. You said it yourself, that's why Fuzzy is making you see the past, cos you're always looking back over your shoulder, thinking about what you've done. Grace worries too, that's how come it's making her look into the future, getting her all stressed about it. You've got a lot in common with her.'

'OK,' I said, 'that makes sense. But I don't want to talk about Grace any more. I want to talk about me and you.'

Asha was wearing an overcoat Simpson had lent her. She had the collar turned up and her hands stuffed into her pockets. The coat came right down to her ankles and it was a bit ridiculous. All I could see of her was her round face, looking up at mine. Her hair piled up so it looked a bit like she had a bird's nest on her head, but in a good way. Brown eyes, cold cheeks I wanted to cup in my hands, sceptical expression.

'I do think about you, Hector,' she said. 'I do. But you and me, we're all how we are, you know? On again, off again, and things nearly happen, but they don't. And you're a worrier and I'm not, you're a geek and I'm not, you are genuinely sometimes phenomenally stupid and I'm not, and it's complicated, isn't it?'

That would have been confusing and probably demoralising if I'd followed it too closely, but I only really heard the first six words. 'You think about me?' I said. 'I think about you too.'

'Yeah,' she said, and her lips twisted into a smirk, and her tone was back to the jaunty, confident Asha I was used to. 'I bet you do. Ew.'

I took her hand.

I wanted to touch her, to make contact skin to skin, because words are unreliable and useless sometimes, and I was planning next to slowly go in for a kiss, aiming for a nice, romantic moment, but I'd forgotten what happened when I touched someone.

I took her hand.

There was about a millisecond in which I thought I saw her lips moving towards a smile, but then all of a sudden

*her mum was worried sick, and Naveen, her brother, looked basically broken with his face in his hands, and Asha was screaming something at him, really letting go,*

*then she was staring into a mirror and weeping. Asha was crying, she looked heartbroken, it was an Asha I'd never seen before.*

She snatched her hand away, and I was back on the beach so suddenly that it felt like I'd fallen down a hole. She screeched a swear word at me as she backed away, furious, clutching her hand as if it was burnt.

'Sorry,' I said, 'sorry, sorry!'

'How dare you!' she yelled.

I put my hands up in front of me, palms outwards, as if I

was warding her off. 'It was an accident,' I said, 'I'm so sorry!'
I took a step towards her.

She was yelling again, but it was different this time because this time it was the Voice, resonant, commanding and irresistible, and she was pointing away, randomly probably, but she was pointing towards the sea so I turned my back on her and started walking and then wading into the water.

It was freezing and horrible but I couldn't stop. I knew

what I was doing and I wanted to stop but I absolutely couldn't stop. I waded deeper and I didn't know how long it would be before the effect of the Voice would wear off. Was I going to have to swim? Was I going to have to keep swimming until I reached Norway, or wherever was off in this direction? Was I going to drown?

'Stop! Come back!'

That was Asha's normal voice and it helped but it didn't do the trick, I was still putting one foot in front of the other moving out into the water, trying to stop myself, unable to. I took another couple of steps, and now I was out of my depth and a wave broke over me, but then Asha called out again, her words half lost on the wind.

'COME BACK!'

That did it. Asha had waded in after me and her Voice had an edge of hysteria to it but it was powerful this time, it seemed to reach right inside my skull and physically pull me, and I turned, thank God, I turned and started swimming, wading, walking back towards her.

I thought she might be laughing at me, or doing a little victory dance or something, but she wasn't, she had her hands over her mouth and her eyes were wet and she was standing knee-deep in the sea.

'I thought you were going to drown,' she croaked. 'I thought I'd killed you.'

We both ran back on to the sand and I was shivering and stamping my feet, and I wanted to hug her but of course I couldn't hug her. 'I didn't mean to see inside your head.' I was shaking my head at the same time as shivering and stamping. I must have looked like an idiot. 'I'm really sorry.'

She was holding her head in both hands now, but she made a breathy sound that was some sort of mixture of crying and laughing. 'You see, I told you,' she said. 'You're just a whole bag of stupid, aren't you?'

'Are you all right?' I said. 'Are you OK?'

She was squeezing her eyes shut. 'Hurts a bit,' she said. Then she shook her head before I could say anything and opened them again. 'I'm fine.'

We were looking right into each other's eyes and we'd sort of apologised so it was actually a tender moment. We might even have kissed then, except first off we'd have had the whole mutant telepathic memory trick again, and second off I did a sneeze that actually bent me in half and almost made me leave the ground and totally left me with my nose running, and then, like it was infectious, Asha did one too.

We ran for the house.

**11.21 a.m.**

#Weird&Proud **I can cope with all the weirdness. It's the little snatches of normal in between, that's the hardest part.**

I squelched through the door with Asha. I was soaked from head to toe, Asha's jeans were soggy and our teeth were chattering but no one even looked at us. I could probably have stripped my trousers off right there and they wouldn't have been distracted. My feelings were all mixed up. I was worried that the Voice was hurting her, and I was a little bit elated that we'd shared a nice moment, even though she'd nearly killed me, and I was also furious with myself for pushing her away, for pushing everyone away, for the past year. So, obviously, I didn't say anything. I just stood there and shivered.

Josh was arguing with Simpson. 'We have to go!' he insisted. 'I don't want Peaches to die.'

Simpson sighed, liked they'd been over this a couple of times already. 'Nor me,' he said, 'obviously.' He waved a hand towards Grace. 'But Bluey here says she can't be sure. She thinks Peaches might die, she also thinks one of you might die.' He looked at her. 'Right?'

Grace looked at Peaches, who was clearly uneasy about the tension in the room. She was turning her head, letting out small whimpers, and her big black eyes moved from Simpson to Josh and back again.

'Yes,' she whispered. 'I'm not completely sure. But I felt the sadness, and I saw . . . something.'

Simpson took a deep breath. 'You saw *something*,' he said. 'Right. So, bottom line, we don't know what's gonna happen, do we? You go now, maybe you save Peaches but one of you catches a bullet. Or you go now, and maybe Bad-Ass Ruby turns up here and kills Peaches because she's pissed off.' He looked at Connor, who was a bit like Peaches actually, turning from Simpson to Josh, big-eyed, biting his lip anxiously. 'Dangerous, you getting the vibe your sister's coming?'

'No,' he said, shaking his head nervously. 'Nothing. Nothing at the moment.'

Simpson smiled at Connor, nodding, doing his muscly, reassuring thing. 'Right, then, we stick to Plan A. You all stay here tonight, you leave first thing tomorrow. Unless the little Dangerous alarm here goes off, in which case you get the hell out immediately.' He didn't even ask if we agreed, that seemed to be that.

He looked at me and Asha, and his lips squashed into a smile. 'What happened to you two? You go swimming with your clothes on?'

I didn't really want to explain. I guessed that Asha didn't want to either. 'Kind of,' I said. I'd noticed a pile of vegetables in the kitchen. 'Can we help with the food?'

Simpson stared at me, well aware that I was avoiding his question. 'Sure,' he said, after a couple of seconds. 'You can do some peeling and chopping. I'll have a look at Vinny. Josh, you're with me. We should have a chat.'

I guessed the chat was going to be about Josh's mum, and I thought that was a good thing.

They went out. Grace and Connor watched TV, Asha and I put our clothes in the drier, then chopped garlic, an onion and some peppers. We were both wearing towels wrapped round us. My legs were cold.

'Don't even like peppers,' said Asha.

'Me neither,' I said. 'See how much we've got in common?'

I really wanted to ask her about what I'd seen inside her head. Those anguished memories. Her mum desperately unhappy, Naveen in pieces, and her so uncharacteristically crushed by sadness. I glanced at her. She was just chopping.

'If you ever want to talk about . . .' I started.

'I don't,' she said.

'I know you don't, but still,' I said. 'You've only got one brother. Maybe you should—'

She cut in, her voice sharp as her knife. 'Hector, I swear, I'll tell you to walk back into the sea.'

So that was the end of that conversation. No sound for a minute except knives on chopping boards. I adjusted my towel, worried it was going to slip off. I felt like I needed to say something to change the mood.

'When you wear a skirt,' I said, 'don't your legs always get cold? Mine are freezing.'

Without even looking, she reached over and patted my bum. 'Don't listen to the haters,' she said. 'You wear what you want.'

We lazed around most of the afternoon, still with that feeling that we were on holiday. Spent more time on the beach, played Monopoly, crowded round Simpson's laptop to see if there was anything relevant in the news. Grace looked at her sketch of Eden, held it over a candle, and set fire to it. She dropped it in the fireplace and watched it burn. I considered asking her about it, but the mood was too mellow and I didn't want to spoil it. She started drawing Josh instead, who was leaning back on the sofa with his notepad on his knees, scribbling.

I was not thinking about our situation, and everyone else was not thinking about our situation too. Ruby on our tail, Doofus and Patronising probably not far behind, Peaches apparently doomed, one of us with a death sentence hanging over our head. Not thinking about it was working pretty well for me.

I was at the other end of the sofa from Josh. Things had gone a bit quiet so I thought I'd risk asking about his writing. 'Is it still a secret?' I said, nodding at his pad.

He didn't even look up. 'Never was a secret,' he said. 'I'm writing a letter to my mum.'

'Right.' I nodded, trying to keep the surprise out of my voice. 'Nice one.'

His eyes stayed on the paper. 'It was Grace's idea,' he muttered, glancing at her. She smiled at him. 'I'm saying stuff I never usually say.'

While we were carefully not thinking about our situation, it seemed like the circumstances were giving us all a little nudge in helpful directions. I was rediscovering my feelings for Asha, and remembering that life outside my bedroom actually had a few advantages, Josh was thinking about his mum, Grace had apparently been thinking about Eden, although I had no idea what that actually meant. It was nice. And Simpson's front room was cosy, with a furry red rug on a stone floor, a shelf full of books on the wall, saggy but comfy armchairs in a rusty, faded print. As it began to get dark, Grace put her sketch away and Josh shoved his letter in his pocket. Simpson lit more candles, turned on a dimmed light in the corner of the room and opened a bottle of wine. We ate spaghetti bolognese, me, Asha and Grace had some wine, and then we worked out where we were sleeping. There were two bedrooms and a little box-room along with the bathroom upstairs. We decided Grace and Asha would share the spare bedroom, Josh, me and Connor would go in Simpson's room, and he said he'd take the box-room, along with Peaches.

'She's downstairs usually,' he said. 'But she'll be right next to me tonight, safe and sound. Everybody happy?'

We all agreed that we were.

'Good. I'm setting my alarm for six o'clock, so try and get some sleep. Night.'

He disappeared into the box-room. For about ten minutes we got in each other's way as we went in and out of the bathroom, back and forth on the little landing, and then I was in my doorway as Asha was in hers. I said, 'Night,' she said, 'If you're going to talk, talk quietly,' Simpson shouted, 'Go to sleep, guys!' and I closed my door.

Connor was in Simpson's bed, me and Josh were in sleeping bags. I burrowed into mine. 'He's a good guy,' I said. 'Simpson. I like him.'

'He's great,' said Connor. 'Why isn't your mum still with him?'

Silence from Josh.

'Stupid question, Con,' I said. 'Good night.'

Darkness, a tense silence, which gradually became a drowsy silence. After a while I could hear the sea hushing and sighing, and that sound became a sleepy song. I felt myself drifting away, and for once I felt confident I wouldn't have any bad dreams.

# DAY FIVE

**04.14 a.m.**

#Weird&Proud **We tried. We failed. Game over.**

There was a sound.

It was the middle of the night and I was buried under heavy layers of sleep. But something had disturbed me.

Someone saying something?

I didn't want to open my eyes, my eyelids were heavy, they felt like they were glued together. Still, I opened them. Just a blurry crack.

Nothing to see.

The darkness had a texture, it was warm and soft, and the sea was quietly, endlessly, hushing and sighing, and I was about to let my eyes close and drift back to sleep when I heard it again.

Connor, muttering.

I felt like I was drifting up out of a deep, dark pond. Connor's words were floating in the darkness above me. *Let me be* . . . something. *Let me be* . . . *Con?* What was he on about? I lay there, still in a fog of sleep, trying to make out his slurred words.

'Let me become.'

I whispered back, not wanting to wake up Josh. 'What?'

His voice became a little louder, a little clearer. But it didn't sound like his voice. It was a small, flat monotone, like he was speaking in an empty room.

'Let me become.'

I rubbed my hand over my face. 'Con? What?'

No answer.

'Connor?'

Still nothing. I yawned. 'Connor,' I whispered. I was confused by his voice. It must be him but it didn't sound like him. 'Is that you?'

And then he said something that woke me up abruptly and completely, like he'd thrown cold water in my face.

He said, 'No.'

I sat up and squinted through the darkness at him lying there on the bed. I swallowed. My voice was small, scared.

'Who is it, then?'

He said, in that flat voice that wasn't his voice, 'Time to go.'

He swung his legs off the bed, and at the same moment there was a crash downstairs. Peaches started barking and Josh stirred and said, 'What?' I scrambled out of my sleeping bag, stumbled over Josh, got to my feet, grabbed the dark shape that was heading for the door.

'Con,' I yelled, 'Connor, wait!'

He tried to shrug me off but I had an arm round his chest and I reached out with my free hand to turn the light on. Another crash downstairs. I was pretty sure someone was hammering the front door, or possibly throwing themselves at it. I was trying not to panic now, because I knew super-strong Bad-Ass Ruby was trying to get in, and Peaches was barking like a mad thing, and Connor had gone weird, and possibly Fuzzy the alien was speaking through him.

'Wait!' I shouted. 'Talk to me!'

Connor turned to look at me. (Another crash from downstairs. Peaches going wild.) His face was ghostly pale.

'*Time to go,*' he repeated.

'No, don't!' I was trying to sound calm and reasonable. Failing. My voice shook and shivered and actually squeaked on the final syllable. 'We'll take you somewhere. Somewhere quiet.'

'No,' he said. '*We like people. We like emotion.*'

Another crash, louder this time. It sounded like the door had just come off its hinges.

I remembered Grace's suggestion a year ago, that the alien was making a sort of nest, that our fear and horror made it feel cosy. It wanted to be in a town, containing just the right number of people. It wanted to be in a little town like Gilpin, surrounded by frightened, panicking teenagers.

The lights went out.

Suddenly we were standing in pitch darkness.

'Hold him!' I told Josh, and Josh stood up and flailed at us in the dark. I pushed Connor into his arms and went to the window, dragged back the curtains, pulled up the sash. I was hoping for ivy or a drainpipe. Nothing, just a straight drop down to the front garden. There was a car out there, exhaust billowing out the back, ghostly white headlights glaring down the lane, fading into the darkness. Ruby must have paid someone, or terrified them into waiting for her.

'Sheets,' Josh shrieked. 'Tie one end to the bed . . .'

'We haven't got time!'

Outside on the landing Simpson was yelling something I couldn't make out, and Peaches was growling like a wild animal. And then I heard Asha. I'd forgotten about her, and even though I was worried that the Voice was hurting her, I thought we were saved.

'STOP!' she commanded.

But something was wrong, because I heard it again, with an edge of fear in it.

'STOP!'

And then a third time, high-pitched and desperate now.

'STOP!'

I flung open the bedroom door, wanting to help Asha, knowing that somehow her Voice had failed. Simpson had a torch and I saw a flickering confusion of black shapes lit by darting shafts of light. Peaches had Ruby's arm and Simpson was grappling with her and Asha and Grace were in the door of their bedroom. I wanted to help but I didn't know how. I was considering diving on top of Ruby but she suddenly threw Simpson off her and he slammed into the wall, and then she got Peaches' head in her hands and Peaches yelped and scrabbled desperately with her paws but Ruby jerked her head violently.

There was a crack.

Ruby dropped Peaches abruptly like she was holding something hot. Peaches fell to the floor with a dull thud and didn't move. Ruby looked down at the body and let out a sound, a gasp that sounded like shock.

Simpson was lying still but his torch was angling up at the ceiling, casting a dim, ghostly light over us all. Him sprawled on the floor, Asha with her hands over her mouth, Grace frozen in the doorway, Peaches on the carpet with her head all bent to one side.

Ruby was wearing earbuds. There was a faint, hissing ssch-ssch-ssch of music coming from them. She looked up and saw me. I watched her take a deep breath.

'Where's that brother of mine?' she said.

Her voice was too loud because she had the music turned up loud in her ears.

I shrugged, as if I didn't know. No point talking to her, she couldn't hear a word.

She took a step towards me.

And then, possibly saving my life, Connor shoved me out of the way and ran on to the landing.

'Don't!' he yelled. 'Don't hurt Peaches!'

It was Connor, it was definitely Connor speaking, high-pitched and scared, it wasn't Fuzzy talking through him.

'Wait!' I shouted, grabbing his arm. 'Don't go with her!'

Without even thinking about it I'd pushed myself between him and her. It wasn't brave, it was more clumsy than anything else. Ruby stepped right up to me, grabbed the T-shirt I'd been wearing in bed and lifted me, one-handed, off my feet.

'I think I might kill you,' she said loudly, but with a hint of confusion, as if it was an idea that had arrived in her head and she wasn't sure what to do with it.

Shouting, or possibly screaming if I'm honest, I flapped at her face, caught hold of a wire, and snatched a bud out of her ear.

I'd hoped after the shop in Middlemiss that Asha wouldn't have to use her Voice again. Then she'd used it twice on the beach, which was totally my fault, and now it was happening again. But we had no choice.

'Asha!' I yelled. 'Try it now!'

Ruby's face twisted into a snarl, but before she could do anything Asha shouted. I heard panic and desperation filling her Voice. It was resonant, it thrummed, it seemed to come from a thousand loudspeakers, it was loud enough to make the whole house vibrate:

'STOP!'

Ruby stopped. The snarl was frozen, showing her gritted teeth, flared nostrils, flinty eyes. But she didn't let go of me, dangling me by my bunched-up T-shirt a few inches off the ground.

'LET GO!'

The Voice wasn't quite as commanding this time, and I thought perhaps I could hear an edge of pain in it, but it still echoed around us, and I'd never been so glad to hear anything before. Except Ruby didn't let go. The music was still jangling through one earbud, distracting her. And the gritted teeth, the flared nostrils, the flinty eyes, they were all signs that she was struggling, that she was fighting it, that Ruby's compulsion to get Connor was as powerful as Asha's Voice.

180

I caught a glimpse of Asha behind her, sinking to her knees, as Ruby opened her mouth and roared in my face, an enraged, wordless, throaty roar, and then I was flying through the air. Ruby threw me past Connor, back through the door of my bedroom. I was actually flying and I had long enough – a fraction of a second – to think 'I'm flying!' and wonder if I was going to go right out of the window that I'd opened, but then I hurtled into Josh, my head smashed into his chest, and we both crashed on to the floor in a tangle of limbs and sleeping bag.

I sat up. Dazed and scared and not even sure at first where the landing was. I was shaking. I could still hear Ruby roaring right in my face. I sat up, thinking she was probably coming for me to finish the job. She was going to kill me. I made a sound which was pretty much a whimper. Everything still black, except for that torchlight. Dark figures. Dark figures moving in front of me. Oh God, was one of them Ruby?

A shape in the doorway. I sort of braced myself and held my breath, frozen, honestly thinking I was about to die. It was a pretty useless reaction, holding my breath, bracing, freezing, but I didn't know what else to do.

And then Grace spoke. 'Are you OK?'

I let my breath out, rubbed my head where it had hit Josh's ribs. Didn't say anything for a moment, just breathed in and out, slowly.

'Where did she go?' I said at last, my voice shaking.

'Peaches is dead,' Grace sobbed.

Josh groaned.

In the silence that followed that, I heard the car outside accelerating away.

Asha was standing behind Grace, leaning against the wall, a hand pressed against her temple. She looked like she was having trouble staying on her feet. 'I slowed her down,' she whispered. 'But she put the earbud back, she took Connor with her. They've both gone. It's over.'

She slid down the wall, her hands on her head.

## 05.26 a.m.

### #Weird&Proud **The teenagers' guide to interrogation: just tell them everything.**

Have you ever buried a dog?

Ever done it before dawn, with the big, lifeless body on the ground next to you covered in a sheet, with someone standing nearby with a powerful torch, with rain spattering in your face and running down your neck, and with the dog's owner digging furiously beside you, grunting and groaning miserably every time he shoves the spade in the earth?

Sadness like a great slow wave.

It was horrible. I dug my spade deep in the ground, puffed a bit, then lifted it, feeling the weight in my arms, shoulders and back. I was cold but sweaty, I was achy, bruised and weary, and the earth was muddy and smelt like dead things.

Simpson just kept going, shovelling the earth like a machine. Josh and me, and Grace when she took a turn, were slower, shakier. Asha was still worn out from using her Voice. She leant on a tree, watching. I glanced at Simpson now and then. He'd hardly said a word. He was probably thinking Peaches' death was down to us. We'd shown up on his doorstep and brought chaos with us.

It was our fault.

We dug a deep hole with crumbling sides, and then Simpson and Josh each took one end of the sheet, and lowered Peaches in. Her body swung and hit the sides and half fell at the end, so that a paw stuck out into the air. We shovelled the earth back in, and by the time we were done birds were singing and the sun was rising over the sea, blood red fingers stretching up into the sky, fading to pink. And my cheeks weren't only wet from the rain.


We sat round the kitchen table in cold, grey light, clutching mugs of tea and coffee. The fuse box was lying on the floor behind me, where Ruby had yanked it off the wall. We'd all tried to apologise to Simpson, but he'd told us to stop.

'It's not your fault,' he'd said. 'It's not even Ruby's fault. This is a whole other thing.'

There was a lot of silence. A lot of watching the sky gradually get lighter. Listening to tea and coffee being slurped.

Simpson sighed, finally. 'Is Connor like a hostage,' he said, 'or did he go willingly?'

Grace's voice was tentative, almost apologetic. 'I think he was trying to save us from Ruby.'

Simpson nodded. 'Yeah. Sounds about right. He's a nice kid. Where d'you think they'll go?' He rubbed his cheek. He had a dark bruise there and his face looked heavy. All of it dragged downwards.

For three or four long seconds it seemed like no one was going to answer. So I had a go.

'Connor, only it wasn't Connor, said this thing to me. He said, "We like people. We like emotion." And I think that was actually the alien talking through him.' I looked around at everyone, worried someone was going to tell me not to be so stupid. No one did. 'So they're going somewhere with people,' I continued.

'Obviously,' Asha muttered.

Simpson nodded. 'The alien likes Gilpin. Must be something about that place.'

'Nice shops,' said Josh, bleakly.

'So Ruby might take Connor back there?' Grace said.

'But Gilpin's probably not the only place in the country that suits it,' I sighed. 'I can't believe it's unique.'

'So they might go absolutely anywhere.' Asha made an impatient tutting sound. 'Brilliant.'

I was worried about Asha. She was slumped in her chair like she'd just run a marathon. Using the Voice against Ruby had drained her.

Josh had his little black box out. He was tapping out a rhythm on the lid with his fingernails.

'Dropped the ball much?' he said.

There was another silence, a tense one this time, broken only by the tap-tap-tap of Josh's nails on the box. It felt like an argument was about to happen. We were weary and shocked and defeated and I'm pretty sure we were all gearing up to start snapping or possibly shouting at each other. And also Josh's fingernails looked like they were finding their way under the lid of the box. I was about to snatch it away from him, which might well have been the start of the shouting, when we heard the cars.

I went to the window. Not cars – military lorries and jeeps, with loud, growly engines, and strained suspensions which clunked and banged on the uneven lane outside. I snapped a picture.

Simpson looked at Josh. He put a hand on his hand, stopping the tapping. He managed a smile.

'Stay strong,' he said.

And then the front door, which was more or less propped up in the doorway since Ruby had forced her way in, was booted open so that it actually crashed down on to the floor.

Black-uniformed soldiers with green-glowing guns burst in.

We were told to put our hands on our heads and our faces on the table. Questions were barked at us while the house was searched. Then Asha, Josh, Grace and me were marched out of the house while Simpson was left there, with a gun pointing at him, and someone still snarling questions at him.

We walked out with soldiers on either side of us, into the cool morning, to find that the sun had climbed out of the sea and the world was full of colour.

One of the lorries was carrying something familiar.

'That's the machine that goes *Boom!*,' said Josh.

'The one that doesn't exist,' said Grace.

The creamy-coloured box with the golf ball, the chrome cylinder attachment and the panel that wasn't currently glowing green. It also had a screen and a console recessed into one side. Why had they brought it with them?

Before we could discuss it any further, Colonel Doofus and Professor Patronising stepped out of a jeep.

Douglas was wearing a ribbed green sweater over his shirt. He had his hands behind his back and his thin, craggy face was red, his lips tightly pursed, like he was angry, like he was having trouble not shouting at us.

He wasted no time. His voice was clipped and tight. 'You fail to cooperate,' he snapped, 'you each go into solitary and when this is over, if you're still alive, you go to a young offender institution. Am I clear?'

We nodded. What else could we do? Kirby was wearing jeans and a black polo neck and her smile had a sneery edge to it. Because we were obnoxious and self-obsessed, and she'd caught us.

'Excellent,' she said, as if we'd made her very happy by saying we didn't want to go to kids' prison. 'Now, we've heard quite a bit about Ruby from a number of traumatised drivers who have helped us to track her. She seems a troubled girl, but I'll be most interested to hear everything you can tell me about Connor. And of course the egg. Especially the egg. They have it, I assume?'

We looked at each other.

Kirby looked from face to face, and her sneery smile faded.

'What?' she said. 'What is it?'

We moved from the drive outside Simpson's house into what they called the Mobile Command Centre. It was basically a truck, but when you got in the back it was like stepping into the future. It was all screens and consoles and glowing lights. We sat on spinny chairs bolted to the floor around a small white table.

'What's that?' asked Josh, pointing at something domed and shiny in the corner.

'Coffee maker,' said Kirby. 'This is fascinating. The creature is inside Connor?'

'Yes,' I snapped. 'So if you get him what are you going to do? Cut him open?'

She tutted impatiently. 'Let me ask you a question,' she said. 'I pointed out to you three days ago the alarming prospect of what we're now officially calling a soft invasion. You remember? Millions of eggs, all over the planet? In the light of that, don't you think you've been criminally irresponsible?'

She stared at me. Cold, green eyes behind those narrow glasses.

I thought she was probably right but at the same time I didn't care, because I was thinking about my friends and all the people I knew from school and yes, actually, I was also thinking about myself.

'You kill that thing,' I said, and my teeth hardly seemed to move apart as I was speaking, 'and you kill Connor, Ruby, us and all the teenagers in Gilpin.'

Douglas was standing by one of the consoles. He came over and looked down at us. He didn't look angry any more, he looked stony-faced and serious, like a man who was weary of making hard decisions.

'I don't want to give an order that will kill teenagers,' he said. 'I have children of my own.'

We all stared at him. This was new. Douglas talking to us sincerely, with sadness, even a hint of guilt, in his voice. It wasn't reassuring though. In fact it was the opposite.

'But the Coordinating Committee have ruled that it may be necessary for me to give that order,' he continued, his voice slow and heavy. 'To send a message.'

For the first time I got a sense of the weight on this man's shoulders. No one answered him. It was clear that there was no discussion to be had, Douglas was just stating a fact. He let his words hang there for a moment, and then he sighed.

'You're no longer relevant. It's time for you to go.'

'Wait,' said Kirby. 'One more thing. In Gilpin there's a teenager who's ageing at an accelerated rate. There's one who appears to be generating electricity. Another who finds that everything he touches begins to rot. I'd like to know what our extra-terrestrial friends have done for you.'

I looked at Asha, Grace and Josh. Asha was being unusually quiet, Grace shrugged, Josh just looked depressed.

'I can see the past,' I said.

Kirby raised her eyebrows. 'The past?'

'I know,' said Josh. 'Rubbish, right?'

'When I touch someone,' I told her, 'I see stuff that's happened to them.'

'And I can sort of sense the future,' said Grace. 'In a blurry way.' She lifted her fringe and revealed her Eye, but she didn't open it.

'You're right,' said Josh, as if Kirby had said something, 'these are the worst powers ever.' He got out his little black box. 'I've got this. My little box of sadness. Don't even ask.'

Kirby gave him a puzzled frown but seemed to decide to leave it for now. She looked at Asha. We all looked at Asha. We waited.

I knew she was still weary, and possibly in pain, but she loves a spotlight, and she always knows when it's her moment. She had her head down, gazing at the table as if there was something interesting there, and she didn't look up for about three seconds. She was enjoying making us wait. And why not? She obviously had by far the best power of the four of us. She was building to it. She slowly lifted her head. She looked Kirby right in the eye and opened her mouth, and I was sure she was about to use the Voice on her.

But I was wrong, she had something much better in mind.

'Superstar,' she sang, '*Been driving in my car, we got pretty far, yes we got pretty far!*'

She belted the words out, loud and tuneless, and Douglas, who was the only one standing, took a couple of hasty steps back. Kirby stared at her, shocked. We all stared at her. All of us shocked.

'*I am the singer,*' she sang, '*that's all I can do!*'

Kirby stood up. 'Right,' she said. 'Thanks . . .'

'*Who is the singer?*' Asha yelled. '*You know who!*'

'Yes, we get the general idea, thank you.' Kirby was talking over her. She looked at me. 'Now you're going to find out what Green Fingers refers to. Goodbye.'

She and Douglas left. Josh put his little box of sadness away. He had a grin on his face.

'OK,' he said, 'that was awesome. But also, you know I said you should be lead singer of The Future? Changed my mind.'

'You're keeping the Voice secret,' Grace murmured.

'Nice,' I nodded. 'But what the hell is Green Fingers?'

Asha took a deep breath, as two soldiers came in. A young blond man, and an unsmiling woman I recognised as Map Girl, who we'd seen in the tent four days ago.

*'You look like my teacher,'* Asha sang, *'it's not your best feature.'*

Back outside, we were held at the side of the lane as the Mobile Command Centre and most of the other vehicles turned or backed up and rumbled away. I saw Colonel Doofus in the passenger seat of the first truck. He looked tired.

When they'd finally all gone, there was just us, the two soldiers, and a jeep left.

'Get in,' said Map Girl.

Asha raised an eyebrow. 'So you can talk? Good to know.'

She looked suspicious. 'I thought you could only sing?' she said.

Asha smiled. 'Nah. I was lying.'

The blond man nodded at the jeep. 'In,' he said.

Asha looked at us. 'Time for us to get out of here?'

Josh laughed. 'Oh, yeah.'

I knew what she was about to do and even though I couldn't see any alternative I was worried. 'Wait,' I said.

She ignored me. She turned back to Map Girl and Blondie. Paused a moment, gathering herself. *'YOU'RE GOING TO DRIVE BACK TO GILPIN WITHOUT US,'* she said. She wasn't shouting, she was doing that persuasive thing she'd done in the shop, that seemed to gently but irresistibly steer you into agreement. She was leaning on the jeep as she did it, her face screwed up with concentration, and possibly pain. *'YOU DON'T NEED TO TELL ANYONE WHAT YOU'RE DOING.'*

They looked confused. Map Girl opened her mouth as if to object, but Blondie was already getting into the jeep. She followed, with an anxious look at us over her shoulder.

*'THANK YOU,'* said Asha, maybe mocking them, maybe thinking it would help in some way.

We stood in the lane and watched the jeep drive away.

Josh pointed at Asha. 'Can I actually seriously marry you?' he said.

She turned round, smiling weakly. 'Smashed it,' she said.

Then she fainted.


**7.32 a.m.**

The soldiers had tilted the door back in its place. We lifted it out of the way, took Asha into the house, replaced it behind us. She was awake again almost immediately, but she was bleary and droopy.

'I'm fine,' she mumbled. Me and Josh were half carrying, half supporting her. She pushed us away then sank into one of Simpson's comfy armchairs.

191

'You're not fine,' I snapped. 'You fainted.'

'Yeah . . .' she breathed.

'You did,' Josh said, as if she was arguing.

I was angry with her because I'd watched her crumple to the ground and I thought she'd died. I was aware it didn't make much sense to be angry with her, and I didn't care. I'd seen Max die last year, and Matt, and I was pretty sure I couldn't actually cope with it happening again. Asha had collapsed and I'd shouted her name as my stomach lurched and I ran towards her, my eyes suddenly wet. Using the Voice had clearly been hurting her for a while and I honestly thought she'd done it once too often and died.

'You can't do the Voice any more!' I was almost shouting at her. It was never a good idea to tell Asha what to do or not do, and never a good idea to shout at her, but these were special circumstances. Special, preventing-death circumstances.

Grace gave Asha a glass of water. She put it right into her hand and closed her fingers round it. Her voice was calm, and probably more effective than mine. 'He's right.'

Asha took a deep breath. She drank half the water, put the glass down, and squashed her fingertips against each side of her head. 'He's not,' she said. We all waited, watching her. 'Hector gets it wrong – big surprise. While I was out, something happened, I got a sense of how it works. What it is, the power has to sort of recharge. It needs a bit of time. This was too soon after Ruby last night, that's all.'

She was lying. Definitely lying. I could see it in the way her eyes slid away from mine and her mouth quirked slightly at the corner. She was almost definitely lying, or at least keeping something to herself. Maybe her power did need to recharge, but there was something more she wasn't telling us.

'So,' she said. 'We're all good.'

She'd got some strength back, and I knew there was no point arguing with her now, but I totally intended to argue with her later.

But meanwhile, we had other things to think about.

I felt terrible, and I knew Josh, Asha and Grace did too. They'd taken Simpson away. We'd turned up at his house, got his dog killed, got him beaten up by Ruby, and now got him arrested by the army. We'd brought him nothing but heartache and trouble.

I found my phone. Jason's phone. Time to be a journalist again. A war correspondent. The least I could do was record what was happening, defy Doofus and Patronising and try to hold them to account.

#GilpinEvent **I'm back! Here's pics of the army coming out in force to arrest me & my mates & search for the aliens. You know? The ones that don't exist.**

I posted that under my own name, rather than the Kurt Wagner alias, because there was no point trying to hide from Doofus any longer. I added the pictures I'd snapped of trucks lining up outside Simpson's house. It wouldn't make any difference, it wouldn't persuade anyone that I was telling the truth, but it made me feel better.

We sat there, and looked at each other.

A long moment. No one saying anything. It was like one of us was about to make a speech but actually I had no idea what to say, and Josh, Asha and Grace obviously had no idea what to say either.

A long, quiet moment.

Maybe it was because Ruby wasn't Hulking out and we weren't in the middle of a car chase, but I remembered at this point how crazy this was. The four of us, four teenagers, trying to deal with this lunatic, lethal, world-changing thing that was happening around us.

I wondered if someone was going to suggest giving up again.

'Sod this,' I said. Not me, I wasn't going to suggest giving up. 'This is the worst moment, right here, this is as bad as it gets.' I didn't think first, I just suddenly started talking. 'We have to get Connor back. For Simpson, for Peaches, for Connor himself.'

I was angry all of a sudden. I felt like I'd been on half power all this time, still wishing I was safely back in my room, pacing up and down, pecking at my keyboard, staying out of harm's way. A couple of days ago, in Gilpin, Kirby told us they'd been mapping social media, identifying and neutralising threats. That was me. Writing sulky blogs, fighting furious trolls online. I'd been neutralised. I'd wasted an entire year of my life like that.

And now I'd had enough.

Asha was about to say something, she was probably going to make some withering comment about me doing pep talks. I talked right over her.

'Check out Simpson's laptop.' I was talking to her and Josh. 'Try and find anything about traffic or police incidents or stuff happening to teenagers.' And then I pointed at Grace before Asha could answer. 'Open your magic Eye,' I said. 'See what you can see. And I touched Ruby,' I said finally. 'I might be able to pick something up.'

Asha snorted, finally getting a chance to speak. 'In her past. You can tell us what she had for lunch yesterday.'

I ignored her. Because I had this anger in me, which was giving me a new energy, a second wind. 'There's no one better qualified than us to find Connor and get him back,' I said. 'So let's do it.' I shrugged and tried a smile. 'Teenage Mutant Fugitives.'

Asha and Josh fired up the laptop. Grace put her elbows on the table, her fingertips on her temples, and looked down. She closed her ordinary eyes and pulled back her fringe. I turned away. What came next felt private.

I closed my own eyes and thought about that moment with Ruby on the landing. When she'd lifted me by my T-shirt her fist had bumped under my chin, and then I'd flapped at her face, brushed her jaw and her ear when I'd grabbed the earbud. Skin on skin. I closed my eyes and tried to empty my mind.

*The taxi-driver looked at her as they pulled up in front of the cottage.*

*'Turn the car round,' she said. 'Keep the engine running. This won't take long.'*

Night-time. Dark countryside flashing past outside. I looked for a landmark, or a road sign, but there was nothing. Ruby was staring at a torn-out page from a road atlas. It was the north-east coast. Whitby and Scarborough to the south, Durham and Newcastle to the north. Her eyes scanned the page, but they didn't stop on one particular place, her finger didn't conveniently rest on a town or a city.

I opened my eyes. Asha and Josh were looking at me. I shook my head. 'Nothing.'

'You know,' said Asha, 'me and Grace, we should leave you two here because you are roughly no help at all.'

She looked at Grace. We all looked at Grace. Her hands were flat on her knees, her head was still bent and her magic Eye was still open, like she was examining the grain of the wood. But she was panting and flinching as if she was in the middle of a nightmare.

'We have to stop this,' said Josh, taking a step towards her.

I put out my arm in front of him. 'Not yet.'

We stared at her. She whimpered, and both Asha and Josh shifted impatiently. They wanted to help her, I wanted to wait. She lifted her head at last, let out a slow breath, and closed her Eye. She was white-faced, trembling.

'Fear,' she said. 'Like falling and falling.' She opened her eyes slowly. 'I saw a castle. A castle by the sea.'

Josh broke a white hydrangea blossom off the bush and laid it on the dishevelled earth over Peaches' grave. It was limp and fragile, it shed petals as he laid it on the ground, but it was the best we could do. He tucked it into the soil a bit, so it wouldn't blow away, and then we got back into Vinny the Van. There was a stink of socks and stale sweat as soon as we opened the doors. Josh backed out of Simpson's garage.

I had the map out. 'Up the coast road.' I pointed at the page. 'Stop when Grace recognises a castle.'

'Yeah,' Josh muttered. 'Cos we should definitely be driving towards the fear.'

Grace was leaning over the back of the seat, looking over my shoulder. 'Even if we find it,' she said, 'they might not be there. They might just have passed it on their way somewhere else. And if they are there – then what?'

'We can do this,' I said. 'Whatever it is you saw, we can deal with it. Ruby's strong but she's just a kid. We're cleverer than her.'

Josh shrugged, as we bumped and rattled over the track. 'And if we're not, Asha can decide it's a proper emergency and she can tell her to jump off the battlements,' he said.

I looked back at Asha. She was lying on the bench seat, eyes closed. But she smiled.

We'd overheard Ruby talking about going to Leeds or Manchester, but surely there'd be roadblocks around the big towns and cities. She'd be looking for smaller places for now, villages like Gilpin that Connor could infect one by one as they moved up the coast. *We like people. We like emotion.* I thought Fuzzy probably wanted somewhere the same size as Gilpin, somewhere where it could create fear and horror without unleashing the kind of full-on chaos that could lead to its own destruction.

We drove up the A174 and the A171. We ate snacks that Simpson had packed for us. They were a bit too healthy. Peanut-butter sandwiches on brown bread. Apples. We looked out at the sea on our right. We kept an eye out for erratic drivers or flashing blue lights. And as the hours passed I felt a gathering sense that we were going the wrong way, doing the wrong thing, wasting our time. We drove in a ragged loop around Middlesbrough and Hartlepool and then headed back towards the coast. I knew that someone was going to say something. That new anger and drive I'd discovered was fading. Hope was fading too.

'Where are we even going?' It was Asha of course,

who eventually spoke up. 'When do we stop and admit we've lost them?'

Josh slowed down, indicated, pulled over. 'If we've lost them,' he said, 'I want to go home.'

We'd been up since four in the morning, we'd been driving for hours, Josh was thinking of his mum, Asha had her own family problems on her mind, all of us except her thought she should never use her Voice again, Grace wasn't exactly insisting that we keep going, and all of us were worried about whatever she'd seen with her magic Eye. Fear, like falling and falling. The sea was on our right, but it didn't bring with it that big wave of optimism that had turned up when we were approaching Simpson's house.

'Peaches is dead,' Asha said. 'Grace reckons one of us is going to die, and she says we're heading for a huge fear-fest. I'm calling it: we tried, we failed, we go home. Because if we don't, this could get so messed up.'

I sighed, looked hopelessly down at the map, looked out to the left. There was a field up ahead, and there was a stand of beech trees in the field. Behind the trees, a long thin pylon was pointing at the clouds.

I pointed. 'I've seen that,' I lied. I was trying to inject some excitement into my voice. 'I think we must be on the right track. Ruby must have been here before she came to us.'

Asha stared at me, frowning. 'Didn't mention it before.'

'It was dark, I wasn't sure.' I was looking at the map again, mostly because I didn't want to look at my friends while I lied to them. I spotted a shape like a little chess piece. I showed Josh.

'There's a castle here.' I put my finger on it. 'Let's get that far at least.'

We drove on in silence, and I knew this was our last chance – we were going to turn round and go home if this wasn't the place. And I'd lied to my friends. Why did I do that? We could have backed off, gone home, avoided the danger of one of us dying. I took a slow breath. I lied to them because I was angry about the year I'd just spent stuck in my room. Basically, I lied because I wanted to take back control of my life.

My phone buzzed. It was a direct message from Dr Lazarus, replying to my tweet about the army showing up outside Simpson's house.

**Where are you now?**

I stared at that for a minute, puzzled, then replied:

**Why?**

The answer arrived quickly:

**Maybe I'll come see for myself. You might convince me it's all true.**

I still thought Dr Lazarus was probably a whole roomful of people working for Doofus, systematically using mockery, sneers and lies to rubbish any stories about aliens or the events in Gilpin. I still thought it was a whole big post-truth operation, smearing honest people, shouting lies loudly and constantly so it was impossible to argue. And if Lazarus was working for Doofus, then obviously I shouldn't tell him where I was. If he wasn't working for Doofus, if he was a genuine spiteful, angry troll who hated me and would happily pass on any information to the authorities, then obviously I still shouldn't tell him where I was.

But in the last few days I'd felt that Lazarus had been helpful, I'd even sensed that he'd been concerned about me. I stared at my phone. I didn't think it would make much difference if I told him. Doofus probably knew where we were anyway.

We were passing a sign that said *Welcome to Seabridge*. I snapped a picture, sent it to Lazarus.

We drove slowly down a narrow high street which had a newsagent, a fish and chip shop, a couple of cafes and an amusement arcade, then we parked in a sandy car park by the beach. Grace and Asha found a loo, while Josh and I walked round Vinny slowly. You could read the whole history of our journey on the bodywork. The scrape Josh made leaving the car park in Gilpin, and then the dents made by Ruby hammering on the side as we escaped; the scuffs and grazes from when we crashed through hedges near Middlemiss; the long raking scratch down the side from the near-miss yesterday morning; the crumpled crater left by Ruby colliding with us soon after.

Josh was patting the van again. I'm pretty sure he was whispering to it in fact.

Grace and Asha came back. The sun was shining and the shops and cottages were mostly in a honey-coloured stone. Doors and window frames were brightly painted in reds, greens and blues. It was like a postcard come to life. We walked from the car park down a lane past shops selling buckets and spades and ice creams and then we stopped.

There was a ruined castle on a grassy hill half a mile away.

'That's it,' Grace whispered. 'That's the castle I saw.'

## 11.32 a.m.

#GilpinEvent **What d'you get when you've got used to mutants? You get zombies. Zombies!**

Two of the castle's walls had half crumbled away, two were in fairly good condition. Scrawled with ivy, pockmarked with holes and craters, but still standing. There was a low tower where those two met. We stared at it for about thirty seconds.

'I hate castles,' said Asha.

We turned away and ignored it. We needed to search the town, and ask around, try to find out if Ruby and Connor were still here or if they'd moved on. There were plenty of teenagers around, loitering on corners, gathering outside the chip shop. We needed to find out if they'd seen Ruby and Connor, and if anything weird was happening locally.

We didn't do any of those things.

'Come on,' said Josh. 'In here.'

He didn't wait, he marched straight into the noisy half-dark of the amusement arcade. We followed. Grace and I made a token effort to look around, among the beat-em-ups and shoot-em-ups and racers. The floor was sticky, the bulbs were tinted so the light was purplish. I jumped at a high-pitched electronic trill, followed by the chunk-chunk-chunk of the change machine. Then we stopped looking round, and somehow the four of us were swaying on a line of motorbikes, and then Josh was sat inside a twirling capsule, and then Asha and I found an ancient Streetfighter II cabinet. Asha destroyed me, kicking, punching, nutting and biting my character, until gobbets of blood flew around the screen and bits of his anatomy flailed helplessly off his body.

We were all still mourning Peaches, and worrying about Simpson. We were probably all still in shock. We were definitely all still aware that time was running out, that Connor was somewhere, possibly nearby, with an alien inside him that would be changing local teenagers.

Whatever, we needed a break.

Josh provided a commentary on the Streetfighter slaughter. 'It's the scissor-grip, he's up in the air, can't do a thing about it, she's biting his head, he can't take much more of this, oh dear his little legs are thrashing around, there it goes, the head's off, it's right off, it's rolling along the floor, it's all over.'

There were plenty of teenagers there, in the purple shadows. Some of them were staring at us, the four strangers, maybe being a bit too loud, a bit overexcited. We ignored them. We were back in holiday mode, like we were only pretending to be on a mission to find Connor, to take him to Burrage, to basically save ourselves and all our friends, like we secretly knew that was way too much for us to handle.

Asha took her hands from the controls and shook them, blew the fingertips that had been beating the buttons. 'Do we even have to leave?' she said. 'In here I'm invincible, no one can touch me.'

On the way out we went past some distorted mirrors, so of course we had to line up and inspect each other. We found them hilarious. Josh was a long, shivering, curving parabola, fragile. Asha opened her mouth to comment and became all mouth and teeth. Grace on the end was small and large as she stepped towards and away from the mirror, and my spindly limbs were long and delicate. I was a stilt-man, ready to walk miles.

We all went out past Grace's mirror, briefly tiny and crushable, then giants, small again, large again. Flickering, interchangeable images. Warped and twisted teenagers were reflected behind us, watching.

We bought fish and chips and found a bench on the promenade, looking out over the beach and the approaching sea. Josh stuffed some chips into his mouth then held the rest up to his nose and inhaled greedily. He made an appreciative humming noise. 'Connor will be sorry he missed this.' I could hardly make out what he was saying. He threw one up to a seagull, which swooped, caught it and flew on.

'How come in two years none of us gets to fly?' I said. 'So not fair.'

We shoved our chip papers into an overflowing bin, ran out on to the beach and started building a sandcastle. There were quite a few teens drifting down there. Maybe there was going to be some sort of early evening, end of summer party out there on the sand. Still we made no effort to question them, we ignored them. My drive to find Connor had faded. We basically stopped being sixteen, Teenage Mutant Fugitives on a mission; we went back to being pretty much ten-year-olds, shouting, pushing and splashing each other, getting really serious about our sandcastle.

It was an extravagant creation. There was a conical pile of sand in the middle with high, thick walls around it, featuring turrets and windows. We made a population of four miniature sand-sculptures inside. Grace inset pebbles along the wall facing the approaching sea. On the highest turret I impaled a boiled sweet wrapper on a toothpick for a flag. It rustled in the breeze.

We dug a deep moat all around the castle, and I stubbornly refused to think about digging a grave for Peaches only a few hours earlier, in the cold grey light before dawn. Stubbornly refused to think about lying to my friends, or about Simpson, Connor, Ruby, Doofus, Patronising. Stubbornly refused to think about Asha hiding something about her power. Shoved all of that away in a dark little corner of my brain and slammed the door on it. We were warm, we were having fun, the sun was shining, the mood was entirely different. I refused to be unhappy.

Maybe if I'd been enjoying myself a bit less, if I'd been a bit more aware of my surroundings, I'd have noticed what was happening.

We stepped inside the castle as the sea arrived. The first tongues of salt water obediently spilt into the moat and ringed the walls. It was gentle at first, nudging and licking the dry sand, then more insistent, splashing against the sides, creating small breaches, splashing over the top. Crowded together, we dug desperately and shored up the undermined walls, sacrificed the high turret to repair a hole. We tiptoed around the trapped sand figures, becoming more involved as the sea ringed us entirely, cutting us off from dry land.

Josh, fully dressed, leapt out from the walls and into the water. 'I'm going to reason with it,' he shouted, and strode out, with the sea lapping over his shoes and above his ankles.

'Take me,' he cried, setting out towards the horizon, 'leave the others, it's me you want.'

The water continued to flood in, around him and through his legs, breaking against his shins. He stopped and stood there, apparently poised somewhere between coming back and wading on out into the North Sea, until a larger wave approached, and galvanised him.

'This was meant to be a truce.' He kicked the wave, returned, climbed back over the diminished walls. 'It's no good,' he shrugged. 'Been nice knowing you.'

But something miraculous happened. The walls held. We all, apart from Josh, kept dry. The sea jostled pointlessly around us for a while, and then began its long retreat. The castle accidentally avoided becoming a glorious failure.

Grace picked a shell out of the walls. 'I'm going to keep this,' she said. 'In a couple of years when I'm at university, when we're all spread out round the country, I'll put it to my ear and in the middle of some small inland city, I'll listen to Josh yelling at the tide.' She dropped the shell into her pocket.

It was getting cooler, and although none of us wanted to, we knew it was time to snap out of holiday mode. I stretched, stepped carefully out of the ruined castle, and looked over at the crowd of teenagers a little way down the beach. There were about a hundred of them now, male and female, aged thirteen to nineteen, and they were just milling around in a tight group. No music, no booze that I could see, no sign of a party starting or a stage being set up. What were they doing there?

It was starting to get a bit creepy.

I was about to say something, I was going to suggest maybe we should move away from those guys, when two kids approached us from the direction of the car park. Two boys, one with a mullet, one good-looking, like a model, both about thirteen. Mullet's skin was a pale, washed out blue, like the sky. There was something white on his bare arm. I looked more closely. It was a cloud, and it was moving. The good-looking one had a pouty mouth, big, girlish eyes, and he was scaly. He had small green scales on his hands and on his neck. It didn't look like a skin disease, it looked like he was turning into a lizard. Or perhaps a snake.

'Connor's here,' I breathed.

'Hey,' said Josh, with a big smile. 'You two seen a guy about your age, in a stripy football shirt? He's probably with his sister.'

We waited. They stood there, looking at us, silent.

'Hello?' said Asha.

'Are you all right?' said Grace.

Then I noticed their faces. Their faces, turned down towards the sand, were slack and empty. They mumbled something, both of them, simultaneously.

'Hey guys,' said Josh. 'Have you gone weird or are you always like this?'

They looked up. 'Find them.'

We stared at them. Scaly boy had sharp teeth and the beginnings of a fork in his tongue.

'Find them.' They were looking straight at us, but their faces didn't change.

'OK, this is bad,' I murmured.

And then blue boy grabbed me. I pushed him away and backed off but he came after me.

'Find them.'

The scaly, good-looking one grabbed Grace. Josh went to help her.

'All right,' said Asha. 'Don't panic. Totally got this.'

She straightened up, put her shoulders back and lifted her chin. Previously when she'd used her power there'd been excitement in her eyes. There wasn't this time. This time I was pretty sure I saw anxiety.

'Don't!' I shouted.

I shoved blue boy again, harder this time, so he stumbled and fell over. Then I helped Josh with the scaly one and we threw him down on top of his friend.

'Don't use your Voice.' I wasn't telling Asha what to do, that never works. I was basically pleading with her. 'We can handle it,' I said.

'My hero,' she sneered. But she didn't use the Voice.

The boys didn't move at first, lying there on the ground looking confused, and then they started to get up, watching us all the time, their lips moving as they continued to mutter, 'Find them.'

A year ago, the egg had woken up all the teenagers in Gilpin in the middle of the night, it had drawn us all down to the square and we'd all started chanting 'Find it', suddenly desperate to know where the egg was.

'It's Fuzzy,' Josh said. 'Fuzzy's trying to stop us finding Connor.'

'Duh,' said Asha.

We backed away, and as we did so I realised that those hundred teenagers further down the beach were looking at us. They weren't milling around any more, they weren't talking to each other, they were just standing there silently. And every one of them was staring at us.

'Er, guys,' I said, trying to keep my voice steady, failing. 'We may have a problem.'

'Whoa.' Josh's voice was low and scared. 'Anyone else getting a bit of a zombie vibe?'

They didn't look angry or curious or stern, they looked sort of concentrated, like the four of us were part of a maths problem. Four strangers plus one hundred locals equals . . .

'If only someone had suggested we give up and go home,' said Asha. 'Oh wait, someone did.'

We backed away slowly at first, like you'd back away from a skittish animal that might charge if it was provoked. The swarm of teenagers sort of swayed, like a field of corn in the wind, and then they all moved at once.

They started walking towards us.

'All right,' said Josh, 'fighting zombies, I mean how cool is that? I have literally been planning for a zombie apocalypse since I was about eight. But also, I don't actually want to die.'

We weren't backing away any more, we were walking fast, straight towards the car park, looking over our shoulders as we went. The two thirteen-year-olds who'd attacked us were swallowed up by the crowd. And they all started to jog.

'Run!' Grace squeaked.

We ran. We broke into a sprint. I've never been much of a runner, and it was difficult on the sand, but terror helped, terror got my legs pumping. But then I saw the second group of teens, in the car park. There were about twenty of them, all pressed up against one side of Vinny. I could see someone with fat, swollen fingers like bananas, someone with what looked like tentacles, someone who seemed to be striped. As we watched they all shoved together, and Josh's mum's battered but brilliant red van teetered.

'No!' Josh yelled.

Made no difference, obviously. They all shoved again and Vinny actually balanced on two wheels for a moment, like it was trying to right itself, before it crashed on to its side with a shattering of glass and a very final-sounding crunch of metal giving way, giving up.

'Vinny,' Josh muttered.

There was no time to mourn. The crowd of twenty mutated teenagers turned to face us.

There was a low rumble of voices chanting 'Find them' behind us, and an answering echo from the group in front of us.

More than a hundred mutated, zombie teens, all after us.

Fear, like falling and falling.

## 2.44 p.m.

### #Anniversary Bad news: It's not just Gilpin any more. Worse news: Did I mention the zombies?

We stopped.

I looked at the mob behind us and the group in front of us. 'Oh God, oh God, oh God.' I was muttering to myself, trying to think and muttering to myself, imagining what they'd do if they caught us, trying not to imagine it.

'Where do we go?' Asha shouted, like we weren't standing right next to her.

Teenagers behind us and ahead of us, nothing but beach and sea in one direction, and in the other . . .

'The castle!' Josh yelped. 'Come on!'

I might have chosen to keep going down the beach, tried to double back into town where maybe there'd be some adults who could help us, or a car we could flag down, but it was too late, Josh, Asha and Grace were sprinting for the castle and I joined them, and who knows, we might have got caught and ripped to pieces if we'd chosen the beach. Panicky thoughts were racing through my head as I ran with my friends towards the castle, chased by two groups of zombified teens, who turned into one great swarm, all of them utterly focused on catching us, all of them chanting, 'Find them.'

'Oh God, oh God, oh God.'

I was muttering again, I couldn't help myself, as we ran towards the steep footpath up to the ruin. And what good was the ruin going to be anyway? It was a ruin! It's not like there was a portcullis and a gate and defenders in turrets with crossbows and vats of boiling oil – it was about as much use as our sandcastle. Panicky thoughts. I was already getting breathless, and I thought I might get a stitch at any moment because I'd had a bellyful of chips, and I was totally unfit because I'd been stuck in my room for a year, wasting my life, all pale and geeky, staring at a computer screen, being neutralised, and like Josh I didn't want to die, I didn't want to die, I didn't want to die.

We'd slowed down, we were all panting audibly, gasping, as we reached the bottom of the footpath. It was dry and pebbly and my trainers slipped as I climbed. There were steep, sandy stretches interspersed with low, shallow steps and there was a bench at a lookout point halfway up. Gasping, I hesitated, looked out at the view. The sea the same colour as the sky, gulls wheeling. I looked back over my shoulder, terrified, thinking how nice it would be, how nice to be in a world where we could all just sit on the bench, look at the view, and chat.

There was a buzzing above our heads. It was a drone. Great. It probably belonged to Doofus and Patronising, which just meant they'd get to watch us being torn to shreds by the mob.

I had a stitch now, I was having trouble breathing and my legs were aching, but I kept going, we all kept going, up the footpath, because we had no choice.

We reached flat ground eventually, and ran through an arch. We were inside the castle walls now, but we were absolutely no safer than before. Scuffed grass, information boards, and a new wooden staircase that led up to the battlements, towards the tower. There was some graffiti by the arch. *CAM LOVES AMES*, in splotchy red spray-paint. Behind us the swarm of zombie teens was still coming, Cam and Ames probably among them, funnelling up the path, stumbling, getting in each other's way, falling now and then, but still coming. We looked at each other, each of us hoping I guess that one of us would have some kind of inspired idea, but no one said anything, and I'd have actually had trouble saying anything because my breath was coming in agonised snatches. It felt like we were deliberately running into a dead end, but we had no choice.

We climbed the staircase.

I stopped at the top. Had to. I needed to get my breath back. We all stopped, chests heaving, leant on the wall and looked out at the view, and ignored the view, watching the mob of teenagers approaching instead.

This was where we'd got to.

Up on a wall in a ruined castle with a sea breeze in our faces and a horde of zombie teens approaching. We'd left Gilpin three days ago. We'd come up with a destination, Burrage, and in completely failing to get there we'd scared people, shoplifted, driven like maniacs, got Peaches killed, got Simpson arrested, and lost Connor. We'd been totally defeated by a thirteen-year-old girl. Asha's power looked like it might be turning on her.

And now apparently our journey was over.

Perhaps Grace had got it wrong, perhaps it wasn't just one of us who was going to die. It could be all of us.

Here. Now.

Fear, like falling and falling.

I took a picture and wrote the tweet while I started to get my breath back. Asha, Grace and Josh were leaning on the wall beside me. I took a deep breath, let it out slowly, wanting my tone to be even.

'I lied about that pylon,' I said. 'Didn't see it in my, you know, vision. Sorry.'

'I knew it,' Asha hissed. 'So now you've got us all killed.'

Josh sighed. 'Least we had chips.' His tone was thoughtful, as if we weren't discussing our own deaths.

Grace was next to me. I looked at her but she didn't say anything. Her mouth was open, she was still taking deep, uneven breaths. It was obviously the wrong time to bring this up, but it was possible that there was never going to be a right time.

'You and Eden,' I said. 'What's that about?'

She stared at me. Like *Really? Are we talking about this now?* 'She's been picking on me,' she said. 'Her and her mates.'

'Why?'

'They've got a problem with me being gay.'

'Right,' I said, nodding, trying to hide my surprise, trying to think of a sensible way to react to this. She was still looking at me. I was still nodding like an idiot. I stopped.

'You're gay?' I said.

She shrugged. 'Mostly. Don't make a whole big thing of it.'

I shook my head, which was at least a change from

214

nodding it. 'Wasn't gonna.' There was nothing good to say coming into my mind. I felt both stupid and guilty. 'Sorry I've been a rubbish friend lately.'

Grace didn't answer that, and Josh looked at me.

'I reckon I turned her gay.'

Asha and Grace both laughed. Breathy, scared, but genuine laughs. 'Yeah, Josh,' Grace smiled. 'It's all about you.'

All of us were amused about that, but there wasn't anything else to say, and our smiles slowly faded. That was the end of that odd little interlude. We looked over the wall, down at the army of approaching teens again. They were nearly at the walls. Inside the tower a stone staircase spiralled steeply up into darkness. We could either go up there or go along the battlements to the low metal guard-rail where the wall crumbled away, see if we could climb down.

I looked at Asha. 'If we go up the tower,' I said, 'they'll have to follow us up the stairs one by one. We can maybe hold them off.'

Asha snorted. 'How long we going to do that for?'

'Anyone got a better idea?' Josh sounded a bit wild, like hysteria was bubbling away beneath the surface. 'Harsh language?'

Grace was still looking over the walls. 'I think they're stopping!' she shouted.

We all looked down. There was some jostling, like the message was reaching them at different times. A whole clump of kids fell over and were stepped on before they got back to their feet. And then they started moving again, but not into the castle, around it instead, circling it.

'Oh my God, it's a siege,' Josh said. 'Think they've got catapults?'

The mass of teenagers thinned out and spread, surrounding the castle. 'Maybe they want to keep us here,' I said, 'while Ruby and Connor go on to wherever they're going next.'

Ruby and Connor stepped out of the tower, like a magic trick. Ruby said, 'Hey Hector, you're not as dumb as you look.'

They were suddenly standing in front of us. Connor looking unhappy, in his stripy Gilpin Hornets football shirt, which had been washed at Simpson's house. Ruby in her sleeveless black T-shirt, which was probably pretty smelly by now, and her skinny black jeans, with earbuds in her ears.

'How'd you even find us?' she said.

Her voice was a bit loud, but she wasn't shouting. She had a hand in her pocket, presumably controlling the volume on the music in her ears.

'Long story,' I told her.

'He lied to us,' Asha said, 'and Grace saw a castle with her magic Eye.'

I shrugged. 'OK, not that long, but Ruby—' I started. I had both hands out, palms down.

She interrupted me, angry, like I'd already said something to piss her off, which surely I hadn't? 'Don't look like the cool kids now,' she snapped. 'Look like you might wet yourselves.'

'OK, cool kids?' I said. 'That's not us.' I was hoping to somehow calm things down, to reason with her.

Josh wasn't. 'You killed Peaches,' he snarled.

Ruby looked at him and winced. She actually winced, like he'd slapped her. 'The dog,' she said. 'Is it dead?'

'Yes,' said Josh. 'She's dead. You made her dead.'

'Ruby,' I said. 'The alien is doing this to you. You don't have to be like this.'

She shook her head irritably, like these words were gnats flying around her face. 'I wanna be like this. It beats sitting on my own at lunch, pretending that's how I like it. Beats being ignored, or hit, or having "Loser" written on my locker. Beats my own mum wishing I'd never been born.'

'Boo-hoo,' said Asha. 'You psycho.'

Ruby looked at her. 'You try and use that Voice on me, I will break you in two.' Her teeth were gritted, her gaze was icy. 'Might do it anyway.'

I actually felt sorry for Ruby. The alien had grabbed her misery, twisted it and weaponised it. But I squashed down my sympathy because there wasn't time for it.

'Connor,' I said. 'Why don't you come over here with us?'

'We're going to go now,' Ruby said. 'Connor says we should stay here, but I wanna head for a city.'

Grace was ignoring Ruby. 'Connor?' Her eyes were on him, her tone gentle, coaxing.

Connor looked at her, biting the inside of his cheek, picking at a fingernail, torn, clearly, between his sister and his new friends. And then there was a shift. His hands dropped to his sides and the muscles of his face relaxed. For a moment, he moved his mouth without making a sound, as if he was practising. Then he spoke.

'No city,' he said, his voice a flat monotone.

'You don't want to go to a city?' I said. 'Why not?'

'Too much.'

'Why did you come to Gilpin?' I said.

I was rubbing my scarred finger, watching Connor. I didn't think he – it – was going to answer. He was looking at the ground between us. Then he lifted his empty face and his eyes seemed to focus on me.

'The taste of the earth,' he said, his tone flat, his voice quiet. 'The drift of the air. Numbers.'

I looked at Ruby. 'That's not Connor speaking,' I said. 'That's the alien.'

'Yeah,' said Ruby. 'So what?' But her voice shook a bit, because you couldn't help but be unsettled, hearing Connor talking like that. 'That thing's been in my head since this started. I don't care what it wants or doesn't want any more,' she insisted, and now she sounded like a petulant thirteen-year-old. 'I'm not going back to Gilpin, I don't even like Gilpin. I want to go to a city.'

And then, like all of a sudden she'd had enough chit-chat, she grabbed hold of Connor. I didn't think, if I had thought about it I might have been too scared to act, but I knew I didn't want Asha trying to use her Voice so I just lunged at Ruby and grabbed her arm.

It was so thin, it was like a twig, how could she be so strong?

My fingers closed all the way around it just below the elbow, I felt her bones and squeezed, and for a moment confused images started to flood me, I felt an overwhelming wave of Ruby's misery and loneliness, but before her memories could suck me in she flung me away with an angry roar. I slammed on to the hard stone and all the breath went out of me but looking up, panting and scared, I could see she'd been shaken by the jolt of memory. She was just standing there, swaying a little, slightly dazed, and that was the moment that Josh stepped forward. He'd got the little black box out of his pocket and he was getting his fingernails under the lid.

'Don't!' I shouted.

He ignored me.

'Eat this, bitch,' he snarled.

And he opened the box in her face.

## 3.21 p.m.

#Anniversary **Imagine Pandora's box, only without the hope.**

Something flew out of the box. It was close to invisible, it had an oily shimmer like a heat-haze, and Josh was screaming. It was despair, fear and concussion all mixed together, all spewing out at once, all latching on to the two people who knew misery intimately. Ruby was staggering back with a look of horror on her face, and Josh was screaming.

He fell to his knees. I jumped to my feet, snatched the box out of his hand and snapped it shut. Ruby looked rooted to the spot and not even angry about it, still reeling from the blast of misery that Josh had unleashed in her face.

Her sadness was still filling me, still making it hard to move, but Josh was on his knees, not screaming any more but on his knees with his face in his hands.

I knelt beside him and put an arm round his shoulders, careful not to let my skin touch his. 'Come on, mate.' I was whispering in his ear. 'Come on, we've got to go.' He didn't move, didn't show any sign that he'd heard. 'Mate?' He was pale, his mouth was open, his eyes were staring, as if there was something terrible just in front of him.

I put my face in front of his, looked him in the eye. My voice was cracking. 'Josh. Look, it's me, Hector. Your best friend. Grace and Asha are here too. You hear me?'

Grace came and knelt beside me, gently pushed me aside and leant her forehead on to Josh's. 'Hey, Josh,' she whispered.

Her face was pressed right up to his. 'We love you. You know that, don't you? We all love you, Josh.'

He let out a long sigh, but he didn't move. I patted his pockets, pulled out the piece of paper from the notepad, gave it to Grace. She forced his hand open and closed it again around the crumpled, lined sheet.

'You've got to deliver this letter to your mum,' I said. 'Remember? You've got to give it to your mum.'

A long moment, and then, finally, Josh looked up.

I let out a breath I hadn't even realised I'd been holding.

'We need you to get up now,' Grace said. 'Can you do that? We have to go.'

His eyes, which had been focused somewhere else, on something else, found Grace.

'Hey,' she said, smiling.

'OK,' he breathed. 'That happened.'

Asha had been watching. When she saw Josh was recovering she put her hands on Connor's shoulders. Her nose was about an inch away from his. 'Connor, you're coming with us!'

I had a moment to wonder if the alien would control Connor, the way it was controlling all those zombie teenagers outside the castle. He blinked three times, and his face twitched. He sniffed. 'Have you had chips?'

Asha looked at Ruby. She was recovering, same as Josh, moving her shoulders, clenching and unclenching her fists. Asha took off her earbuds.

'Asha . . .' I said.

She ignored me of course. A moment. That anxious look on her face, mixed with determination. She didn't do the

221

full-on, imperious Voice, she did the persuasive one, that maybe took less effort.

'STAY THERE.'

Ruby had her teeth bared in fury, but she couldn't move. Asha stumbled away from her, and I half caught her.

'Are you all right?'

She nodded, panting, looking far from all right.

We were all set to go, but Grace walked right up to Ruby.

'Doesn't have to be this way,' she said. 'We want to help you.'

I don't know if Ruby could have answered, but she didn't. Grace hesitated a moment, Asha snapped, 'Come on,' and then we ran. Grace helped Asha and Josh stumbled along beside me at first, with my arm supporting him, then he shrugged me off and kept going without any help. It felt like we'd been running for three solid days, since Ruby chased us from the clubhouse, along the river, to the car park in the woods.

Down the stairs, through the arch and straight into a bunch of besieging teenagers. I was all ready for a fight, I could see Asha was desperately preparing to use the Voice, but Grace was observant as ever. 'It's all right!' she shouted. And it was all right. I lowered my fists, Asha let out a deep breath. The teens were confused, they looked anxious, and they were totally harmless. They weren't zombies any more.

A girl in a pink T-shirt and too much make-up looked at me blearily, like she'd had a couple too many shots.

'What happened?' she croaked.

There was ice on her fingertips and on her eyelashes. She lifted her hand and watched snow form on her palm.

'Why am I so cold?'

'I'm sorry,' I said uselessly, and other than that we ignored her, we pushed past and kept running down the footpath. I was thinking we'd get down to the High Street, jump in a car and beg them to take us somewhere, or get a taxi if we could find one and use the money Simpson had given us, or even get a bus if there was one. Anything to get out of Seabridge.

We ran, slipped, stumbled and actually slid down the steep path. It might have been fun if it hadn't been desperate and panicky. The car park was ahead, the van on its side, its roof facing us.

'They killed Vinny!' Connor squeaked.

So unfair. Such a totally undignified way for that brilliant vehicle to finish up. We got on to the flat again, and I looked back. Ruby wasn't following. She was up at the top of the footpath, standing in the arch of the castle wall, just waiting there, watching us. Something dark and angular above her head. The drone.

We kept moving, not running any more because we weren't physically up to it, got to the edge of the car park. I paused, panting again. Maybe I'd be a bit fitter at the end of this. If I wasn't dead.

'What are we going to . . . actually . . . do?' I gasped.

A car pulled into the car park at speed, braked hard and skidded side on to us, showering sand at us. The driver leant over and pushed a door open.

'Need a lift?' he said.

Asha peered at the driver. 'Wait,' she said, 'is that . . .'

I was staring at him. 'No,' I stammered, my voice small,

confused. I was shaking my head. 'What?' This couldn't be right. How had this happened?

I was frozen, because I was staring at Jason, I was staring at my brother. I was staring at him sitting behind the wheel in a big Audi in a car park in Seabridge.

'How . . .' I started.

Asha shoved me in the back. 'Questions later,' she growled.

She was right, obviously. I got in the passenger seat. Asha, Grace, Josh and Connor all squashed into the back. It was a tight fit.

'All in?' Jason said.

Asha slammed the door and shoved her knee into the back of my seat. 'How come you get the passenger seat?' she said.

Jason manoeuvred around the fallen campervan, nosed towards the exit of the car park, and then accelerated down the High Street, where adults were beginning to come out, looking up at the castle, wondering what all those teenagers were doing up there, wondering what was wrong with them, wondering what on earth was going on.

'What's going on?' I said to Jason. 'What the hell? I've hardly seen you for a year and now . . . suddenly . . . what?' I was shocked, I felt actually, properly dazed, I didn't even have the words to express my confusion. I sort of wanted to give him a hug but I also wanted to sit him down and basically interrogate him.

He glanced at me, looked back at the road. 'I came up north to find you. About a year ago you kind of saved my life,' he said. 'Remember? I told you I owed you one. So here I am.'

'OK,' I said. 'But how—'

He interrupted, impatient, like this should have been obvious: 'I'm Dr Lazarus,' he said. 'You didn't work that out?'

I didn't answer at first. We were leaving Seabridge. Past the arcade, the cafes, the fish and chip shop, the newsagent, back into the countryside. I didn't answer at first because I couldn't find the words. Dr Lazarus, who'd mocked me and insulted me and trashed every word I'd put online for the last year.

'No,' I said finally. 'I didn't work that out. He – you – said some horrible things. On Twitter, on your blog ...'

'I was in a bad place for a while.'

'Uncle Pete's?'

'No, idiot, I was in a bad place in my head. But I was basically trying to help.'

'By calling me stupid?'

Asha leant forward and put a hand on my shoulder. 'To be fair,' she said, 'you are as stupid as a bag of sticks.'

'You two need to talk,' Grace said. 'But should we decide where we're going first?'

'Yeah,' said Asha. 'Grace is right. No one cares about your whole big family feud. Where we going? You got a plan, Jase?'

He didn't hesitate: 'No,' he said. 'But you guys always have a plan, right?'

So we told him about Burrage. The tiny village in Northumberland, the worst holiday ever.

'Oh my God,' said Jason, 'I remember that. It was terrible.'

Squeezed into the car, driving nowhere in particular for now except away from Seabridge, we discussed it. We'd left Ruby behind, it would take her a while to find someone to drive her, and we were in a new vehicle, which meant Doofus and Patronising shouldn't be able to track us. Our priority was to stay away from Ruby and keep Connor away from teenagers until Fuzzy finally arrived, which would surely be soon.

It felt like, miraculously, we were back on track. We had a chance of doing this.

'Fine,' said Jason. 'Let's do that. Drive to Burrage, capital of Where the Hell Am I? Yes?'

We all agreed. It was maybe the first time since this had started that we'd all been on the same page.

Jason turned on to an A road, and put his foot down.

**3.48 p.m.**

#Anniversary **That moment when you think everything's finally come together, and then you find out No, it really hasn't.**

I looked over my shoulder. Grace was squashed up next to Josh, who was staring out of the window. She had an arm round his shoulders.

'How you feeling, mate?' I said.

He didn't answer, just kept looking out of the window.

'I'm fine, thanks for asking,' said Asha. 'Except I'm really not, cos Connor is basically on my lap.' Connor tried to wriggle away from her which didn't work at all. 'Stop wriggling!' she shouted. 'How about we pull over and I sit up front?'

'Let's get some distance between us and Seabridge first,' said Jason. He indicated, moved into the fast lane, accelerated.

I was briefly pressed back into my soft leather seat. I was driving in a big, shiny car with my brother. I'd worried that he might never fully recover from last year's events, that we might never be able to relax and spend time together again. And now here we were. Not exactly relaxed, but still.

'Where'd you get the car?' I said. It was all leather in different shades of brown, and screens and dials and digital read-outs like the cockpit of a jet.

'It's Uncle Pete's.' Jason made it sound like this was obvious, as he stared out of the window, not looking at me.

This was a bit surprising. Last I remembered, all Uncle Pete could afford was an old VW Golf. 'He's traded up,' I said.

Jason drummed his fingers on the wheel. 'Want to tell me what's been happening?' he said. 'Your tweets aren't exactly informative. Can I see the egg?'

'I'm Connor,' said Connor. 'Hello. And there's no egg. Are you Hector's brother?'

'You know when you talk?' Asha said. 'Your whole body moves. Could you not talk?'

'Wait,' said Jason, 'there's no egg?'

So we told him what had happened in Gilpin, and what had been going on since we left. I tried to tell him in a controlled, step-by-step sort of way – this happened, and then that happened, and because of that the next thing

227

happened. As far as I was concerned it was my story. It started with me being shut in my room stuck in front of my computer for a year, and it all led up to me feeling like I was taking control of my life again, in the car with my long-lost brother. Yay me.

Connor had different ideas, he seemed to think it was his story, and he kept interrupting with excited comments and corrections, and Asha snapped at me because apparently it wasn't all about me, and she snapped at Connor because apparently it wasn't all about him either, and also because his bum was literally vibrating on her lap because he was so excited. Grace occasionally tried to calm things down but all three of us ignored her.

I glanced over at Josh and realised he'd looked away from the window. He still had the precious letter scrunched in his hand but he had half a smile on his face. I stopped worrying about clarifying for them all how it was basically my story. All I wanted at that moment, was to encourage Josh's smile.

'Connor,' I said, 'is your bum actually vibrating? Yes, or no?'

'No!' he squealed.

'Yes, it is,' said Asha. 'Tell him to stop.'

'Connor—' I began.

'I heard!'

And then there was a sound that I couldn't identify, and when I looked round I thought Josh was crying, but it turned out he'd done a short, snorty sort of laugh.

'So anyway,' I told Jason, 'that's more or less what's been going on. And just now, Josh opened his little box of sadness which probably saved our lives but it was really horrible for him.'

'But now he's laughing because Asha thinks my bum's vibrating,' said Connor happily.

'I didn't even mention your shoulder blade digging into my boob,' said Asha.

'I can't help it!' Connor was leaning away from Asha now, his voice squeaky and apologetic, and I snorted with laughter too.

'Your sister was right,' Josh said. 'We're definitely the cool kids.'

It was a good feeling. We had a buzz going, a happy mood developing. It felt like we might have snatched a victory when defeat had basically turned up, surrounded us and was about to dismember and devour us zombie-style. It definitely felt like we were on the right track now, and there could actually be a good outcome to this journey we were on.

And then the car made a weird noise.

It was a grinding, coughing noise and it was followed by a judder that made us all lurch forwards in our seats.

'Jason . . .'

He looked at his dials. 'Petrol,' he said. 'Damn!'

'Seriously?' Asha squawked. 'We've run out of petrol? Does stupid run in your family?'

Jason seemed to be speaking through gritted teeth. 'I was in a hurry,' he said. 'You remember I rescued you, right?'

'Some rescue.'

Jason took a left. 'Running on fumes,' he muttered. He took another left, down a lane lined on either side by tall hedges, then, as the car spluttered and coughed, he pulled in at a layby.

We sat there, in the stationary car, and for about ten seconds no one spoke. We were all slowly readjusting, realising that we hadn't quite won yet after all. And I was worrying. I was worrying that something wasn't quite right. Jason was a bit stiff, a bit uneasy. Why was that?

He finally sighed. 'We passed a petrol station about a mile back,' he said.

'And you didn't stop?' Asha was almost shouting at him.

He ignored her. 'I'll go and get some.'

'I'll come with you,' I said.

He looked at me sharply, like he was going to argue, but he seemed to change his mind. 'Fine,' he shrugged.

We didn't wait to discuss it, or hear any more abuse from Asha. 'Won't be long,' I said. We got out of the car before anyone could say anything, and we set off.

It might have been nice, in other circumstances, to spend time with my brother. With him at Uncle Pete's and me shut in my room, we were almost like two strangers. Back when the world went insane the first time, a year ago, the egg had started turning him into some sort of insect. It had made him a bit crazy too, and eventually he'd used a rusty knife to try to cut a wing off his shoulder. After coming out of hospital he'd stayed well away from Gilpin, and hadn't been keen on being visited.

He had his phone out, and his fingers were moving over the screen. 'Who you texting?' I said.

'Promised Mum and Dad I'd tell them if I found you. Don't worry, I'm not saying where we are.'

I felt a pang of guilt about having been out of touch for so long, but I squashed it down. After all, this was going to end soon, one way or another. If Fuzzy popped out of Connor and we all survived, then we'd all go back to normal. And this time I didn't intend 'normal' to involve me being stuck in my room for a year like a crazy hermit.

'So,' I said. We were walking fast, almost running but not quite, which meant that I was almost out of breath but not quite. 'How've you been?'

No answer, just the sound of us both taking quick breaths, and cars rushing past us now that we were on the A road. I looked at him. He glanced at me. Glanced away.

'Sorry I haven't seen you for so long,' he said, finally. 'And sorry about the whole Dr Lazarus thing. But it was only because I want what's best for you, I hope you get that, Hector. Whatever happens, I want what's best for you.'

'Yeah,' I said, 'of course I get that.' I was a bit puzzled by his tone. A bit bothered by it too. I heard regret and guilt echoing in his voice and that was OK, but it was also slightly worrying. *Whatever happens?* What did that mean?

He didn't speak for a minute. A motorbike whined past us and I got a stink of exhaust. 'I hated everything about what happened last year,' he said. 'I was feeling horrible before that thing, the egg, even turned up, and somehow it knew. It took the way I was feeling and made it worse, and it turned it into something . . . physical.'

I nodded. He was right. That's exactly how the egg worked last year, and how Fuzzy was working this year. It interacted in some way with a teenager's mood or personality, then took that raw material and made something warped and physical out of it.

'So I was happy the government was trying to cover it up,' Jason continued. 'I was completely onside with that, because I wanted to pretend it had never happened. You and other people blogging and tweeting, you just wouldn't let it go. So I responded. I said it was all rubbish, I said you were either deluded or inventing the whole thing.' He shrugged. 'Sorry.'

A helicopter clattered overhead. I looked up into the gathering gloom and watched it heading away, back towards Seabridge. That was the second time he'd apologised in two minutes and I knew he wanted me to tell him it was fine, but I was having trouble forgiving him. He'd kind of helped to ruin my life for the past year.

'We should get a move on,' I said.

We broke into a jog, and stopped talking for a while. At the petrol station Jason bought a canister and filled it with petrol, while I got some sandwiches and drinks. I got a box of French Fancies seeing as they'd gone down so well last time. As we came out, a convoy of army trucks passed on the A road, heading for Seabridge. One of them was the Mobile Command Centre we'd last seen outside Simpson's house. I wondered if Kirby was in there, using the coffee machine. Perhaps she'd been in the helicopter.

'Hope they get Ruby,' I said. 'If they lock her up it's better for us and probably better for her too.'

'Yeah, about that,' said Jason. 'You've told me what you've been doing, but you haven't really explained why you've been doing it. Why not just leave it all to those people we met last year? Douglas and Kirby?'

We couldn't jog now, Jason was lugging the canister of petrol, I was swinging a heavy carrier bag, but we were walking as fast as we could.

'We can't trust them!' I said. 'They'll do whatever it takes to stop the alien from coming back—'

Jason interrupted. 'Which is a good thing.'

'But if they damage or kill the creature that's inside Connor then everyone who's been affected by it will die! All the teenagers in Seabridge, all the teenagers in Gilpin, plus Asha, Grace, Josh, Connor, Ruby. Me.'

'And if you let it hatch, or whatever it wants to do, then that's like giving up, isn't it? That says, Come on down, we'll be your nursery.'

He sounded like Doofus. And it was a decent argument too, because I didn't want more eggs coming back. But I didn't want me and my friends to die either. Surely there had to be another option?

'They won't let teenagers die,' he insisted. 'They've been studying this for a year, preparing.'

I stopped and stared at him, properly uneasy now. The tone of voice was still worrying me. So was the Audi. And the texting.

'How do you know that?' I said.

He stopped too. Shrugged. 'Stands to reason, doesn't it? The point is, Douglas and Kirby are basically trying to stop an invasion. A soft invasion. Shouldn't we get behind that? I think we should.'

I stared at him another moment as the truth slowly sank in. My brother. Unbelievable.

He saw it in my face, he saw that I knew.

'Hector . . .' he began.

I dropped the bag of sandwiches and water and ran. That phrase 'a soft invasion', that was Kirby's phrase. Jason had betrayed us. He'd said it himself, I'd heard him, he'd said he was completely onside with the government. Kirby and Douglas had convinced him no one would die, and they'd sent him out to look for me. That's why he was driving a shiny new car, that's why he'd been texting.

My own brother had betrayed me.

I sprinted down the A road and round the corner. I had no idea whether Jason was following me and I didn't care. I turned down the hedge-lined lane and saw a black jeep and a van parked alongside Jason's Audi. Black-uniformed soldiers on the road. No sign of Asha, Grace, Josh or Connor. I stopped, started thinking about backing up, but they'd seen me. One was pointing his gun at me, dark, swampy green light bleeding from its muzzle; two of them were running towards me and I knew it was over, there was no way out this time, it was all over.

Jason came up beside me, panting.

'I did this for you, Hector, it's for the best. You've lost sight of what you're doing.'

I swung round to face him. 'I want to punch you in your face right now,' I snarled, my teary voice breaking.

'Hector . . .' he started.

And then I did, even though he was blurry because my

eyes were wet, I punched him in the face. The first soldier ran up to me shouting something, and I didn't listen, I just jumped on Jason. I was breathless and furious and my heart was hurting, and I grabbed his hand. I gritted my teeth, still snarling, as his memories washed into me and he started to yell. I didn't let go, I held on tighter.

*He was standing there, all black and leathery, with blue-black wings unfurled behind his shoulders. He was hunched, like he was carrying a burden, and his face was all twisted and desperate like he was in terrible pain. He lifted a knife up to his shoulder.*

This was the first memory that came. It was a year old but it was fresh and vibrant like it had happened yesterday. My rage started to fade, but the first soldier was wrestling with me and I was still clutching Jason's arm.

The second soldier was Map Girl. I dimly saw her stop a couple of steps away from us.

She smiled, raised her gun and shot me.

**4.52 p.m.**

Green light, a whoosh like an email being sent, and my stomach knotted as if someone had got hold of my internal organs and was wringing them out. I croaked a hoarse, agonised gasp, let go of Jason, let go of the soldier, and fell on the ground.

All of that happened in about half a second.

I took a bit longer to lift myself up on all fours and throw up.

It wasn't just my stomach, my brain was scrambling too. I looked up at Map Girl and tried to speak but only confused, scared sounds came out. It was like I'd forgotten how to use words. I stuttered and choked and gagged.

She was still smiling. And she was raising the gun again.

I saw Jason's shoes. He was saying something. He was shouting and shoving Map Girl away from me. I had no idea what was going on. I tipped over on my side and closed my eyes.

Sounds came back first. A rumbling that I thought was inside my skull, to go with my throbbing headache. Then movement. A steady vibration. Then a pain in my back. Some sort of sharp ridge under my shoulder blades. Sound, movement, pain. It was like I was putting the world together, piece by piece. I tried to move and found that I couldn't. My arms were . . . what? Tied up? Handcuffed? I lifted my chin off my chest and opened my eyes.

Asha was opposite me. She had something on her face. Grace was next to her. She had something on her head. I turned, slowly. Josh was next to me.

'Hey, mate,' he said, bright and smiley, like I was knocking on his front door on an ordinary day. 'So, we're totally screwed.'

We were, as far as I could tell, in a box. We were handcuffed to our seats, in a box.

I turned my head the other way. There was a soldier sitting facing us with one of those customised guns on his lap.

'Are we . . .?' My throat was dry. I coughed, which hurt my head, tried again. 'Are we . . . in a box?'

Asha made a sound. She rolled her eyes. She was wearing a gag, but I could still feel the word 'stupid' radiating off her.

'We're in the back of a van,' Grace said. She had some sort of tight bandana pulled down over her forehead, covering her third eye.

'Connor?' I said.

'Not here,' said Josh. 'Unless he's hiding.' He looked from side to side. 'Which he isn't.'

'Where are we going?'

Grace shook her head. 'We don't know. Are you all right? What happened to you?'

I told them about the green gun, what it did. I'd been holding on to Jason, seeing his memories, and then all of a sudden, when Map Girl shot me, it stopped. No more memories. It was like my power had been turned off. And it had made me as sick as a very sick dog. I was getting a little bit clearer. Like Grace said, we were in the back of a van. The rumble I'd heard was engine noise. We were handcuffed to our seats. That pain in my back was the top of my seat digging into my spine.

Josh looked at me, made sure he had my attention. 'You know when Ruby killed Peaches and took Connor, and then the army arrested Simpson?' he said. 'You know you reckoned that was the worst moment?'

I nodded.

'Spoke too soon,' he said.

I sighed.

'Also,' he said, 'your brother? Total dick.'

No one spoke much after that. I was still recovering, Asha was gagged, Grace was her usual quiet, watchful self, Josh was sunk deep in his own thoughts. We drove. We listened to the echoey grumble of the engine. The soldier watched us, bored, silent, his hands always on his gun. Occasionally, accidentally, I'd catch Asha or Grace's eye. I thought Asha looked angry, although it was hard to tell. Grace looked sad. Our eyes would meet, then flick away, like we were embarrassed, like we hardly knew each other. I took deep breaths of stale, van air, slowly feeling a bit more human.

And also feeling, basically, despair.

They had Connor. They'd do some experiments on him and sooner or later they'd damage Fuzzy or kill him and we'd die. We'd all die. I couldn't see any other likely outcome.

Time passed. Maybe two hours. Everything ached, and I was thirsty, and now that the nausea had ebbed away I was starting to feel hungry too. I was pretty sure we'd been on a motorway for a while, going fast and steady, and then we'd gone more slowly on smaller roads, stopping and starting. And now we'd been going slowly and bumpily for a while, perhaps down a lane. We stopped briefly and I heard shouts. We crept forward a little further, and then we finally stopped again. The engine was turned off.

There were voices, there was movement outside, and with a clunk and a creak the back of the van was opened up. Fresh air rushed in and I took a deep breath of it, relieved, sitting up, stretching my spine, moving my shoulders back. Hard to see what was going on outside. It was dark, but the dusty yellow beams of spotlights lit up a dirt road, long sheds and a high fence.

I screwed up my eyes against the dazzle. Two dark shapes were slowly coming into focus. Colonel Doofus and Professor Patronising.

Kirby smiled. First proper smile I'd seen from her this year. She knew she'd won.

'Welcome to Green Fingers,' she said.

We were taken to a small brick building, and shown into a bare room where folding wooden chairs were lined up against the walls. One dark window. The chairs were unfolded and we sat down in a line. A bored-looking guard leant next to the door holding a gun across his chest. None of us bothered trying to talk to him. Asha was still gagged and we were all still handcuffed.

I dropped my head on to my shoulder and rolled my neck right round, feeling stiff, feeling restless. Silence, except for our breathing. There was nothing to hear, nothing to see. The walls were pale yellow. There were bits of Blu Tack by the door where a poster had probably been pulled down, and there was a corkboard on the wall opposite, with some things that looked like receipts pinned to it. Above Josh's head there was a postcard of a flower with long, pink petals. I wondered if it had been overlooked, or if someone had left it there deliberately, in an effort to brighten the place up.

After a few minutes Kirby and Douglas came in. They stood in front of us, like a couple of teachers with a very small class.

'So you've finally come to our Safeguarding Centre,' said Kirby, her voice bright and cheerful. 'Goodness knows you've been threatened with it often enough. You know what it used to be, don't you?'

She looked at us, waiting, as if she really expected us to speculate.

'A garden centre,' I said flatly. Grace had guessed it, back when I'd first told them about the file I'd seen on the desk.

'That's right,' Kirby exclaimed, in the satisfied tone of someone who's told a good joke. 'Who'd have thought it?' She looked round at us, as if she expected some sort of reaction. 'We can't stay long,' she continued. 'Connor of course is our main concern.'

'What's going on with that gun?' I nodded at the soldier by the door.

Kirby smiled. 'Yes, we're quite proud of that,' she said. She had a weakness for explaining things, especially if it involved showing off. 'The prenatal creature produces a form of radiation which, as you know, disrupts your metabolic pathway and alters your genetic code. That gun emits a pulse of electromagnetic energy which interrupts the creature's signal, creating interference, temporarily neutralising the effect. And thus temporarily removing your power.'

'It half killed me,' I said. 'Is it even legal?'

'Emergency powers,' Douglas growled. 'Your rights are suspended indefinitely. Everything is legal.'

Kirby smiled again. 'Which is how all Gilpin's teenagers happen to be gathered in a garden centre,' she said. 'Like a collection of exotic plants.'

Usually her smile seemed false, but tonight it made her cheeks bunch up and it reached her eyes – it was definitely genuine. It was the smile of someone who'd been involved in a long game, and had been losing it, but had managed to pull off an unlikely, last-minute win.

I glanced at the receipts again, and at the postcard of the pink flower, and I thought about the ordinary world, that had been suspended along with our rights. I felt homesick for that place, a place where you might pin a receipt for some gooseberry bushes up on a corkboard.

'Tomorrow, my assistants are going to question you,' Kirby continued. 'We want to know everything you can tell us about Connor. If you cooperate, you'll be allowed to see your parents. They've been told that the teenagers of Gilpin have been brought here to avoid a repeat of last year's hysteria. They think it's a sort of holiday with therapy.'

'Rather than a prison with torture,' said Josh.

Douglas stepped forward. I sensed he'd been impatient for Kirby to stop talking. His hands behind his back, his eyes squinting as if into sunlight.

'There'll be no torture here,' he snapped. 'We're conducting urgent scientific research, but we will maintain civilised standards of behaviour.'

'Until you kill us by killing the alien,' I said.

He stared at me, but he didn't answer. That was the most scary thing. Not what he said, what he failed to say.

'We'll remove your handcuffs, the gag and the bandana,' he continued. He looked at Asha. 'All guards around you will be wearing noise-cancelling headphones. Any attempt by any of you to use your mutation in an offensive manner will be met by force. Do you understand?'

We didn't answer. 'Have you got Ruby too?' I said.

He hesitated. His eyes narrowed a fraction. Then he turned and walked out.

Kirby was about to go too.

'She'll come for her brother.'

She smiled once more. It was a tight smile this time, with no humour behind it at all. Just anger.

'We'll be ready,' she said.

She turned and walked away too.

# DAY SIX

**8.33 a.m.**

I had a good night's sleep. Maybe I shouldn't have done, lying on my back under a thin blanket on a creaky camp-bed, basically in prison, with Josh breathing heavily in another bed a few feet away. But the thing about being in prison is you feel safe and secure. No one's after you, because they've already got you. Ruby was probably on her way, but I didn't have to worry about that because I wasn't standing between her and her brother any more. Me, Asha, Josh and Grace were, as Kirby had pointed out a couple of days ago, irrelevant.

Game over.

Turns out losing is quite a nice, peaceful feeling.

The other reason I slept like a baby was no phone. I find it kind of relaxing when I don't have to worry about what to say to my worldwide army of followers on social media. It's dipped from millions down to hundreds of thousands but still, all those demanding, angry, sceptical, anxious, curious, accusing people are a weight and a responsibility. I felt lighter without them hanging round my neck.

One more reason my sleep was all deep and dreamless: Grace's prediction that one of was going to die had been hovering in the air around all of us like a black cloud, like a whole separate little box of sadness, ever since she'd first said it. Loss, like a great empty pit. It seemed like she'd got that wrong. It had looked like it might be Asha, but now she had no reason to use her Voice. Of course there was still an excellent chance that Professor Patronising would kill Fuzzy, so in fact we'd all die. That was still a bit of a worry, but the fact that it was now out of our hands was oddly comforting.

'D'you reckon they're dissecting Connor?' Josh murmured.

I hadn't even realised he was awake.

'No!' I said. 'Don't say that.' I turned over, and the campbed squeaked and shifted. Now, of course, I couldn't get that idea out of my mind.

He was lying on his back, yawning. 'Sorry,' he said. 'Bad joke.'

'I sort of believed what Doofus said about civilised standards of behaviour,' I told him. 'And if they try and get it out, we'll know about it anyway, cos we'll probably all die.' I started yawning on the word 'die', so it lasted for ages.

He sat up. 'Well, I want breakfast first,' he announced.

I realised I was starving. We hadn't eaten a thing since the fish and chips in Seabridge.

Josh got up and opened the door. There was a soldier there, wearing headphones. 'Full English!' Josh yelled. 'It's a human right!'

We washed in a plain shower block which smelt of antiseptic, and dressed in bright red T-shirts and grey tracksuit bottoms that had been left folded on top of our lockers. The garden centre had been prepared for the teenagers of Gilpin. Shower block, uniforms, kitchens, high, razor wire fences. It had all been set up, waiting for us, a couple of miles outside town, on the road to Glydegate. Our government. Hiding the truth, and tucking us away in a camp which officially didn't even exist.

Asha and Grace emerged at the same time we did. Asha marched straight up to a soldier.

'I don't wear tracksuits,' she snapped. 'Where's my clothes?'

He stared at her, unmoved, obviously not hearing a word and not particularly wanting to.

She looked at me and Josh. 'I hate garden centres,' she said.

Josh was patting his pockets. 'Where's my letter?' he said to himself. Then he looked up at the soldier, and suddenly he was shouting. 'Where's my letter?'

He marched up to the soldier, who shoved him in the chest, took a step back and raised his gun.

'All right, all right!' I got between them. 'Josh, they're going to question us, we'll ask then, OK?'

The soldier nodded to us to follow and headed towards a long, low shed. We followed, Josh muttering angrily to himself. Through double doors, past an area where there probably used to be tills and bags of sweets for sale. We'd been kept apart from the main population of the camp so far.

It looked like we were about to meet them. There was a big room up ahead, full of kids.

It felt like school. I heard chatter and the tink-tink of cutlery on plates as we approached. I could just about imagine people were discussing double History and who'd been doing what, with who, on Saturday night. Through a sliding door and into the hall, which was actually a greenhouse. Trestle tables and folding chairs had been lined up, and there were Suzie and Freddie, Rufus, Kayleigh and her brother Kieran, Amber, Arshad, Zahra, Sam and everyone else. There was Eden, with her tight little group of mates. They were all eating, but they slowly stopped and looked round when we came in. Everyone did. A hush slowly fell. About a hundred kids silently stared at us. Which was embarrassing.

'Hey,' said Asha. She gave a little wave.

She's hard to embarrass, Asha.

Freddie shouted, 'Where've you been?'

Rufus said, 'Hi', a couple of kids waved back. They all studied us, obviously wondering what kind of mutations we had.

'So . . . can anyone fly?' said Asha.

It was just like school. Apart from the black-uniformed soldiers spaced around the room. And apart from the fact that all the colour had been leached out of Suzie so she was albino, even her hair was white, and Freddie had long, curving claws which made it hard for him to hold cutlery, Rufus seemed to be about eight feet tall and Sam had an electric light show buzzing round his body. Zahra suddenly laughed at something her neighbour had said, and as she laughed water sprayed off

246

her like she was a fountain. Last year Kayleigh had had transparent skin, and she'd looked like something out of a horror movie. This year I couldn't see anything visibly wrong with her, which was a small relief. She was talking to Kieran. But then she looked away from her brother and kept talking, non-stop, even while she was trying to eat and drink. So it was just like school, except that it was bizarre, and also sinister, and actually nothing at all like school.

And Eden? She had her head down, focusing on her plate. I wondered what was wrong with her.

We sat at a table with Arshad and Amber. Arshad had had X-ray vision last year, but not in a good way. He saw through his own eyelids, saw right through people's bodies. This year his eyes were way too big, they were bulging, cartoonish orbs in his face.

'Whoa,' said Asha. 'That is a look.'

Arshad turned his head towards her voice. 'Can't see you,' he said. 'Can only see stuff about half a mile away.'

We all looked at Amber. Couldn't help it, it was basically the first question you had to ask. She lifted up her hands, showed us her webbed fingers.

Josh, still preoccupied, looked unimpressed. 'Is that it?' he said. 'Guess you got off lightly.'

She smiled and pulled down her collar to show gills. 'I can breathe underwater.' She looked really pleased with herself.

Josh nodded. 'Well played.'

Breakfast was cereal and toast, and Josh complained about the lack of bacon. We talked about what had happened to us, what had happened to everyone else, and who was in the hospital wing (Livvy Read, who was ageing at a dangerous rate, and Danny White, who made things rot when he touched them). We found out there was a so-called games room with a TV, an Xbox and an old pool table, there was football on a patch of grass which had become a pitch, and there were some half-hearted school books all stacked up in a classroom that everyone ignored. We wanted to talk to everyone, Asha was about to peel off and join some mates, and I definitely hadn't had enough to eat, when the soldiers came and told us we needed 'debriefing'.

I snorted. 'You mean interrogating, right?'

No answer.

We were taken back to the small brick building and separated, and all of a sudden I was back in the bare room with the postcard of the pink flower. On my own this time. Two chairs on either side of a desk. Still air, a dusty smell, the shouts of some kids outside playing football. I didn't sit down, I looked out the window instead, and found that if I twisted my neck a bit I could see a corner of the pitch. I drummed the glass with my fingernails. I wanted to be outside, running up the wing, selfishly hogging the ball, charging towards the goal, in a world where aliens didn't exist and the government was something to do with taxes and foreign policy and nothing to do with barbed wire fences and killing teenagers.

Kirby came in. Of course she did. It had to be her. She took out a pad of lined paper and laid a pen on it.

'Terribly busy,' she chirped, like a teacher with a lot of books to mark. 'But I've always got time for you, Hector. Where shall we begin?'

'With Josh,' I said. 'He had a letter in his pocket, it was important. Where are our clothes?'

'Burnt,' she said. 'Sorry. Now, I'd like to know what you've been doing.'

I could have got angry with her, but what good would it have done? I sat down opposite her and I just told her everything. Straight off. Because why not? Maybe after that I could go out and kick a football around with my mates. I told her about the powers each of us had, how and when they'd emerged, the different times we'd used them. She looked surprised by my cooperation, but she didn't interrupt, she just made notes. Small handwriting, leaning sharply to the right. I told her about the zombies of Seabridge and I finished up by telling her how the alien had spoken to me, through Connor. That made her put down her pen. Her tongue actually emerged and licked her upper lip.

I told her about *Let me become*. I said it didn't want to go to a city, because that was *Too much*. I told her about *The taste of the earth*, *The drift of the air*, *Numbers*. I was sure that every word I said was being recorded, but Kirby had her pen in her hand again, she was writing down each phrase in capitals, as if she needed them there, on paper, in front of her.

She looked down at them, studied them, like she'd written a poem.

'Environment,' she said, more to herself than to me. 'The taste of the earth refers to the particular composition of the

249

soil in Gilpin; the drift of the air is radiation; numbers means population.' She looked up and caught my eye, and for a moment she was speaking to me as if to a colleague. 'It all comes together in Gilpin, in the geographical centre. This confirms what we thought.'

I nodded seriously, like I was a colleague, like my interest was scientific and not in any way personal.

'Yeah,' I said. 'Good. Also, are you planning to kill whatever's inside Connor, and basically murder us all?'

She stared at me, and there was a sort of emptiness about her pale face. Red hair pulled back, steady green eyes behind her narrow glasses. No hint of a smile or a sneer.

My stomach knotted. It was just like when Doofus had failed to answer me when I'd said he was going to kill us by killing the alien. 'That looks like a yes,' I said.

She seemed to recover herself. She shook her head quickly, and found some vestige of a smile. 'No, no,' she said. 'No, that's not our plan. However,' she tapped her pen on her pad, 'as I said to you once before, there can be no guarantees, Hector. The situation is serious, and it is fluid.'

Well, that wasn't even a tiny bit reassuring. We sat there in that little room, opposite each other, on either side of the desk.

'Anyway,' she said eventually. 'Thank you.' She stood up. 'You can go when you're ready.'

And then she left and I sat there some more, alone again, and thinking.

It was no good. Losing might be peaceful, but we couldn't give up, not if that meant relying on Doofus and Patronising to keep us safe. They'd pretty much confirmed they were prepared to let us all die. We needed a plan.

No sign of Josh when I left that room. He'd have heard what happened to his letter and I wanted to see how he was, but he'd gone missing.

So I went and looked for Asha instead. I needed to find her because she was part of the plan I was coming up with, which was likely to involve her using the Voice. So I had to know what she was hiding. I tried our dormitory and found her on her way out.

'Asha,' I said. 'Can we talk?'

She looked impatient. 'I know this is a weird concept for you, Hector,' she said, 'but I've got about a hundred friends to catch up with.'

She was about to push straight past me, but I didn't move. Ever since she'd fainted, I'd been waiting for the right time to bring this up, and I was pretty sure the right time was right now. 'I've got, possibly, a plan,' I told her, 'but you're lying about something, and I have to know the truth.'

That stopped her. She hesitated, caught between storming out and discussing this thing she obviously didn't want to discuss. Her lips moved like she wanted to snap some angry comment at me, but nothing came out.

'Please?' I said.

It was a bit like when Grace said *Please*, before any of this had started, when they all persuaded me to leave my bedroom. It worked this time too. Asha and I sat in her room. Her on her bed, me on Grace's, right opposite her. I almost felt pleased, because the fact I'd seen there was something wrong and no one else had felt like evidence that I was close to her, that I still had a connection with her. But I was also scared, because I could see she was scared.

She'd been looking at her knees, but finally she looked up.

'I'm the one who's going to die,' she sighed.

I opened my mouth. Closed it again. Shook my head.

'No,' I stumbled, eventually.

'Actually, yes,' she said. 'It all came together somehow after I fainted, like while I was out I got a proper snapshot of what's going on in my skull. Good news: like I told you, I can keep doing the Voice, as long as I leave time for it to recharge. Bad news: it's a proper strain up here,' she was tapping her head. 'A strain on the brain. It's busting blood vessels and damaging synapses or neurons or whatever the hell they are, and I think I'll have a full-on stroke or something if I keep doing it.'

I was shaking my head again. 'How do you even know?'

She shrugged. 'I feel it. With a bit of luck it'll repair and be good as new if Fuzzy appears and we all go back to normal. But I don't know how much more I can use it before ... something permanent happens. Which is why I reckon I'm the one who's going to die. Happy now?'

We were sitting opposite each other, our knees almost touching. I felt physically sick. This was like Max, it was like Max all over again. My best friend dying was like losing a part of myself, and now Asha was telling me she was next. I shook my head, like I could just say no, like if I said it firmly enough I could change the horrible reality that was facing us. I wanted to go and sit beside her and put an arm round her but I wasn't sure if she'd welcome that.

'Hey, stupid, I'm not dead yet!'

She always had an effective voice, Asha, even before she had the Voice. I sat up, sort of shook myself. 'Sorry,' I said.

'Tell me about your plan.'

So I told her about the plan that might save all the teens we knew, and a whole lot that we didn't know, but might kill her.

And then we just sat there, and looked at each other, and wondered what to do.


I played football, that's what I did. It wasn't part of the plan I'd come up with, I just felt like it.

I wasn't on the wing, but I was in the midfield with tall Rufus and sparky Sam, and amphibian Amber was up front with nightmare Freddie, which was great because no one dared to go near those claws, and it was fun. Our quest to take Connor and Fuzzy to the middle of nowhere had totally failed, death was hanging over all of us, but especially Asha, my brother had betrayed me, Simpson was arrested, Peaches was dead, and Vinny the Van was lying on its side in a car park in Seabridge. But there were mates here, and there was plenty of food, my parents finally knew I was safe, and maybe there was some way Asha could avoid using the Voice again. That's what I was telling myself.

No one was going to die today. No one even looked like they might be about to die. Not Asha, not Livvy or Danny in the hospital wing. No one. I was just playing football, and trying hard not to think about anything else.

I had the ball at my feet, I was choosing between a short pass and a jinking run, and was about to give the jinking run a go, because obviously, when I heard the humming.

I looked at tall Rufus, who I was about to not pass the ball to. 'What's that?' I said.

And then there was a muffled *Boom!* and I fell to my knees. And tall Rufus fell to his knees. And sparky Sam, amphibian Amber, nightmare Freddie and every other teenager in sight fell to their knees.

My insides were knotting. It was a sharp, tight pain that felt like it was yanking me into my own navel. I was gasping in agony.

I rolled over on to my back. I wanted my mum, I

wanted Dad, I wanted Asha.

And then the pain stopped.

Just like that it stopped and I was lying on my back, panting, looking up at the bright, white sky, only slowly working out that I was still alive.

Tall Rufus was next to me. He was already getting carefully back up. 'What,' I gasped, 'was that?'

'Happens once or twice a day,' he said. 'The doctors say they don't know why. They're probably lying.' He took the ball, and ran off towards the goal.

I finally saw Josh at dinner. He was bent over his plate not looking at anyone.

'Hey, mate,' I said, sitting down next to him.

No answer. Grace came and sat on the other side of him.

'I'm sorry about your letter,' she said.

Still nothing. He stabbed a piece of chicken like it had looked at him wrong.

I balanced some peas on my fork. I was quite pleased to be able to focus on Josh for a minute, not to think about Asha. 'Don't blame you for being angry,' I said. 'That letter had super-powers.'

He looked at me. His look said *What the hell are you talking about?*

'It brought you back yesterday, after you opened the box, when we couldn't reach you.' I put my peas in my mouth because they were about to fall off the fork, and spoke through them. 'Thing is though, it wasn't the piece of paper that did that. It was the words.'

Grace put her hand on his chest, over his heart. He had to

put down an overloaded forkful of chicken. 'It was the feelings,' she said. 'Just talk to her. Talk to your mum.'

He put the chicken in his mouth, chewed it, swallowed. 'All right,' he said finally. 'Enough with the therapy. I'm trying to eat here.'

So I changed the subject. 'You heard the hum and the boom, right?' I said. 'Before we all got the massive stomach cramps? It was that machine again, the one that made me fall in the river.'

Josh nodded. 'Never did find out what it's for,' he said.

I told him and Grace what I thought it was for, and then I told them about my plan, and then finally I took a deep breath and told them about Asha.

Grace just stared at me for about three seconds, then jumped up with a harsh scrape of her chair and hurried off to find her. We followed. She was at a table with albino Suzie, talkative Kayleigh, amphibious Amber and some other girls.

Grace hugged her and Asha smiled but shook her head like she didn't want to talk about it. Not now at least, at a table full of people.

'Hey, Hector,' Kayleigh whispered, 'Josh, what's up, we've been hearing all about everything, Ruby and Connor, eh, wow, it's been so boring here, good to get some new people, I was saying, wasn't I, Asha, good to get new people . . .'

Her voice was hoarse and quiet, barely audible, and had a hint of desperation in it. She had a jug of water and a glass next to her and she started drinking as she was speaking, spilling it everywhere but lubricating her throat.

A woman in a white coat came up to the table. 'Come on, Kayleigh,' she said. 'Time for treatment.'

Kayleigh put down her glass. 'So, yeah, I'm off then, see you tomorrow, guys, this is wild, right, but it's going to stop soon, isn't it? Isn't it, Grace? Is that right? Is it going to stop? Is it?'

Grace was lingering by Asha but Kayleigh seemed to desperately want reassurance, and to believe that we might be able to offer it. So Grace walked with her as she was led away, still talking, still asking that question – 'Is it going to stop though? Is it, Grace?' – with that hint of desperation swelling up so it was starting to sound like hysteria.

'Yes,' I heard Grace say. 'Yes, Kayleigh, it's going to stop soon.'

'They drug her overnight,' Suzie told us. 'So she can sleep, and her throat gets a rest.'

Then Kayleigh and the woman in the white coat had gone, and Grace was left standing by the table where Eden and her mates were sitting. She didn't move. She just stood there and looked at them like she was wondering what to do next.

So I went over and joined her, because she'd said Eden had been picking on her and I hadn't even noticed for a whole year. She ignored me. She said, 'Hey, Eden.'

Eden looked up. She wore her blonde hair short, in a way that a load of Year Eleven and Twelve girls had copied, she had a splodge of eyeliner in the corners of her eyes, Egyptian style, which had also been copied. I'd heard someone say she'd had her lips injected to make them fuller, but that was probably just gossip. Anyway, you didn't really notice her hair or her eyes or her lips today. Because she was spiky. She had little tiny spikes and big spikes about three inches long erupting all over her skin.

'Is that right?' she said. 'What you told Kayleigh? Is it going to stop soon? D'you know something?'

Grace's eyes moved slowly over Eden's spiky face, over her spiky hands. 'You called me a freak,' she said finally. Her tone was calm, like they were discussing something completely neutral. 'D'you remember? You were all over Instagram having a go at me. And every time you saw me you said, "Still freaky, Grace?" Funny that, isn't it? Looking at you, now.'

She wasn't helping my guilt. I'd been addicted to social media for the past year, but I'd still somehow managed to miss Eden cyber-bullying Grace. Too preoccupied with my self-important dreams of being a journalist, while avoiding cardboard and battling trolls.

Eden stared at Grace. Grace looked back. Eden had a hand over her mouth and it looked like she was chewing a nail.

'Thing is, Eden, you're not a freak. You're just different. Same as me, same as all of us. And here's the thing – different's fine.' She was about to go, but then she hesitated. 'Mean and stupid aren't fine, though,' she said. 'They're kind of pathetic, to be honest.'

She didn't wait for an answer to that, she walked away. Which left me standing at the table, which felt a bit awkward. So I gave Eden my best hard stare, and then I followed Grace.

Asha was finishing the dry flapjack they'd given us for

pudding. Her eyes flicked over towards Eden, back to Grace. 'All right?'

Grace nodded.

'Got your back,' Asha said.

'I've got all the rest of you.' Josh pointed, to clarify. 'Front, top, bottom.'

'But actually,' Grace told Asha, 'you're way more important right now.'

Asha nodded and smiled. 'Course I am.' She put down her flapjack. 'Let's skip right over *why didn't you tell us, and oh my God you might die.*' She looked at me. 'You want to talk about the hum and the boom, right?'

Grace sighed. 'We're coming back to *why didn't you tell us and oh my God you might die,*' she said. 'But we do need to talk about that machine. First they use it to search for the egg, then they bring it along when they're chasing us. And now they've got Connor, and they're using it again.'

'I think they were using it to track him,' I said. 'And now I reckon they're using it to examine him. And every time they use it Fuzzy feels threatened, which means we all basically nearly die.'

Josh nodded. 'Which is why,' he said, 'Hector's got a genius plan.'

'Yeah,' said Asha. 'And his plans always go so well.'

'I'm only interested if it doesn't involve you using the Voice.' Grace's own voice was suddenly loud and shaky.

Asha shook her head. 'Can't see any way to avoid it,' she said gently. 'And if we do nothing, I'm probably dead anyway.'

I took a slow breath, thinking about that game of football

and wishing it could have continued in a normal way, with no one nearly dying.

Josh didn't wait for me to finish my slow breath. 'Long story short,' he said, 'we have to rescue Con one way or another, or us and all our mates are toast. Right, Hector?'

I didn't answer, so Asha answered for me.

'Right,' she said. 'We totally have to rescue Connor.'

# DAY SEVEN

**5.00 a.m.**

The alarm on my watch went off. It was early morning, but it felt like the middle of the night. I sat up, opened my eyes slowly.

Josh rolled on to his side and muttered, 'Bacon.' It wasn't a code word, he was still asleep. I shook him, whispered it was time. He yawned.

We were still in the little two-bedroom block, because maybe they didn't have room for us anywhere else. That was helpful. There were only four rooms, with a narrow corridor down the middle. Asha and Grace were opposite us, there was a loo and a little utility room on either side of the main door. And outside the main door there was a guard, armed with one of those nasty, power-dampening puke-guns.

There was a quiet knock, and Asha and Grace came in.

'Hector,' Josh was pulling on his T-shirt. 'Mate, it's the middle of the night and two hot girls have just come in our bedroom. I think they want our bodies.'

Asha smiled sweetly at him. 'I'll use my Voice on you,' she said. 'I'll make you stand on your head in the corner and sing Beyonce songs till you faint. It'll be worth the risk.'

Josh started humming 'All the Single Ladies'. He either really was over losing the letter or, more likely, doing a good job of pretending he was.

'Can we focus?' I whispered. I looked at Grace. 'You ready?'

She sighed, pushed her fringe off her forehead, closed her eyes. And opened her third Eye. We didn't want to turn on any lights, and our mobiles had been taken away, so we were sitting in almost complete darkness, but I could still imagine that blue-green Eye, the colour of the sea, moving over us. Josh stopped humming. I could more than imagine the Eye, I could feel it when it landed on me. It felt like feathery fingers trailing down my face. I shivered and breathed in sharply.

'I think I see him,' Grace said. 'I think we're going to find Connor.'

'Yes!' Josh, beside me, did a little fist pump.

'But . . .'

She sat back, and I felt rather than saw her closing her third Eye, opening her ordinary, human eyes.

We waited.

'Fear, again,' she said. 'Loss.' She swallowed, and there was a tremor in her voice. 'Death.'

I looked at Asha, looked at Josh and Grace. 'Are we all up for this?' I said. 'Are we going to do it? Because we could just go back to bed.'

'For Peaches,' said Josh. 'And Simpson, wherever he is.'

'And for Connor,' said Grace.

'And for me,' said Asha. 'I don't want to die but I'm up

for risking it, because those morons couldn't care less what happens to us. Let's do this.'

## Part One of My Genius Plan: Get Out of Our Dormitory

I stood at the main door, looked back over my shoulder at my friends. Then I knocked to warn the guard I was coming, and opened it. I was hoping he'd be bored and sleepy, or perhaps even actually asleep, but as the door swung out he wheeled round to face me, backed off fast and raised his gun. He was in black body armour, his eyes were cold and hard, there was a coiled quality to him, like he was on the verge of attacking me.

What had they told him? I felt like a terrorist.

'Don't move,' he barked, too loud, because of his headphones.

I raised both hands, palms up in front of my chest. 'Not gonna,' I said. 'It's my mate Josh, he's sick.'

He was well out of reach and his gun was pointing straight at my chest. Definitely not bored or sleepy. Definitely not actually asleep. He looked highly trained, alert and suspicious. Also, he hadn't heard a word I'd just said.

'Back inside,' he snapped.

I stood there like an idiot, trying to think of something to say. Failing. Was my plan over before it had even started? I tried to look more worried, which was easy because I thought I was probably about to be shot. I gestured behind me, I shouted: 'Josh. My mate. Sick.' I rubbed my stomach to indicate illness, but it probably just made me look hungry.

I was all ready to give up, I was going to back up and close the door behind me, when Grace pushed me out of the way. She was crying. 'Please,' she said. Was she actually crying? The soldier took a small step forward. Asha was the actor, but if he'd seen her he'd probably have shot on sight. Everyone knew about her Voice. As far as they knew there was nothing dangerous about Grace. Or me. I could see the past? So what?

'What?' he said. 'What's wrong?'

Grace pointed behind her.

The guy looked torn for a moment. He had a radio, but he probably didn't want to report that he was spooked by a tearful sixteen-year-old girl. He pointed the gun at me. 'You, back off. Go in the bedroom with the other girl, close the door.' He indicated Grace. 'You. Show me.'

Well, it was progress at least. We were getting him inside. I went back in. Asha was waiting in the corridor.

'You were rubbish,' she said.

We went into her and Grace's room. The soldier was still waiting outside, cautious.

'Shut the door!' he shouted.

I shut the door, but Asha and I leant up against it, listening to Grace and the man coming in, heading for the other bedroom. Josh had volunteered to open his little box of sadness again, but we'd all said no. Too risky. Last time it had seemed to share itself between him and Ruby, drawn to their personalities, their characters. What if this time it all focused on Josh? I felt like he might not survive that.

So Asha and I leant against the door, listening. Footsteps,

Asha's breathing. The warm, just-out-of-bed scent of her, the distracting closeness of her.

'Now,' she whispered.

I opened the door. The soldier was in the corridor with his back to us, looking into our room. He'd heard nothing because of his headphones. Grace was in front of him, saying something about Josh, waving her hands around, distracting him.

I took a deep breath. Then I reached out one hand to his bare neck, one to his headphones.

I slapped my hand on to his neck and grabbed his headphones, aiming to yank them off his head, while Asha used her Voice. But he twisted, his reactions way quicker than I'd expected, and the headphones didn't come fully off. I kept my palm pressed against his bare skin as the gun went off, firing a bright green pulse at the ceiling, and then he let go of it and went for me with his teeth bared in a snarl of fury and the heel of his hand aiming for my chin.

I was pretty sure this SAS maniac was going to break my neck.

*Numbers and letters. Like a keyboard, but it wasn't a keyboard. This guy's finger pressing them. 4705J.*

I had no idea what that was, but it made him pause, confused, staring at me like *What the hell just happened?* He was quick, though, I saw his face reset, focus back on me. His hand went for my throat. I kept my palm pressed against his neck.

*A face. High definition, like it was right there in front of me. It was a young guy, smiling and chatting, saying something about sand that was making us both laugh. We were in a vehicle, it was rumbling and jolting along a road. It was gloomy in there but this guy's face was bright and I felt a surge of affection for him.*

*There was an enormous BANG!*

*I was flung into the air.*

*Screams. It was me, I was screaming. Gouts of flame, a burst of heat. Body parts. The troop carrier was a ruined shell. There was smoke, gunfire, panicky yelling.*

The soldier gasped and staggered back and my hand fell away from his neck. A long moment, nothing to hear except both of us panting. His gaze slowly refocusing again. It settled on me, standing in front of him, shaking.

And now there was murder in his eyes.

Grace saved me. She pulled the headphones off his head and shouted 'Now!'

Asha yelled, 'STOP!'

The soldier stopped. His face was still twisted in fury, he still looked like he wanted to rip my head right off my shoulders. But he stopped.

I was shaking, knowing I'd just seen his mate die and him narrowly escape death. I was shaking like I'd been in that armoured car with them. 'I'm sorry,' I said, 'I'm so sorry.'

But even as I said it, I was looking at the lanyard hanging round his neck. On an impulse I took it off him and shoved it in my pocket.

'GO IN THE BEDROOM,' Asha commanded in her gentler, persuasive Voice. 'LIE DOWN. STAY THERE FOR AN HOUR.'

He did as he was told, brushing past Josh who was coming out. I watched him go, feeling horrible.

'Are you all right?' Grace asked Asha.

She nodded. She was leaning against the wall, her palm pressed against her temple, taking deep breaths. 'Golden,' she murmured. 'Just don't ask me to do it again any time soon.'

'We're not going to ask you to do it again at all,' I said. 'That's it, never again.'

'Right,' said Josh, flexing his shoulders with a worried look at Asha. 'Let's go rescue Dangerous Connor. We get him somewhere quiet, Fuzzy comes out, and you're OK.' He nodded at Asha. 'Livvy and Danny are OK, everyone's happy.'

I was starting to feel something, a sort of faint electric buzz in the air.

'Fuzzy's coming,' I said. 'We need to move fast, because whatever Doofus and Patronising are going to do, they're going to do it soon.'


**5.11 a.m.**

*Part Two of My Genius Plan: Find Connor*

We came out of our little building, looked around cautiously. The night was moonless, which was helpful, and cold, which wasn't. I immediately wished I'd pulled a sweater over my red T-shirt, but there was no way I was going back into my bedroom, where the soldier was lying on my bed. So I just shivered. To the left, next to the football field, was the dark shape of the dormitory, where everyone was sleeping. The hospital wing beside it, and the rooms where we'd been questioned. Straight ahead of us was the former greenhouse, where we'd eaten. Off to the right, a little brick building. Maybe an office.

As we watched, a shadow appeared along the side of the dormitory. It was a sentry. We crouched, silent. He walked up the side of the building, then around the corner and along the front. He paused there for a minute, under a dim light, scanning the area, then he disappeared down the other side. He seemed to be wide-awake and focused, like the guy we'd just dealt with, but he also seemed to be the only security. No searchlights, no patrols. Doofus and Patronising had got complacent.

'They've totally underestimated us,' Josh breathed, sounding offended.

'Good,' I said. 'They think we're a bunch of scared, helpless kids. So we find Connor, we rescue Connor, we get the hell out.'

'But how do we even know he's here?' Asha whispered.

'Because Kirby's here,' I said. 'And because if they keep him here they know he's not infecting anyone else.' I tried to sound confident, but I was looking around, not seeing anywhere likely, feeling worried.

'All right, genius, where is he, then?' said Asha, seeming to read my mind.

'I'm pretty sure I saw us finding him.' Grace sounded confused, worried. 'He must be here.'

'There might be more guards,' I said. 'We can't just wander round the place randomly.'

We just stood there, not moving, looking around like idiots, like we were waiting for Connor to come up and say hi.

'Great plan,' Asha muttered. 'One of your best.'

'OK,' I said, pointing at the greenhouse. 'We've eaten in there, so that can't be it.' I pointed at the dormitory. 'Everyone's sleeping in there, so that can't be it. Hospital bit's right up next to it, I doubt they've got him there, and we've all been in the building where they questioned us. That leaves . . .' I couldn't stop doubt entering my voice. '. . . That place.'

I pointed at the little brick building.

Asha laughed. 'Right,' she said. 'Major research centre stuffed full of big shiny machines, plus a whole team of scientists and a squad of soldiers checking out full-on alien invasion, all squashed together into that shed.'

I was losing patience. 'Got a better idea?' I snapped.

She looked surprised. Said nothing.

'Didn't think so,' I sneered.

'Way to ruin the mood,' Josh murmured.

'Mood wasn't great, anyway,' I said.

The soldier reappeared along the side of the dormitory and we went quiet again while we watched him, waiting for him to disappear from sight. I felt bad. We were meant to be a team. Teenage Mutant Fugitives. And now there was a whole bad-tempered, tense silence hanging over us. I'd snapped at Asha because I was worried sick about her, because I thought she was possibly going to die, so now I was annoyed with myself, and I was also remembering what Josh had said a couple of days ago. *You ever noticed that you're always bickering? You know what that means, don't you?* I mostly knew that I didn't want Asha to die.

The soldier by the dormitory disappeared from sight.

'So,' I said, 'we sticking to the plan?'

'We have to,' said Grace. And she put out her hand, palm down, between us. Josh laid his on top of hers. I sort of hovered my hand over Josh's. I looked at Asha.

'Sorry,' I said.

She put her hand over mine and shrugged. 'Whatever.'

'We're family,' said Josh. 'Can't have you falling out, it gives me horrible flashbacks to my parents. For the win, guys.'

We lifted our hands, a bit half-hearted, and then he and Grace jogged off towards the dormitory. He looked back over his shoulder. 'Nobody die,' he said.

Asha and I watched them go.

I tried to sound optimistic, upbeat. 'Let's check it out then,' I said.

Asha turned to me. 'Talk to me like that again, and you're on your own,' she snapped.

I held up both hands. 'OK.'

We headed for the little brick building that didn't look anything like a place where scientists might study and experiment on potential aliens. The silence wasn't exactly bad-tempered any more but it was definitely still tense.

So I stopped. We'd only taken a couple of steps but I stopped in the dark under a clear sky full of stars. I was properly cold, I thought I might be about to sneeze, and every shadow looked like it might be a sentry.

But I stopped because suddenly something seemed more important than Connor and Fuzzy and soldiers.

'Hey,' I said.

Asha stopped too. 'What?'

'I'm sorry I snapped at you.'

'You already said that.'

I took a slow breath. 'But I just wanted to say – there's no one I'd rather be risking my life with.'

Silence. I couldn't see her face in the dark. I started to feel a bit stupid, standing there, wondering if she was going to even bother to answer. Finally she spoke, her tone flat.

'Wow. I feel all warm inside.'

'I mean it,' I persisted. 'I really wanted to say that. In case one of us does die, or anything. Because on the beach at Simpson's house . . .'

'When I nearly killed you.'

'I'd have kissed you then, if I could have kissed you.'

She tutted. 'Come on, Hector,' she said. 'We need to go.'

I didn't move. Cool breeze. Some distant animal noise, maybe a fox.

'Would that have been OK?' I said. 'If I'd kissed you?'

Another silence. I felt like I could sense the world turning beneath my feet as I waited. I was half holding my breath but I was also kind of enjoying this moment, in a bit of a masochistic way, this exciting, tingling sense of something almost happening with my ex-girlfriend.

Asha Kamala, literally the girl of my dreams.

'Ask me again,' she said eventually, 'when this is over.'

And then she turned and walked away. So I followed her.

## Part Three of My Genius Plan: Diversion

We kept half an eye on the dormitory, and froze when we saw the soldier appear. As soon as he walked round the other side of the dorm we ran, crouching, towards the brick building. I put out a hand, stopped Asha abruptly. We could see round the other side of the building now, and there was a sentry there, all in black, leaning against the wall. We stopped. He was a good sign, because if there was a guard it meant there was something worth guarding.

We waited.

Josh and Grace were meant to be in the dorm, persuading our friends to start a riot. They were supposed to create a whole, massive diversion, and – Part Four of the plan – we nip in, find Connor and rescue him while everyone's busy. It lacked a bit of detail – it lacked any detail at all – but it was the best I could do.

But nothing was happening. No distraction. Maybe our friends didn't want to riot, maybe they preferred to stay in bed. Maybe the scary, SAS-style, combat-ready sentry had caught Josh and Grace. Maybe something else had happened that we couldn't even predict. It wasn't like my genius plan was actually in fact remotely genius.

I looked at Asha. She shrugged. I sighed. That was it, sighing and shrugging, that was all we had to offer.

And then the soldier straightened up suddenly. He took a step forwards. I thought for a moment that he'd seen us, but he was looking away from us, like he'd heard something. He walked away quickly, towards the fence.

I had no idea what he'd heard, but I didn't hesitate. 'Now,' I said.

We ran to the door. The building was low and square, and the whole thing was only about the size of a classroom. The bricks were pink and new, there were no windows, and the door appeared to be metal. In fact up close it looked more like a bunker than part of a garden centre.

'This is a bit weird,' I said.

Asha shrugged. 'Maybe it's got electrics in it. A generator or something.'

She tried the door. Locked of course. If the guard turned round he'd probably see us. If he came back he'd walk right into us. And what had he heard? An owl? A fox? Someone else with a whole different genius plan?

I got the lanyard out, slid it into a slot over the lock. There was a click, and a little green light came on. We looked at each other. Asha's eyes were wide open, her lips were parted, and I thought I saw a slight tremble in them. I was pretty sure my face looked exactly the same.

My whole body was telling me to walk away, or run away. To get the hell out of there.

Asha nodded.

I tried a smile, which came out crooked.

Then I opened the door, and we went in.


**5.26 a.m.**

No one there.

Thank God, there was no one there.

It was an empty room. The air-conditioning was humming,

and there was a slight, static tingle in the air, as if maybe somewhere, some sort of sophisticated technology was whirring away. There was a desk with a computer and a phone on it, a couple of chairs round a low table. Nothing else.

'Don't have another tantrum,' said Asha, 'but this doesn't look promising.'

It made no sense. Why was there a guard on an empty room? And if Connor wasn't here, where was he?

'I don't get it,' I said.

We walked round the walls of the room, looking for a door, or a slot where I could use the lanyard. Nothing. I wound up at the desk. Computer. Phone.

'Well, this is all going tits up,' said Asha. 'Number one, we're totally in the wrong place. Number two, no riot.'

And then, right on cue, Part Three of my plan happened. An alarm went off. It was loud and sudden, a two-tone whine suddenly blaring. I flinched, put my hands over my ears. There were shouts and screams outside, there was the crash of a window breaking.

Voices from somewhere, footsteps. Where were they coming from? It sounded like it was beneath us.

'Behind the desk!' I whispered urgently.

We dived behind the desk as a door clicked open and I glimpsed two soldiers, one of them speaking into a radio, calling in reinforcements. They opened the outside door, ran out. Josh and Grace had done their job, they'd got a riot started, creating a diversion, getting some soldiers out of our way. Two soldiers, to be precise, but I guessed that was better than nothing.

Another click.

The invisible door had closed.

We stayed behind the desk after the soldiers had gone, because that made sense, in case they came back, or more of them appeared. But maybe we stayed there longer than we needed to, because it was easy, just keeping still, hiding, not doing anything. It was easy, and it felt safe. It felt a lot safer than going through that invisible door.

The alarm stopped abruptly, and Asha stood up, like that was a signal.

I stood up beside her, because staying crouching down by her ankles would have been weird.

'OK,' she said. 'Door.'

But there was no sign of it. Wherever it was, it was part of the wall, its edges somehow hidden. There was no way through from this side. But that was ridiculous, there had to be a way through from this side.

I was back at the desk again. Computer. Phone.

4705J.

I closed my eyes, remembering the flash I'd had when I touched the soldier's neck. I pressed the numbers and the letter on the computer keyboard. Nothing. I tried it on the phone. 4705, then 5 again for the J. Still nothing.

I picked up the phone.

'What you doing?' said Asha. 'Calling your mum?'

I pressed the numbers once more.

4705J.

There was a click.

It didn't come from the phone, it came from . . .

'Look' said Asha. 'The wall!'

An invisible door had clicked open. It had been entirely flush with the wall, but now it was ajar.

## Part Four of My Genius Plan: Rescue

There was a lift behind the door, and stairs leading down into darkness. I looked at Asha and, in spite of my nerves, in spite of the fact my genius plan was already going wrong and was probably totally going to fail, I was grinning.

'It's all underground.' I felt like an excited kid. Asha looked unimpressed. I needed Josh here, he'd get it. 'I bet it's a full-on, secret, James-Bond-style, super-villain's underground lair.'

'Yay,' said Asha, without any enthusiasm at all. 'You coming then?'

We headed down the stairs.

The hum of the air-conditioning got louder. The static tingle of whatever the hell it was got more obvious, so I felt like my skin was itching. I couldn't quite believe it. That first day, by the river, Doofus had told us: 'This year, we're prepared.' They'd prepared the green guns and the machine that went Boom!, they'd prepared this camp, to lock us up, and they'd prepared a whole laboratory, out in the middle of nowhere, underground, to study the alien. To work out how to respond to the alien.

There was a corridor at the bottom of the stairs. Fluorescent lights, a white and pale blue colour scheme, like a hospital. Connor would be down here. Professor Patronising and a team of scientists would be down here. Possibly Doofus and definitely a whole bunch of soldiers would be down here. I had no idea what to do next, except I knew that I absolutely didn't want Asha to use the Voice. My genius plan didn't give us any more pointers.

We stood there, at the bottom of the stairs, hesitating, confused, like we'd accidentally walked into the wrong house.

I went up to the first door on the left. It was plain white, with a panel of frosted glass. I listened. Couldn't hear anything.

Asha reached past me, opened the door, turned on the light and walked right in.

I'd sort of been planning to be a bit more cautious, but OK, I thought. I followed her.

There was a computer, papers all over a desk, a load of filing cabinets. I was staring mostly at the computer. I had a really strong urge to sit down and start tweeting.

**Secret underground lab! Teens being held and experimented on! Welcoming committee for ET!**

Everything I wanted to say sounded like a headline on some wacky website. Of course no one believed me when I tweeted and blogged about this stuff. Why would they? It was impossible. Completely impossible and, at the same time, completely true.

'Ha!'

I jumped and looked at Asha. She'd got a file out of a filing cabinet and was grinning at it.

'I am officially dangerous. To be handled with extreme caution. Oh yes.' She read on: 'Subject's voice has a coercive, apparently irresistible effect. Query stimulation of basal ganglia, research indicated, query EEG, MRI, extracellular analysis.' She looked up. 'They want to poke around inside my brain.'

'You should be proud,' I said. 'You could get Kirby a Nobel Prize.'

She made a dismissive noise. 'Let's go.'

We left the room, closed the door quietly behind us, pretty much tiptoed to the door opposite.

Which opened as we approached it.

Kirby came out.

Narrow face and narrow glasses, as ever. Cheekbones you could cut yourself on, red hair pulled back severely. Her lips were twisted into a snarl.

'You think you're clever?' she snapped, like we were in the middle of a conversation. She looked furious. Her cheeks were quivering, nostrils flared, eyes screwed up. I could see why, to be fair. She was basically holding the most exciting scientific breakthrough in history, and we wanted to snatch it out of her hands. 'You're on CCTV,' she said. 'You triggered three different motion sensors, the disturbance in the dormitory will be dealt with in no time. You're not just obnoxious and self-obsessed, you're also utterly predictable.'

'Shut up!' Asha barked.

Kirby, also known as Professor Patronising, gave us her most patronising smile. She indicated her ears. Small buds were visible, nestled inside each.

'I don't think so,' she said.

I almost laughed. Kirby thought Asha was using the Voice but she wasn't, she was just being Asha. Then two soldiers appeared from the room behind her, carrying their green-glowing guns. I didn't feel like laughing any more.

'Shoot them,' she barked.

She stepped aside to let the soldiers into the corridor, and then she stepped back into the doorway. Apparently she wanted to watch. Asha and I backed up, back towards the stairs, but there was no way in the narrow space that we could avoid the guns. The soldiers were wearing earbuds too. They were cold-eyed and grim, two more from the black body armour, SAS-style platoon. We weren't going to be able to reason with them.

I badly wanted to hold Asha's hand, but I knew I couldn't hold her hand.

'Don't,' I whispered, uselessly.

I heard Asha hold her breath. There was a sound from Kirby. Possibly a chuckle.

The two soldiers raised their guns, and pointed them at our chests. I closed my eyes.

## 5.38 a.m.

The soldiers paused.

At first I thought they were sadistically stringing it out, making us wait. But they were looking past us, behind us.

I turned round.

A slight, dark figure was coming down the stairs.

Skinny black jeans with white, thready holes at the knees. Sleeveless black T-shirt with a white creepy-crawly print on it. Dyed black hair, chopped short.

Ruby got to the bottom of the stairs, looked at me and Asha, glanced at the soldiers, then looked at us again.

'I want my brother,' she said. Her voice was a snarl with a tremble in it, a hint of a whine. For the first time since this had started I could see the scared, lonely thirteen-year-old inside the angry, super-strong ninja. Like us, she'd been running for days, but unlike us she'd been alone the whole time. Connor had told us he was her only friend. She'd thought she'd got him back, but he'd been snatched away again. 'Where is he?' she said. 'Where's Connor?'

I remembered the guard hearing something, heading out towards the fence. He must have heard Ruby. And she must have dealt with him. And now bizarrely she was going to, maybe, if we were lucky, save us.

I pointed my thumb back over my shoulder at the soldiers.

'They've got him,' I said.

Asha and I stepped aside as Ruby marched forwards, her face tense and set like she was trying not to lose it.

The soldiers moved their guns off us, trained them on her. One of them was half a step ahead of the other.

'Stay there,' he said. 'Don't move.'

She kept walking.

'I mean it.'

She didn't stop.

'Shoot her!' Kirby shrieked.

The soldier was probably not long back from Afghanistan, or somewhere like that. And he was staring at a young girl who looked like she might be about to cry. She looked feeble.

I liked that he ignored Kirby. I thought underneath the whole cold-eyed, grim, SAS thing, he might even be a good bloke.

He should have listened to her, though.

Ruby stepped right up in his face and as he put an arm out, maybe to shove her back, she pulled back her right elbow, splayed her hand and jerked her palm into his stomach, like a piston. He flew back down the corridor, like he was on elastic, letting out a long, explosive 'Uhhhhh'. It was partly surprise, partly all the air leaving his body at once. His gun clattered on to the floor.

'Where's Connor!' Ruby shouted after him.

That was pointless, he wasn't going to be saying anything for a while. His mate took several steps back, keeping his gun trained on Ruby.

Then he shot her in the chest.

Dark green light flashed into Ruby with a whoosh. She stumbled, bent over, made a choking sound. A long second, and then she straightened slowly, and took a step forward.

He shot her again.

She staggered and wailed as the green light hit her. She didn't sound anything like a super-strong, evil, Terminator-style avenger. She bent over again, hands on her knees, panting.

'Stop there,' said the soldier, through gritted teeth.

She straightened up slowly, painfully.

'I want my brother,' she coughed.

I was seriously impressed, and also worried for her, and also glad that it was her getting shot and not me or Asha. She stumbled towards the soldier and as he shot her a third time, point-blank straight into her, she fell on him, thrusting both her hands at his chest.

He slammed into the floor and I saw his head bounce. He didn't move.

Ruby sank to her knees and threw up.

Kirby was back in her office, on her mobile. I ignored her, knelt down beside Ruby who it turned out wasn't the Big Bad after all, she was a miserable, sick kid, who was skating close to despair.

'It's horrible,' I said, 'but it wears off. You'll be all right.'

'Where's Connor?' she whispered.

I looked up at Asha.

'We're on it,' she said.

In her office, Kirby was shouting into her phone. There were four more doors, two on each side. I opened the first on the right – it was a loo. Opposite was a room with sofas and a TV, maybe somewhere for the guards to relax. The last two doors had locks on.

'Should have started here,' I said.

I tried my lanyard on the last door on the right. It didn't work. I banged on the door. 'Connor, you there?'

I realised Asha wasn't beside me, she was back by the first dazed soldier, grabbing another lanyard from around his neck.

She threw it to me. 'Try this.'

How much time did we have? Minutes, at most, before Kirby got help or the two soldiers recovered. Asha collected their guns while I slid the lanyard into the door. Green light. I opened up.

It was a pale blue and white cube. There was a bed and bedside table, a small TV on a bracket on the wall, a couple of books. It was Connor's room I guessed, or his cell, but there was no one there. I turned to the last door, slid the lanyard in, kicked it open.

This room was much bigger than any of the others, and one whole wall was a bank of machines. I saw test tubes of blood being agitated, X-ray pictures pinned up on light boxes, monitors showing what looked like a whole range of body scans. I saw a creamy white box with a chrome cylinder attachment and a large golf ball on top surrounded by aerials, and a panel on its sloping side that wasn't currently glowing. I guessed if it was glowing, I'd be on my knees, retching.

And I saw Connor.

He was about to slide under a thick white tube for some sort of scan, but when he saw me he sat up and started pulling sensors off his chest and forehead. Unbelievably, he smiled.

'You came!' he said. 'You found me! I knew you would!'

I might have smiled back at him, I'd definitely have said something, but there were three adults in the room with him, two doctors and another soldier, and his gun was swinging towards me. But he wasn't wearing earbuds.

'Don't, Asha!' I shouted, as I leapt towards him. But I knew I wasn't going to reach him in time, and I knew what Asha was going to do.

'PUT IT DOWN!'

He looked surprised, downright shocked, but he did as he was told.

Connor swung his legs off the platform he was sitting on. 'That's Asha,' he told the soldier. 'She rocks.'

She sank down to her knees, looking like she was about to faint again. I picked up a chair, a whole swivel chair with a metal pedestal, and crashed it down on to the machine.

Connor got up slowly. 'So, I think Fuzzy's coming,' he said.

'I know he is,' I told him. I knelt by Asha. 'Can you walk?'

She didn't say anything, she just looked at me like she didn't know who I was. For a moment I couldn't move, I couldn't even think.

'Asha?'

No answer, just that dazed, confused look. I wanted to shout for Kirby to call an ambulance, but I knew that wouldn't do any good. The only thing that might help was Fuzzy coming, and everyone losing their powers, going back to normal.

I helped her up. Connor wasn't up to running either. We left the room and moved into the corridor slowly, like it was school and there was a teacher watching. One of the soldiers was stirring. Ruby was on her feet but still bent over, leaning on the wall with a hand on her stomach. We were basically a bunch of casualties. I didn't see how we were going to get out.

'Ruby!' Now Connor ran, awkwardly, just a few steps to get up beside her. He hugged her. 'Are you OK? What happened?' He looked at us accusingly. His smile had vanished. 'What did you do to her?'

'Not us,' I snapped. 'These guys.' I pointed at the soldiers on the floor. 'Come on, come on, gotta go, you said it yourself: Fuzzy!'

Connor looked like he knew there was going to be an argument. 'Ruby's coming too,' he said.

Asha stared at him, slowly working out who he was. 'Connor, right?' she murmured, like she was sleepy. 'Random.'

Connor looked from her to me. 'What's wrong with her?'

I couldn't bear to say it, to put it into words. I could hardly bear to think it. Her brain was giving up. Blood vessels, synapses, neurons, all bursting or shutting down and possibly doing permanent damage. I might have lost my friend. All that energy, humour, personality – vanished. I couldn't afford to have that thought in my head because it meant I couldn't function. Part of me still wanted to turn her over to the doctors here, beg them to help, but I knew the best possible treatment for her was Fuzzy hatching out of Connor. And that meant getting out of here.

'Ruby just saved us,' I told Connor. 'You can bring her along. Now move!'

Ruby straightened up slowly, painfully. Glared at Asha. 'I don't like you,' she said.

'No one cares,' I snapped. 'Just don't punch her.' I led Asha towards the stairs.

Connor put one of Ruby's arms over his shoulder, and followed us. There was no sign of Kirby and that was probably just as well, I wasn't going to forget her ordering soldiers to shoot us.

Back up the stairs, shuffling awkwardly, and out of the door.

Fuzzy was going to hatch imminently, we were doing our desperate, daredevil escape in slow motion, and Asha should probably be in intensive care. I had my strongest urge yet to stop and give up but I didn't because this was all Patronising and Doofus's fault, and they couldn't help, and they wouldn't if they could. We had to get as far away from them as possible.

I was muttering to myself, 'If Fuzzy hatches, Asha will be fine.' Repeating it like a mantra. 'If Fuzzy hatches, Asha will be fine.' Like if I said it often enough it would be true.

It felt like it should be morning, but that was still another hour away. It felt like it should be still and quiet, but it wasn't. Over by the dormitory there were screams, flashes of green light, that distinctive whooshing sound. It was hard to see in the dark, but it looked like the black shapes of soldiers were successfully rounding up our friends, herding them together.

Ruby took her arm off Connor's shoulder, standing a little more steadily, still leaning on him.

'Can you show us where you came in?' I asked her. 'Cos we have to get out of here right now.'

'What,' said Josh, 'without us?' He and Grace appeared from the side of the building, where they'd been waiting. He glared at Ruby. 'What's she doing here?'

'She's coming with us,' said Connor. 'She can be a Teenage Mutant Fugitive.' He looked at Ruby. 'It's a thing.'

Josh shook his head. 'Nope. No way. Not having it.'

Ruby's voice shook. 'I'm sorry I killed the dog.'

'She had a name,' Josh snarled. 'Peaches.'

'I'm sorry,' Ruby said again. 'There's something wrong inside me.'

Grace stepped forward. She was the one who right from the start had been trying to reach out to Ruby, who'd understood that what was happening wasn't her fault. Or wasn't entirely her fault.

She pointed a finger in Ruby's face. 'You're coming with us,' she said. She glanced at Josh. 'If you don't like it, you can stay here.' Then she saw Asha for the first time. She was swaying, her eyes unfocused. 'Asha!' It was almost a scream. She looked at me, mouthed a question. 'Is she OK?'

'She will be,' I whispered, trying to sound a lot more confident than I actually felt. 'When Fuzzy hatches, she'll be fine. Let's get out of here.'

We set off towards the fence. Still moving slowly.

'What are we doing?' said Asha.

'Going for a . . . like a . . . walk,' I said.

'Hate walks,' Asha muttered.

Grace walked beside her, holding her hand. On the other side of the cold, dark field the whooshing sounds and the gouts of green light had stopped and teenagers were coughing and retching. I thought I could hear the high-pitched, never-ending babble of Kayleigh's voice. Soldiers barked commands.

We staggered on, into the shadows.

**5.44 a.m.**

This was mad.

We shuffled across the grass, through a jagged hole in the fence and into the trees.

This was complete madness.

Where did we think we were going? I was really cold, there was a greyness to the light which suggested dawn was coming, and this was ridiculous. We were just stumbling through the trees with no destination in mind.

My genius plan had been all about rescuing Connor and it had sort of accidentally succeeded, but I had no idea what to do next and nor did anyone else.

'Wait!' I gasped. I stopped. 'Where are we even going?'

They all stopped too.

'Yeah,' said Asha. 'That's what I want to know.'

Everyone was panting, but Connor had a hand on his stomach, like he was feeling sick, and Asha had a hand on her forehead, like she was feeling dazed. And then Ruby sank down on to one knee. I remembered how I'd felt after being hit once by the green puke-gun, how long it had taken me to recover. Ruby had been hit three times.

Grace actually lifted my hand and put it on Asha's shoulder. Then she knelt beside Ruby. 'You OK?' she said.

Ruby didn't answer. She looked up, saw Connor, and he came over beside her.

I was moving, restless, almost hopping from foot to foot. 'We're not safe here,' I said.

Grace's tone was gentle and coaxing, like a mum with a distressed child.

'You've been lonely,' she said, 'haven't you?'

'I'm always lonely,' Ruby muttered.

'It's true,' said Connor. 'She is.'

'I get that,' said Grace.

Ruby gave her that sneer she'd perfected. 'No, you don't.'

'My dad died,' Grace said. 'Everyone called me Silent Grace for a whole year. This year's not been brilliant either. I promise you, I get it.'

'Doesn't matter,' Josh snarled. He was looking from Asha to Connor to Ruby, and like me he was aware of this situation getting out of our control. He needed to let his anger out. 'It's no excuse for killing Peaches.'

'I didn't mean to,' Ruby moaned. 'I didn't even want to. Everything went narrow and focused and it felt like I was being carried by this huge wave.'

'It wasn't your fault,' Grace said. She glared at Josh, separating each word: 'It wasn't her fault.'

'Why's everyone arguing?' Asha muttered. 'We're mates, aren't we? Aren't we mates?'

'Yeah, Asha.' I tried to make my voice light and relaxed. 'That's right, we're all mates. Everything's fine.'

'Why's your voice all weird?' she said. 'And what are we even doing here?'

She was looking anxious and I didn't blame her and I was trying to find an answer, but then we heard the pursuit. I swivelled round – there were black shapes sprinting through the undergrowth only about a hundred metres behind us. Torch beams angled through the trees, and overhead there was the whir of a drone.

'Come on, come on!' I yelled 'Let's go!'

We got moving again, jogging now, me and Josh helping Asha, Connor and Grace helping Ruby, but still with no idea where we were going. We didn't have a chance, we were going to get caught for sure.

We came out on a road. 'Maybe split up?' I panted.

There was a car coming. It probably contained Doofus and a squad of SAS commandos all wanting payback for me inflicting post-traumatic stress, and Asha using her Voice and Ruby throwing them around the corridor like an emo ninja barely out of primary school.

'What do we do?' squeaked Connor. 'What do we do?'

What we did was nothing. The car was coming too fast, we were caught in its headlights, and meanwhile the army was close behind. So we froze.

We just waited to get caught basically.

The car screeched to a stop right next to us. And for the second time in a couple of days, my brother kicked the door open and said, 'Need a lift?'

Obviously a whole lot of shock and surprise and *What the hell are you doing here?* kicked off in my head, but I thrust all that to one side, bent down, put my head in the car and yelled, 'Piss off!'

And I put everything into it, so my voice was almost like Asha's Voice, because seriously, did he think I was ever in my entire life going to forgive him or speak to him or get in a car with him again?

Which would have been fine, but Josh pressed a hand on my bum and a hand between my shoulders, shoved me into the passenger seat then jumped on to my lap, while Asha, Grace, Ruby and Connor all climbed into the back seat.

Car doors slammed and Connor shouted, 'Go, go, go!'

Jason accelerated away, just as the first figures burst out of the trees.

'Don't even try to talk to me,' I snapped.

'Fine. Won't say a word,' said Jason.

'And don't betray us this time,' Josh added, 'or Ruby will literally rip bits off you.'

'Good,' I said, to Jason.

'Where are we going?' Asha asked.

'Move, move, I can't breathe!' Josh squashed himself against the door and pushed me towards my brother.

'Burrage?' he said, to Asha.

'What's the difference,' I sneered. 'Whatever we say you're going to turn us over to Douglas.'

'What's Burrage?' Asha said.

'I've warned him,' Josh said. 'Ruby would totally do it.'

'Anyone?' said Jason, with a sigh in his voice. 'Where we actually going?'

'Can we make it quick?' Connor said. 'Because . . . Fuzzy.'

No one spoke for a moment. And then Grace said, 'I've got an idea.'

Jason took us back into Gilpin. He drove up the hill leading towards the school, then half a mile or so along Horngate, passing really close to our house, where our parents were, presumably, sleeping. Down Crook Lane.

Dawn was breaking, the heavy grey sky scribbled with pink, as we bumped down the track towards Max's house. The house where my best friend had turned into a ghost, and saved my life, and died. The house where it had all started last year, and where it had all ended, in the garden, when the egg cracked open and the alien emerged.

Except it hadn't ended, and at the moment it seemed like perhaps it never would.

We pulled up outside.

Connor opened the car door, let out a gasp of pain and fell on to the road.

**6.27 a.m.**

Josh and I tumbled out of the car. Jason was saying something, but I ignored him. Connor was standing up gingerly, both hands pressed against his stomach.

'I'm all right,' he panted. 'I think. Except it felt like someone punched me.'

We kicked through long grass and wriggling weeds to get to the front door. It was locked. I looked up at the bathroom window that I'd climbed through, twice, a year ago. That wasn't going to be necessary this time. A ground-floor window had been smashed. Jason climbed through first, so I made sure I went in last, avoiding a few shards and spikes still embedded in the frame.

And as soon as we were inside, Grace said, 'You two need to talk.'

'No we don't,' I snapped.

Asha looked sleepily from me to Jason. 'Hey, Jason,' she said. 'Hector's been worried about you.'

I'd reminded her she only had one brother, I'd basically told her she shouldn't give up on Naveen. And now here we were, me and Jason. I looked at Connor.

'I'm OK.' He smiled uncertainly. 'Sort of.'

Grace led him and everybody else out. So Jason and me were left in Max's front room, awkward and silent, like a couple of near-strangers who don't much like the look of each other.

The room was like a ghost of its old self. I sat on the arm of a sofa with no cushions and a torn seat, looking at empty shelves on the wall next to where the TV used to be. There was a cool, fresh-air smell from the broken window, but it was combined with damp and a whiff of urine.

This was the room where Max and me used to play on his Xbox and watch The Simpsons, where his mum sometimes brought us fish fingers and oven chips, where we'd once got into trouble for making a big, room-sized den out of chairs, a mattress and sheets dragged from his bedroom.

Sadness was like a weight in my chest.

I missed Max. I missed my friend.

And now I was wondering if I'd lost Asha too.

'Hector,' Jason said.

And my lying, trolling, betraying brother expected me to forgive him? Don't think so.

'I've got a foot-long scar on my back. I know what this thing can do.'

That wasn't going to work. Except I knew how that memory haunted him because I'd seen it in 3D hi-res when I attacked him outside Seabridge. But that didn't excuse what he'd done.

'You were crappy to me all year as Dr so-called Lazarus.' My voice was vibrating with emotion. This was my brother,

293

who I loved, how could he do this to me?' And then you turn me over to Douglas and Kirby, who chuck me in prison.'

'Mum and Dad turned up at Uncle Pete's.' He was trying to do calm, soothing, but his voice was tight and sharp. He was angry too. Why was he angry? 'They said you'd gone missing, they showed me the note you wrote. Mum was crying, Dad was worried sick, they were both in pieces. "See you soon, I hope"? You get that made it sound like you might not be coming back? Did you even think about how that would make them feel?'

I didn't answer that.

'So they said, "Find your brother." I didn't know where to start, but then Douglas got in touch.'

'And you saluted and said, "Yes sir, I'll catch him for you, and I'll get Connor for you too. You can dissect him and kill my brother, that'll be fine."'

'When did you get so self-righteous, Hector?' Jason was almost shouting at me now. 'Douglas promised me he'd do everything possible to make sure no teenagers died. But he also told me we have to stop this whole soft invasion.'

'You can't trust him!' I was shouting right back at him. 'And you especially can't trust Kirby! Killing every teenager in Gilpin, and now Seabridge too, isn't a price worth paying to maybe, possibly, get the aliens to leave us alone.'

Jason took a slow breath. The quiet between us felt more tense than the shouting. I could hear movement in Max's kitchen, and I realised my friends had probably heard the whole argument. I wondered what Asha was making of it. I didn't want to be with Jason, I wanted to be with her.

He spoke again. Quietly, calmly. 'When they shot you, right in front of me, everything changed. You come first. Of course you do.' He paused, took another breath, like he was trying to work out what to say. 'But I'm still basically terrified by this idea of an invasion.' He shrugged. 'I mean, aren't you?'

I could have said yes to that but I didn't. I stared at him instead. He stared back at me. I realised he'd done what he thought was for the best, just like I had. And the truth is, I still had no idea which one of us had actually done the right thing.

I should probably have tried to find something to say, something to mend what was broken between us. But I didn't.

'Whatever,' I snapped.

I walked out, hoping he wouldn't follow, hoping he'd just disappear. I found the others in the kitchen.

Josh glanced at me cautiously. 'Kissed and made up?'

I made a face.

Asha sighed. 'I haven't seen Naveen for ... I can't remember how long,' she said.

Naveen and Asha had been in Max's front room exactly a year ago. And he'd hit her. Then Naveen had come into this kitchen and tried to kill me. Asha was unguarded now, vulnerable, and it felt intrusive and unfair but I could totally see how much she missed her brother. I wanted to talk about it with her but I couldn't talk about it with her. Fear that we might never get her back lurched inside me, made me feel physically sick, but I squashed it down.

I was looking for something to say to her, but then Connor suddenly staggered and bent over as if he'd been stabbed in the stomach and let out a long, rattling breath.

'It hurts,' he gasped.

Ruby and Grace started to sit him down but he shook them off.

'It wants to be outside.'

Just like last year, when Old Hector had taken us all out into Max's back garden and we'd watched the egg hatch. We went out through the glass doors at the end of the kitchen, and we stood in the long grass.

There was a buzzing sound. A spindly drone was wobbling in the air above us. It was flying low, presumably wanting a good look at us.

'I don't believe it!' I said. 'Jason's told them where we are.'

'Probably not him,' Josh muttered. 'Bet they were tracking the car.'

He was searching on the ground. He found a stone, then crouched. His bent arm swung backwards, he paused a moment, a fierce, wound-up quality to him, and then his arm, elbow and wrist snapped forwards and the stone flew up into the air and hit the drone. It wobbled, whined angrily, then crashed to the ground.

Josh punched the air. 'He shoots, he scores!'

Connor actually clapped. 'That was so cool!' he said. He was grinning like nothing was wrong at all. 'Get us.' He looked all right now, he had that goofy, likeable smile on his face that he always seemed to have when you saw him in a corridor or on the way to school. He knew something was wrong with Asha but he didn't know what, so he thought everything was basically OK. 'We're brilliant, aren't we? I know this has been all weird and horrible, this week, but look, I've got my sister back and here we are, all together. So you know, thanks, guys, you're honestly the best. Teenage Mutant—'

There was a loud hum.

Connor sat down abruptly in the grass.

We were all staring, Ruby gasped, we must have looked worried, but he was still smiling. 'No, I'm fine,' he said. Ruby had a hand on his shoulder. 'It's OK, Rubes, I think I'm—'

There was a Boom!

Connor cried out and we all made anguished sounds too, buckling, sinking to our knees, grabbing our stomachs where that tight, sharp little fist of pain was clenching internal organs. I gritted my teeth. That machine must be nearby. That panel on its side must be glowing a swampy green. I was pretty sure I knew what was happening. They'd decided to go ahead and kill the creature inside Connor before it emerged, and by doing that they were going to kill us too.

This time they weren't going to stop.

My vision was rippling, getting darker. I felt like I was fading away, and as I faded I dimly heard another sound, a sort of roar over the hum, and I assumed that was the machine intensifying, but then I heard something else,

A crash!

The humming stopped. Cut off abruptly.

The pain stopped too. It was like someone had lifted their boot off my stomach.

I was lying on my back, like I was on the football pitch yesterday, blinking up at the pale early morning sky, recovering slowly. I sat up gingerly. Took some slow breaths. Asha, Grace, Ruby and Josh were tentatively sitting up too.

'Everyone OK?' I said.

Josh got to his feet, staggered over to the low wall, looked over it.

'Go, Jason,' he said. 'He rammed his car right into their machine.'

Connor was still on his back on the grass. He whimpered.

And then he was hit by at least three simultaneous pulses of dark green light. Asha and Ruby were hit too. More whooshes, more flashes of green, dogs barked and commands were yelled. I threw myself on the ground and a pulse of green fizzed over my head.

And then silence. The whooshing had stopped. I had my face pressed into the ground. I heard Asha or Ruby or both of them retching.

'Continue suppressing fire!'

Douglas's harsh, grating voice had an edge of desperation in it. But no one responded. No one fired. I looked up, tentative, and I saw that something impossible was happening. Again.

All around us black-clad soldiers had their guns trained on Connor. But those soldiers were rising into the air as if they were on invisible strings – their feet were off the ground and they were dangling. Guns dropped out of hands, there were panicky shouts, and they kept rising till they were maybe ten feet in the air and then they just hung there.

Connor arched suddenly, convulsively. Only his heels and his skull were on the ground, and the air above his stomach went hazy and blurred.

The air parted above this blur. It parted like something was pulling aside curtains.

And a wet and flickering shape emerged.

It was dark, darker than the morning sunshine around it, and it had no clear edges and no feeling of actually, in a concrete sense, being there at all.

But it was there.

Something was there.

The cold, still presence from my nightmares.

A dog whined, I heard gasps, and a soldier, hanging in the air above me, started praying in a shaky whisper. There were too many impossible things happening at once. The creature was coming out of Connor. Its mother was coming out of a gap in the air.

Douglas and Kirby were by the house, and they had their feet planted on the ground. The alien had somehow levitated all the soldiers, but it had ignored them, because it assumed they weren't dangerous.

Douglas took out a pistol and raised it. His teeth were gritted and his eyes were wide, I didn't know if he was scared or angry or both, but I leapt desperately between him and Connor. A little voice in my head said I might be about to die but I didn't care, I couldn't stop myself.

I yelled at the creature hovering above Connor's agonisingly arched body. 'Don't come back!'

I didn't know what I was doing, but a rage erupted out of me. This alien had killed Max and Matt last year, it had brought horror and fear with it again this year, it had damaged Asha, put kids in hospital, brought the weight of the army down on us and right now it seemed to be torturing Connor.

'Please!' I walked towards it as I yelled. Every last atom in my body was shrinking away from it, wanted to turn and run, but I walked towards it. My voice was hoarse but loud and filled with passion, it was a rubbish imitation of Asha's Voice. 'Please, don't ever come back!'

The dark, flickering thing, hovering over Connor, here and not here, shimmering, altered its shape. I couldn't see what it was doing, but I could feel what it was doing.

It was turning towards me.

I stopped. I was shaking and I wanted to throw up or run away, but I stood still. And we looked at each other. Last year the creature had come out of the egg and it had had Max's face, and Matt's face, and my face. This year it had appeared in my nightmares before it had arrived in Gilpin. I felt that somehow, because of how closely I'd been involved with it, this alien thing knew me.

*We give you gifts*, it said.

The voice came from Connor, but it wasn't his. It was harsh and grating, and sounded like Connor's throat was contorted as well as his body.

'We don't want them.' My own voice was cracking but I wasn't yelling any more, I was trying to be as clear as I possibly could. 'We don't want your gifts. We don't want you.'

It made a hissing sound. It might have been an exhalation of breath. It might have been the word *So*.

The blur above Connor's agonisingly raised stomach clarified. Something was there. Something with long, darkly glittering limbs, unfolding, and dabbling in the fresh air. It shifted and shimmered and it had a face, something like a face, with a hint of Connor, a hint of Ruby. Fuzzy. It had shifted out of Connor. He finally collapsed back on to the grass and it squatted over him. Grotesque, fragile, newborn.

Its mother hovered above it.

'Please,' I said. 'Never again.'

The dark, wet, flickering thing, the presence that wasn't by ordinary definitions present, scooped up the creature that had emerged from Connor.

*Never again*. The words were mumbled quietly, like an afterthought, like a sigh.

Was it agreeing with what I'd said, or just repeating it?

Was there a hint of a questioning uplift in the tone? The six words it had spoken and that one sibilant sound would be endlessly analysed in the future, but the truth is it was impossible to say what that alien consciousness was thinking. Impossible to imagine.

It turned away from me. It hung there for a moment, then retreated back into the fissure it had created in the air.

It dwindled.

And the fissure closed.

The soldiers dropped to the ground, like ripe apples falling from a tree. They groaned and swore, and sat up slowly.

Connor didn't sit up.

He didn't move.

He lay limp and still on the grass.


**6.55 a.m.**

I leapt towards him and grabbed his wrist. Ruby, Asha, Grace and Josh joined me.

Someone was shouting, 'Medic!', Ruby was weeping, Grace was holding her, Josh was pulling his box of sadness out of a pocket.

I gripped Connor's wrist. Asha was right beside me and it was too soon to see how she was but she was alive at least. This must be the death Grace had seen on the moor, back when our journey was just beginning. This was the horrible sense of loss she had described, like a great empty pit. But I wasn't having it.

The alien had gone, which meant, if it was like last year, we'd lose our so-called gifts very soon, but maybe there was still time.

Josh yanked up Connor's white T-shirt and pressed the box, which had somehow healed his concussion, against his pale, bare chest.

And I clutched Connor's wrist.

Closed my eyes.

I saw darkness, but I looked into the darkness.

I saw fog, but I kept looking.

*Simpson, a big, reassuring presence, called him Dangerous Connor and he laughed. Peaches' big, black eyes looked up at him while he rubbed her shaggy head, scratching behind her ears. I felt her soft hair, I smelt dog.*

*Then Connor's mum, in a grey suit and a smart shirt, her face all clenched with anger, was shouting at Ruby, who was stomping off. A slammed door, like a gunshot.*

It wasn't clear, it wasn't immersive hi-res 3D, but I kept gripping Connor's wrist tightly.

*Ruby was in her bedroom, muttering and swearing to herself, her face clenched in misery so she looked like a younger version of her mum.*

I focused on her, I focused. I wouldn't let the image change because she needed him, Ruby needed her brother.

*There he was, in the doorway, and Ruby said his name. She looked at him standing there and she said, 'Connor.'*

I said it too, in Max's garden, I heard my own whisper.

'Connor.'

I was only dimly aware of Josh, of Asha, Grace and Ruby standing near me. I pushed all that away, so it was just Ruby and Connor in the bedroom, and me there too, but none of it clear or sharp, all of it swimming in front of my eyes.

Ruby spoke to him again, an imploring note in her voice. She said: 'Connor?'

He was there in the doorway and he looked unsure, like he didn't know whether to step in with her or step back, into the shadows outside the bedroom, into the darkness.

Ruby was crying now, her mascara running down her cheeks, and he was hesitating in the doorway.

Was this a memory, or something else? I'd never spoken in one of these visions before. How could I? I wasn't actually there.

But I was there in Ruby's bedroom, I was in front of him, looking into his eyes, and I held out my hand and spoke to him.

'Don't leave us, Connor. Please.'

Nothing happened.

And then nothing continued to happen.

And now I saw nothing, not light, not dark, just a clear, cool sense of nothing at all.

There was a long, strangled sigh. I didn't know where it came from. Possibly me. Suddenly I was on my back in the long grass again and I was still clutching Connor's wrist tightly, like someone was trying to pull me away from him.

In fact, someone was trying to pull him away from me.

'Ow,' he said.

I opened my eyes.

My fist was clenched around Connor's wrist and he was trying to pull himself free.

Grace didn't say anything, she just flung her arms round Asha, who looked surprised, but pleased.

'I did it,' Josh declared, grinning, holding up his little box of sadness like a trophy. 'Got all the hurt, squashed it all in here, saved the actual day. You're welcome, mate.'

Surely Josh's box only worked on him? I thought it was me, I was pretty sure I'd saved Connor's life by going right inside his head and actually in real time speaking to him.

But to be honest, who cared?

I sat up, smiled weakly at Connor. 'Nice one,' I said.

He was white-faced and his eyes looked like they weren't focused, but he managed a trembly smile back.

'I know, right?' he whispered.

'Were you going towards a bright light?' said Josh, excited. 'Was there a tunnel and a choir and angels?'

I turned to Asha, who was extricating herself from Grace's arms. I was opening my mouth trying to find words, but words weren't coming. 'Asha?' I managed her name, no more than that.

'OK,' she said, slowly. 'You fell in the river. Very funny. Everything after that ... it's a bit hazy. But I was probably awesome, right?'

'Definitely,' I said.

I took a deep breath, and got unsteadily to my feet. The garden was full of soldiers, and Douglas and Kirby were still standing outside the door from the kitchen, Kirby watching us sourly, Douglas looking troubled, like a man who was used to being in control finding that he wasn't even slightly in control. I started swaying, and Asha put a hand on my shoulder.

'You OK, Fish Boy?'

'I need to see if Jason's all right,' I said. 'I need to talk to him.' Then I hesitated, looked at her. 'And you need to talk to Naveen.'

She looked puzzled by that, but she didn't snap at me, which felt like a step in the right direction.

I shrugged. 'Brothers, right?' Then I stumbled away, towards the low wall, climbed over it.

The golf ball had fallen off the machine, the cylinder was crushed, the screen had a spider-web of cracks on its surface, and the front of the Audi was crumpled like a giant had squashed it in his hand. The airbag had deployed though, and Jason was sitting on the ground, leaning on the driver's door while a medic shone a torch into his eyes.

'Is he all right?'

'Concussed,' said the medic. 'Look after him a minute.'

She hurried off and Jason looked at me woozily. 'That was some punch,' he said.

'No,' I said. 'The punch was a couple of days ago. You just crashed the car.'

He nodded, then looked like he regretted moving his head. 'Right,' he murmured. He ran his fingertips over his forehead, looking confused. 'Are we good though?'

He was having trouble keeping his eyes focused on me, but he was trying.

'Yes,' I said. I nodded for both of us. 'We're good.' I even tried a smile. 'I've only got one brother, haven't I?'

The medic came back carrying a stretcher with a nurse, and she reassured me Jason was fine, so I promised him I'd see him soon and I went back to the garden. Kirby was trying to take charge. One soldier had a broken leg and two had sprained ankles, but she obviously thought she had enough men left to carry on bullying us.

'For now you'll return to Green Fingers,' she said. 'While we prepare charges against you. Emergency powers still apply.'

Josh ignored her completely. He was searching his pockets for his little box of sadness. He looked at me. 'It's gone.'

Grace was standing with Ruby and Connor, like she was looking out for them, but she had her fingers under her fringe, feeling her forehead. I was pretty sure it would be smooth by now, the Eye would have vanished. When the aliens went, all the mutations went with them.

We clustered together in the middle of the lawn. Me, Asha, Grace and Josh, with Ruby and Connor.

Douglas was talking to Kirby. They seemed to be arguing. I was getting impatient, wondering why we were all just standing there, like these two had any authority over us. If we all left, how could they stop us? Surely they wouldn't shoot those guns at us again? And even if they did, perhaps they wouldn't have any effect. I was about to suggest we did that, climbed over the wall, got the hell out of there, when Kirby finally looked over at us.

'We're going to keep you interned,' Kirby said. She was

basically repeating herself, but there was a strain in her voice, as if even she wasn't quite convinced by what she was saying. 'Until CoCom has decided how to move forward.'

I almost laughed at her. 'What?' I said. 'Because you think your Coordinating Committee might keep lying? After all this?'

I turned away because I didn't even want to look at her and, as if they had somehow teleported into Max's garden, I saw my parents pushing past soldiers as they came out of the house. I left our little cluster and ran across the lawn to meet them, and there was Josh's mum behind them, with Simpson, and Mrs Kamala behind them, with Dr Thompson. And suddenly it was like a party in the garden, a party with a lot of kissing and hugging and wordless sounds of surprise and pleasure, and half-asked questions beginning with 'Where?' and 'What?', and a load of confused, surly soldiers just standing around watching like uninvited guests, unsure what to do.

I saw Josh hugging his mum. 'I wrote you a letter,' he told her, with a crack in his voice. 'I wanted to give it to you.'

She looked a bit confused, and Simpson smiled that reassuring smile of his and said, 'I saw it, it was like a book he was writing. Where is it, big man?'

Josh shook his head. 'I haven't got it. They burnt it.'

His mum, clearly puzzled by this, touched his face. 'I'm not a big reader anyway.' She smiled. 'Why don't you just tell me what it said?'

So, as far as I could tell, he did, or he started to at least, but none of us really wanted to be in Max's garden, surrounded by soldiers.

My parents and Simpson and Dr Thompson finally turned on Douglas and Kirby.

'We're all going now,' Simpson said. 'What you going to do about that?'

Kirby began to speak, but Douglas interrupted.

'Nothing,' he said. 'Go home. For God's sake, just go back to your homes.' You could hear the weariness in his voice, and also an edge of relief, like a weight had been lifted off him. He knew he didn't have much choice, and he knew that the danger was over for another year, and possibly for ever. I had a feeling that whatever the Coordinating Committee did next, they'd be doing it without Colonel Douglas.

Kirby wasn't looking at Simpson, or any of the adults, she was looking at me and my friends. She had dark rings under her eyes, her whole face seemed to be sagging.

'You don't know what you've done,' she said.

I nodded. It was true, we didn't.

'I guess we'll see,' I said.

'Your actions have been incredibly irresponsible,' she snapped.

'So has your face,' said Josh.

I laughed. I'd been about to tell her that everyone was alive, and the aliens had gone, and that was a pretty good result, but I didn't bother. Josh had covered it.

On our way out of Max's front door we met Ruby and Connor's parents. Jason had called Mum just before he rammed the Audi into the machine, and she'd called everyone else. So there they were, on the crazy-paving path to the door.

Connor's mum gasped and put a hand over her mouth

when she saw us. Connor, who'd got a bit of colour back in his face, ran to her and hugged her tight. 'I died!' he announced. His dad had a hand on Connor's shoulder but was looking past him at Ruby, who was hanging back, standing next to Grace. He put out an arm, inviting her into their embrace. She hesitated a minute, then stepped in and stood stiffly while her father's arm went around her shoulders, pulling her towards them.

That was nice. Not gushing or anything, but nice. I didn't exactly have a tear in my eye though, because I just wanted to get home. Leave Connor and Ruby to their awkward reunion, leave Josh to his, leave Grace and even Asha and spend some time alone in my room, recovering. I'd come down for dinner. Maybe Dad could make another lasagne, maybe I'd be allowed a beer.

I got in the back of our car. Sighed, and closed my eyes. Dad got behind the wheel and started the engine. Surely all the questions could wait till tomorrow?

Mum, in the passenger seat, twisted round.

'Where's Jason?' she said.

'And where the hell have you been?' said Dad. 'Start at the beginning and keep going. What on earth's been going on?'

'This time,' said Mum, 'we want to know everything.'

# ANOTHER DAY

**2.46 p.m.**

We weren't sitting in the square outside *Love Bites*, and we weren't sipping milkshakes in *Shake!*. We were staying out of town because it was jammed with giant vans with satellite dishes on top, and it was full of reporters roaming in predatory packs who stopped anyone, but especially teenagers, to shove a microphone and a camera in their face and bark questions at them about aliens.

The reporters' voices were half excited, half scared, half completely incredulous, and if that doesn't add up it's because that's the way the world is now. It's different. Since the announcement from the Prime Minister, the impossible has become the possible. It's officially our new reality.

So we were staying out of town for a while, because everyone knew it all started with teenagers in Gilpin, and the whole entire world's attention was focused here. We were hiding basically, in Asha's house, and Josh was on the leather sofa necking Diet Coke while he tried to persuade Asha that we'd actually genuinely discussed starting a band, Grace was rolling her eyes, and I was on my phone.

I was pleased to be able to get at my laptop again, and to have my phone back, but I'd made a definite decision to do less blogging and tweeting and general social media. I'd spent a whole year obsessed with it, and I'd finally worked out it was all a step away from real, proper life which meant that basically, mostly, it was a complete waste of time and effort. I'd had enough of that because of precisely this: sitting in Asha's house with my best mates. This felt like a much better way to spend time.

I did want to send one tweet though, now that the news was out, and finally no one could deny the truth any more. I sent this one for all the trolls who'd spent so long sneering at me, chucking all sorts of horrible abuse at me, calling me an idiot and a liar.

**Told you so.**

'You're keeping quiet.' Asha all of a sudden turned on me. 'Bet you think you're totally the hero, right?'

I smiled, shrugged. Busted.

'Ha!' said Asha. 'Knew it! I might have forgotten basically the whole of the last week, but I've had it properly explained to me by everyone, and it was me, OK? Get used to it. I had the best powers, and I nearly died, so I was heroine of this whole last week. End of.'

We were living in a different world, but at the same time it was the same world. Asha had had a full check-up and was apparently fine, apart from the gap in her memory, Connor had made a full recovery, Jason was out of hospital. Everything was slipping back into normality, like it did this time last year. School was starting in a week's time. Year Twelve, the beginning of A levels. I was nagging my parents about driving lessons when I turned seventeen. Jason was going to retake his exams and look for a job.

And this year, I was ready for ordinary life. I was looking forward to it. I wasn't going to need to convince anyone that the impossible had visited Gilpin, because everyone knew. And I wasn't going to let myself be paralysed by worries about my future, because I was hoping to enjoy the present. It felt pretty good, to be honest.

Josh and Grace got on Asha's mum's computer, finding a game Josh swore was brilliant. Me and Asha moved into the kitchen. She opened the oven to get the pizza out. Warm air and a whiff of hot dough. I found the plates, but I stopped her as she started cutting.

I put a hand on her hand.

She laid the knife down. Turned and faced me, with a twist of a smile on her face.

'So you've forgotten what you said?'

We were close together in the small kitchen.

She shrugged. 'I said I was the heroine.'

'No, before that.' I took a deep breath. 'See the thing is, we actually sort of had a moment a couple of days ago. I mean you nearly killed me but apart from that it was really nice, and you're probably not even going to believe me, but later I asked you if it would have been all right if we'd kissed, and you said . . .'

She interrupted, nodding slowly. 'Ask me again when all this is over.'

I stared.

'Memory's coming back,' she said. 'In patches.' Her hazel eyes, smiling, mocking, direct, were gazing right into mine.

I nodded.

'Go on, then,' she said. 'Ask me.'

# Acknowledgements

Thanks again to my lovely agent Jo Unwin, and to my excellent new editor, Rachel Wade, who made the whole process so pleasant. And thanks again to Bimpe Alliu for more wonderful work bringing my words to life.

Thanks also to Sally Corcos, Holly Illis, Julius Nicholson and Martin Riley for their comments, criticisms, suggestions and (in some cases) cups of tea.